BRIDES OF WATERLOO

Love forged on the battlefield

Meet Mary Endacott, a radical schoolmistress,
Sarah Latymor, a darling of the *ton*, and
Catherine 'Rose' Tatton, a society lady
with no memories of her past.

Three very different women united
in a fight for their lives, their reputations
and the men they love.

With war raging around them, the biggest battle
these women face is protecting their hearts
from three notorious soldiers…

Will Mary be able to resist Colonel Lord Randall?
Find out in

A Lady for Lord Randall
by
Sarah Mallory

Discover how pampered Lady Sarah
handles rakish Major Bartlett in

A Mistress for Major Bartlett
by
Annie Burrows

What will happen when Major Flint
helps Lady Catherine 'Rose' Tatton
discover her past? Find out in

AUTHOR NOTE

Why settle for one hero when you can have a whole bunch? That was the idea behind Randall's Rogues—a crack artillery unit with brilliant but maverick officers (all handsome devils, of course) brought together by one very special leader: Justin Latymor, Colonel Lord Randall. And so the *Brides of Waterloo* mini-series was born! *A Lady for Lord Randall* is the first of three romantic adventures commemorating the Battle of Waterloo, which took place on 18th June 1815.

Randall is a professional soldier with no time for romance—until he meets the fiercely independent Mary Endacott. Against all rational judgement they are drawn together in the heady days before Waterloo, but can they ever find lasting happiness when their lives, their outlooks and even their principles are so very different?

The summer of 1815 was a momentous time. Napoleon was set to dominate Europe; Britain and the Allies were making one final stand against him. It would be nice to think that if Randall's Rogues had ever existed they would have played their part in helping the Allies to victory on that day.

Working on this trilogy with Annie Burrows and Louise Allen has been immensely enjoyable and I learned even more about my craft—so thank you, ladies. Thanks also to Jos van Loo for his Belgian insider knowledge. Finally I am indebted to Trevor Rutter, whose battlefield tour of Waterloo was such an inspiration. Trevor was also extremely generous with his advice and encouragement while I was writing this book. If there are any errors in the battle scenes then they are entirely my own.

I do hope you enjoy reading this book—do contact me to let me know. You can find me at www.sarahmallory.com

A LADY FOR LORD RANDALL

Sarah Mallory

MILLS & BOON

Published in Great Britain 2015
by Mills & Boon, an imprint of Harlequin (UK) Limited,
Eton House, 18-24 Paradise Road, Richmond, Surrey, TW9 1SR

© 2015 Sarah Mallory

ISBN: 978-0-263-24777-0

Harlequin (UK) Limited's policy is to use papers that are natural,
renewable and recyclable products and made from wood grown in
sustainable forests. The logging and manufacturing processes conform
to the legal environmental regulations of the country of origin.

Printed and bound in Spain
by CPI, Barcelona

Sarah Mallory was born in the West Country and now lives on the beautiful Yorkshire moors. She has been writing for more than three decades—mainly historical romances set in the Georgian and Regency period. She has won several awards for her writing, most recently the Romantic Novelists' Association RoNA Rose Award in 2012 (*The Dangerous Lord Darrington*) and 2013 (*Beneath the Major's Scars*).

Books by Sarah Mallory

Mills & Boon® Historical Romance and Mills & Boon® Historical *Undone!* eBook

Brides of Waterloo

A Lady for Lord Randall

The Notorious Coale Brothers

Beneath the Major's Scars
Behind the Rake's Wicked Wager
The Tantalising Miss Coale (Undone!)

Linked by Character

Lady Beneath the Veil
At the Highwayman's Pleasure

Stand-Alone Novels

The Earl's Runaway Bride
Disgrace and Desire
To Catch a Husband...
One Snowy Regency Christmas
Snowbound with the Notorious Rake
The Dangerous Lord Darrington
Bought for Revenge
The Scarlet Gown
Never Trust a Rebel

M&B *Castonbury Park* Regency mini-series

The Illegitimate Montague

**Visit the author profile page
at millsandboon.co.uk for more titles**

Peter O'Toole (1932–2013)
An inspiration for many romantic heroes
including Randall, my very own rogue male.

Chapter One

Randall glanced at the clock. Had it only been an hour since they had arrived at the Bentincks'? It felt longer. He was not naturally sociable, preferring the company of a few close friends to parties such as this where the room was crowded with strangers, but he knew he must try to make himself agreeable, for his sister Hattie's sake. The Bentincks were a cheerful couple whose children had flown the nest and who now liked to fill their time and their house with interesting young people. The problem was, their idea of interesting was not Randall's. Hattie had explained that the Bentincks' house would be full of intellectuals, artists and atheists.

'And tradesmen, too, no doubt,' he had retorted.

'They are invited because of their intelligence, not their rank,' she told him and gave a little trill of laughter when Randall grimaced at the idea. 'You must come, they will be quite delighted to have an earl, a real live peer of the realm in their midst. And a soldier, to boot.'

'And does the Bishop approve of you and Graveney attending these parties?' he had asked her, thinking of her husband, the rural dean.

Hattie's eyes had twinkled merrily at that.

'Not at all, but Theo loves to go there, he approaches these evenings with all the zeal of a missionary. As he says, what is the point of always preaching to the converted?'

Observing his brother-in-law across the Bentincks' drawing room, Randall could well believe it. Theo Graveney was involved in a lively discussion with a group of gentlemen in loose coats and untidy hair. Arms were flying and voices were raised as the debate grew ever more heated.

Randall's gaze moved on. Most of the guests were writers or scholars, he guessed, his eyes dwelling on one or two shabbily dressed men with ink stains on their fingers. There were no military men present, save himself, the rest of the party being made up of tradesmen, artists and even a couple of French *émigrés*. They were all gathered in little groups, engaged in animated conversation. There was a smattering of women amongst the crowd, some of them pretty, in a blowsy sort of way, and all giving their opinions as decidedly as the men.

Randall disliked such loud, overbearing society and he had retreated as soon as he could to a quiet corner. He had known how it would be and he should have remained at Somervil. Oh, Mrs Bentinck had greeted him warmly enough, but her first comment had warned him just what to expect from the evening:

'We are very informal here, my lord, and stand on no ceremony. I shall make no introductions, you must take your chances like the rest of the guests.'

She had carried Hattie away then, leaving Randall to mingle as he wished. But Randall did not wish. With Bonaparte even now marching through France and the country on the verge of war again, he was not to be distracted with idle conversation. His sister came up and handed him a glass of wine.

'Well, Randall, what do you think of our little gathering?'

'*Little* gathering, Hattie? Such a number would be considered a crush even in the Latymor town house.'

'They travel from far and wide to attend the Bentincks' soirées,' she said proudly.

'That may be so, but it is not to my taste,' muttered Randall. 'I am a soldier, plain and simple.' A shout from the far corner caught their attention and he glanced to where a group of young men were now arguing noisily. 'I have no patience with artistic tantrums.'

'Pray do not be tiresome, Justin, there are more than just artists here, and plenty to entertain, if you are not too high in the instep.' Hattie patted his arm, murmuring as she prepared to move away, 'You should relax and enjoy yourself, dear brother. You are a man of the world, so I trust you not be shocked by the company we keep.'

Randall knew he could not stay in one spot all evening and he began to stroll around the room, listening to the conversations, but joining in with very few of them. He had not worn his uniform, but began to think he would have been more at home if he had done so. At least then it would have been plain what his role was and he would not have been asked for his opinion on so-and-so's latest stanzas, or if he had read some new and profound religious tract. He was wondering how soon he could possibly retire without giving offence when a soft, musical voice sounded at his elbow.

'You look a little lost, sir.'

He turned, vexed to find himself addressed by a woman he did not know. But he should not be surprised at such brazen behaviour, given the company gathered here tonight. He could not recall seeing her before amongst the crowd, for there was certainly nothing blowsy about her. She was neatly dressed in a gown of cream muslin with her dark hair swept up on her head, unrelieved by ribbons or flowers. She carried herself with an assurance that seemed odd in one so young— she looked about two-and-twenty, the same age as his sister Sarah. The woman was regarding him with a humorous twinkle in her green eyes and he found himself wanting to respond with a smile. Impossible, of course. One did not encourage such persons. Still, he replied more politely that he was wont to do.

'Not lost. Merely daydreaming.'

'I have not seen you here before. I am Mary Endacott, I am presently staying here. Mrs Bentinck is my cousin.'

She waited, clearly expecting him to introduce himself.

'I'm Randall,' he said shortly, rather taken aback by such forwardness.

Her brows went up. 'The earl, Harriett's brother?'

'You are surprised, ma'am?'

His cold tone should have depressed any pretension, but Mary Endacott merely laughed at him.

'Well, yes, I am. I would not have seen this as your normal milieu. The company is a little... radical.'

'I arrived at short notice today.'

'Ah, so you had no choice but to attend.'

He said carefully, 'I am very happy to be here.'

'But you would rather not socialise with us. I have been watching you, my lord, and you do not look to be enjoying yourself.'

'That is because my mind is occupied elsewhere.'

'On the forthcoming confrontation with Napoleon, perhaps?'

'Amongst other things.'

She nodded. 'It does seem rather frivolous to be discussing art and philosophy when the fate of Europe hangs in the balance.'

'Just so.' He glanced at her fingers, which were holding her closed fan. The right hand was folded over the left so he could not see any ring, but she had such poise and confidence that he guessed she was a married woman. He glanced about the room. 'Which of these gentlemen is your husband?'

'Oh, I am not married.' She chuckled. 'Actually, that applies to a number of the women here tonight, but in my case I am not in a *union* with anyone, either. Many here are opposed to the concept of marriage,' she explained. 'No church ceremony can bind a man and woman together, only love can do that. Love, and a commonality of intellectual interests, of course.'

Her eyes were fixed on his face and he had the impression she was trying to shock him.

'And is that your conviction, too?'

He had the satisfaction of seeing that his blunt question had discomposed her, but then he was a little sorry when she looked away from him.

'It is what I was brought up to believe.'

He said, 'It would require a great deal of trust on the woman's part, I think, to enter into such a union without the blessing of the church. She would not have the protection of the man's name.'

'She would not become his property, either. The current law is a scandalous state of affairs and has serious disadvantages for a woman.'

He inclined his head.

'Very true, Miss Endacott.'

A female of decided opinions. Not his type at all.

'Ah, Mary, so you have met my brother.'

He had not seen Harriett come up, but now she linked arms with Miss Endacott.

'We introduced ourselves,' he said shortly.

'I would not have thought that necessary,' said Harriett. 'Did you not recognise the nose, Mary? All the Latymors have it, and any number of villagers, too, thanks to Papa. At home one could never walk through Chalfont Magna without encountering at least two of his by-blows. Oh, there is no need for you to look daggers at me, Randall, Mary knows all about our father's dissolute ways.

We are very old friends, you see. We were at Miss Burchell's Academy together.'

He relaxed, just a little. So the forward Miss Endacott was one of Harriett's free-thinking school friends.

'That explains a great deal,' he murmured.

Harriett's eyes twinkled. 'Has Mary outraged you with her radical ideas? Her parents were great admirers of Mrs Godwin—Mary Wollstonecraft—hence her name.'

Miss Endacott chuckled, a soft, warm sound that was very pleasing to the ear.

'I certainly tried to be outrageous, Hattie, but your brother would not rise to the bait.'

'Well, you know he is a soldier, and commands a company of rogues, so he is most likely unshockable.'

With two pairs of eyes fixed upon him, two laughing faces turned up to his, Randall felt ill at ease. He gave a little nod and left them. By God, he would prefer to face a charge by French cavalry than these teasing women! He passed Theo, who was at the centre of a group of clerics and rather surprisingly arguing for Catholic emancipation, and moved on to a group of young men who were discussing the Lake poets, but he was thankful when Mr Bentinck came up and carried him away.

'You do not look to be enjoying yourself, my lord.'

'I confess I have little in common with your guests,' replied Randall carefully 'I came to please my sister.'

'Ah, yes. Mrs Graveney.' His host nodded. 'She may prefer not to be known as Lady Harriett these days but she is very proud of *you*, you know. She likes the fact that you followed your grandfather into the artillery rather than buying a commission. Well, sir, there are fellows over here whose conversation might be more to your taste.'

Bentinck took him across to a cluster of tradesmen who were eager for news of Bonaparte. Randall stayed for a while, discussing the latest situation and how it might affect their business, before moving on.

The good dinner his sister had provided at Somervil, plus the Bentincks' excellent wines, were having an effect. Randall felt more relaxed, more able to participate in the conversations, but even as he did so, he found his eyes straying to Mary Endacott as she moved around the room. Her figure was very good and she had a natural grace. He liked the way the swing of her hips set the thin skirts of her muslin gown fluttering in the most alluring fashion as she walked. When she passed close to him he stepped away from the group he was with to talk to her.

'You are not enamoured of any of the discussions, Miss Endacott?'

'On the contrary, I find them all fascinating, but a heated debate on theology with Mr Graveney has left me sadly thirsty.'

'Allow me.' He accompanied her to the table at the side of the room, where an array of jugs and decanters were set out. He filled two wine glasses and held one out to her.

'Thank you,' she said. 'I am sure you are more used to raising a finger and having a servant wait upon you.'

'Trying to put me to the blush, Miss Endacott? You will not succeed.' He followed her to a vacant sofa and sat down beside her. 'I am a soldier and accustomed to much rougher conditions than these.'

She laughed.

'Of course you are. Hattie has told me all about Randall's Rogues, the raff and scaff of the military gathered into one troop. Men it is impossible to place elsewhere. If you had not taken them most would have been hanged by now.' She sipped at the wine. 'I do not approve of war, but your efforts in this case are admirable; you have turned them into a formidable unit. From the despatches I read in the newspapers they acquitted themselves well in the Peninsula.'

'They are all good artillerymen.'

'Perhaps they have a good colonel.'

Randall shrugged.

'I demand only two things, Miss Endacott, unquestioning obedience and loyalty.'

She shook her head at him.

'Loyalty I can understand, but unquestioning obedience? I do not think I could give anyone that.' She gave a little shrug and smiled at him. 'Nevertheless, I have to congratulate you on your success, sir. To take such unpromising material and turn them into a crack artillery troop is no mean feat.'

'A man's background is nothing to me, as long as he can fight.'

'But how does one control such men?' she asked him.

'Iron discipline. The lash and the rope. When a man joins the Rogues he knows it is his last chance.'

He saw the disapproval in her eyes.

'That is a brutal way to go on, my lord.'

'It is necessary. In war a man must know he can rely on his comrades.'

'I would there were no wars and no need for armies.'

'That is a dream of all reasonable beings, madam.'

He leaned back, watching the changing emotions flicker across her countenance.

She said a little wistfully, 'My father was a great supporter of the revolution in France, and of

Bonaparte, at first. Papa thought he would uphold democracy, until he proclaimed himself emperor and began to overrun Europe.'

'Thus, until the world is at peace we shall always need soldiers, Miss Endacott.'

'We shall indeed. But this is dismal talk, Lord Randall, surely there must be a more entertaining topic?'

'Yes, you,' he said, surprising himself, but it was worth it to see the becoming blush spread over her cheeks.

'No, no, I am not entertaining at all.'

'Will you not let me be the judge of that?' She shook her head and looked as if she might leave him, so he said quickly, 'Very well, what would you like to discuss? Let us agree that I shall allow you to choose the first topic for discussion. You must then allow me my choice.'

She leaned back against the arm of the sofa and regarded him, a faint smile playing at the edges of her mouth.

'Very well. I would like to know what persuaded the great Earl Randall to attend the party tonight.'

'That is simple: my sister asked me.'

'Even though you clearly do not approve of us?'

'Even so. I am only here for one week and did not wish to spend an evening apart from Harriett.'

'Hattie always said you were the best of the

Latymors.' She observed his surprise and her smile grew. 'You must remember I have been Hattie's friend since our schooldays, Lord Randall. I am aware that your mother, the countess, was outraged when Harriett returned from school with her head full of independent ideas. Our intentions were very much the same, you see. We both wished to make our own way in the world and declared we would never marry. It must have been a relief when Hattie fell head over heels in love with Theophilus three years ago.'

'It was. Graveney had a comfortable independence and my mother was too relieved to see her daughter respectably married to protest at her new son-in-law's rather unconventional views.'

Randall was surprised that he should talk so freely. It was not his habit to discuss his family with anyone, but there was an elusive charm about this woman that put him at his ease.

'Quite...' she nodded '...and they have lived happily in Sussex ever since, unconcerned that Harriett's family disapprove of the match.'

'I do not disapprove,' said Randall mildly. 'For my part I have no objection to Graveney. He is a decade older than I am and we have little in common, but I like the fact that he has made no effort to ingratiate himself with the family and he is not afraid to speak his mind.'

'You do not object to that?' she asked, her brows raised.

'No, I respect it. And I am content that the fellow can support Harriett and make her happy.' He paused. 'Now what have I said to make you smile?'

'Hattie told me you were very different from the rest of the Latymors.'

'Oh?' He stiffened. 'May I ask what she has said about our family?'

'She did not imply any criticism,' she replied quickly. 'Merely that you are more tolerant than the others. I expect that comes from being a soldier and away so much. I believe your mama, Lady Randall, runs the house and estates at Chalfont Magna in your absence and looks after your younger brothers?'

'Yes, they are twins and still at Eton.'

'How old are they now, fourteen? I have no doubt they are very proud of you.'

'I do not know, I hardly see them. I have been on campaign for most of their lives.'

'That is very sad, they could learn so much from you. Have you no thoughts of leaving the army and going home, taking your place as head of the household?'

Home. Randall considered Chalfont Abbey. Had he ever felt at home there? His mother ran everything like clockwork and he had always been happy to let her do so. He felt a little spurt of irritation. How dare the woman question him in this way?

'I have a job to do, Miss Endacott. Perhaps you do not understand that I have a duty to my men and my country.'

'Of course I understand that, but perhaps, when this campaign is over, you might decide to stay at Chalfont. I am sure your mama would welcome your support.'

'I doubt it. She has always managed very well without me.'

Even as he said it he was not sure it was true. This last short visit to Chalfont had shown him that she was growing older. She left more of the work to the stewards now.

'What of the rest of your family? Harriett tells me your oldest sister is in Europe.'

'Yes.'

'You do not approve?'

He frowned. This young woman was too perceptive for comfort. He knew he could snub her, but he was enjoying talking to her, more so than anyone else he had met this evening. She spoke again, saying in a reflective voice, 'From what Harriett has told me about Augusta I am sure she was eager to follow the *ton* to Paris.'

'She was and her doting husband indulged her. My mother sent my youngest sister Sarah with them, knowing she would be thrown in the way of eligible young men and hoping she might be induced to accept one of them.' He gave a little huff of amusement. 'My mother thinks that at two-and-twenty Sarah is running out of time to find a husband.'

Again Miss Endacott gave that warm gurgle of laughter.

'Yes, she is practically on the shelf!'

'But her twin is unmarried—did you know there are two sets of twins in our family?' he asked. 'My mother has seven surviving children of which I am the eldest. Our father was very productive.'

His jaw tightened. The old earl had been well known for his insatiable appetite, not just for his wife but for any woman.

'Yes, I did know Sarah had a twin brother, but when it comes to marriage it is very different for a man.' Miss Endacott's voice interrupted his bitter thoughts. 'Gideon will be free to do very much as he pleases. How is he enjoying his new cavalry regiment, by the by?'

'I have no idea, he does not correspond with me.'

'If you will excuse my saying so, Lord Randall, you do not seem a very close family, but I believe that is the way amongst the nobility.'

'And what do you know of the nobility, Miss Endacott?'

He spoke frostily and saw her visibly withdraw from him.

'Now I have offended you,' she said quietly. 'I had best leave you—'

A moment ago he had been wishing her at Hades, but as she made to rise he put out a hand to stop her.

'We had a bargain, Miss Endacott.' The faint lift of an eyebrow told him she would dispute it and he tried for a softer note. 'Please, ma'am, stay and talk to me.'

The distant look faded from her countenance and she sank back on the sofa, waiting expectantly for him to begin.

'Do you make a long stay with the Bentincks, Miss Endcaott?'

'Two weeks only. A pity because I would have liked to see more of Harriett.'

'Then why not stay longer? I am sure if Mrs Bentinck cannot put you up my sister would be delighted to do so.'

'She has already suggested it, but it cannot be, I am afraid. Business calls me away.' She saw his puzzled look and laughed. 'I am not a lady of leisure, my lord. I have to earn my living. If I were a scholar perhaps, or a poet or an author, then I might remain in Sussex and be busy with my pen.'

'Oh? Are you in trade?'

That disturbing twinkle lit her eyes again.

'Why, yes, of a sort. I must get back to my girls or—' she corrected herself, a mischievous smile lilting on her lips, 'my *ladies*, as I call them.'

A young man lounged up and laughingly asked Miss Endcaott to come and support him in an argument with his friends. When Randall bridled, incensed at being interrupted, the lady rested one hand on his arm.

'You are not used to such freedom of manners, sir, but remember, no one here knows who you are.' She rose. 'Forgive me, I had best go, I have spent far too long with you already.' Her eyes twinkled and she said mischievously, 'My reputation would be quite ruined, you know, if I had one!'

Randall watched her walk away. He was intrigued. Who in heaven's name was Mary Endacott? Not a scholar, she had said, but in trade. He regarded her retreating form thoughtfully. She had joined a group of gentlemen and was quite at her ease with them, laughing at their jokes and making a riposte of her own. She was not pretty in the conventional sense, but certainly attractive enough for the gentlemen around her to be captivated.

Some sort of trade. Involving *ladies*. And she had said she had no reputation to be ruined. Suddenly his sister's words came back to him: *'I trust you not to be shocked by the company we keep.'*

Good God! His eyes narrowed. Was that what Hattie meant?

Mary tried to concentrate upon the conversation that was going on around her, but all she could think of was Lord Randall's blue eyes and lean, handsome face. When she had seen him standing alone at the side of the room she had decided to take pity on him, knowing that the Bentincks' unorthodox soirée would be a little daunting to a strange gentleman, and this man clearly *was* a gentleman. At first glance he looked quite slender and it was only when she drew closer that she realised it was his height that made him look perfectly proportioned. She had noted immediately the fashionably short hair—brown and sun streaked—and the exquisite tailoring of his coat. The dark blue Bath superfine fitted across those broad shoulders without a crease, its severity relieved by a white quilted waistcoat and the snowy white linen at his throat and wrists. He would be accustomed to society parties where the guests all knew one another and introductions would be carried out for any newcomer, to make sure their rank was acknowledged and understood. In an effort to put this stranger at his ease she had made the first move, only to have him look down his aristocratic nose at her. He had fixed her with that cool, aloof gaze and informed her that he was Randall, Harriett's haughty and very proper brother.

Mary remembered the letters Harriett had received from him while they were at Miss Burchell's Academy. Always short and to the point, advising Harriett of news—their mother's removal to Worthing for a little sea bathing when she was recovering from influenza, their father's ill health, his own promotion within an artillery regiment. Nothing chatty, nothing warm or comforting for his little sister miles away from the family home.

A servant had always been dispatched to take Harriett home so Mary had never met Justin Latymor and by the time the girls left Miss Burchell's Academy he was a career soldier, not even selling out when his father died and he became the sixth Earl Randall. That Harriett was fond of her big brother was beyond doubt. She said he was the only one who had not lectured her upon her marriage to Theophilus Graveney, but Mary had built up an image of a cold, stiff-backed man, lacking in humour.

And so he had been, when she had first approached him. Or should she say accosted him? His tall frame was rigidly upright and he looked so hard and unmovable he might have been hewn from a single oak. He was clearly not accustomed to young ladies introducing themselves. Yet there was a sensitivity around those sculpted lips and there had been warmth and the suspicion of a gleam in those blue, blue eyes when he had spoken to Hattie. She had seen it, too, when he had surprised her by stepping aside to engage her in conversation.

'You are allowing yourself to be dazzled by a title,' she told herself sternly. 'Shameful for one who believes in a meritocracy.'

Yet she could not get the thought of the earl out of her head. It did not help that whenever she looked about he seemed to be watching her. The idea brought an unaccustomed heat to her cheeks. It was so long since she had blushed that she had thought herself too old for such frivolity, but now she found that even at four-and-twenty a young lady could find herself attracted to a man. And not just any man, an earl, no less!

'Mary, what are you smiling at?'

Mrs Bentinck's voice brought her out of her reverie. Mary looked up. Her companions were huddled together to read an article in a recent edition of Cobbett's *Political Register*, a publication that was known to induce indignation or outrage, but never laughter.

'Oh, an old joke,' she said swiftly. 'My mind was wandering.'

Mrs Bentinck patted her arm. 'What you need

is sustenance. Everyone will be leaving soon and we will then have a little supper.'

She went off to see her guests out and Mary moved across to join Harriett, who was beckoning to her from the sofa.

'We have been invited to stay to sup with you,' she said, pulling Mary down beside her.

'Oh.' Mary found her gaze once more drifting to the tall figure of the earl standing before the fire. 'But, Lord Randall must be exhausted if he only reached you today—'

'Nonsense,' said Harriett bracingly. 'My brother is a hardened soldier and quite capable of staying up all night, if necessary, is that not so, Justin?'

Mary had thought the earl deep in conversation with Mr Graveney, but he turned his head and she found herself once more subjected to that piercing blue gaze.

'Indeed it is, but it will be no hardship to spend a little more time here and in such delightful company.'

'Why, Justin, that is quite the prettiest thing I have ever heard you say,' declared Harriett, quite shocked.

Mary felt her friend's speculative glance turned upon her and quickly looked away, busying herself with smoothing the wrinkles from her long gloves. When everyone else had left they went into the dining room where supper was set out, comprising cold meats, fruit and wine. Since informality was the order of the day Mary chose a seat between her cousin and Harriett. This put her as far as possible from Randall, which she thought safest for her peace of mind, so it was in horror that she realised her old school friend was rising from her seat, saying cheerfully, 'Brother, dear, would you be kind enough to change places with me? I think I have a slight chill and would much prefer to sit a little closer to the fire.'

The next moment the earl was lowering his long frame on to the chair beside her. She tried to keep her eyes fixed upon her plate, but it was impossible not to look at his lean, muscled legs as he took his place. The black-stockinet pantaloons clung tightly to his thighs and she felt herself growing quite hot with embarrassment as her imagination rioted. Mary closed her eyes. Good heavens, she was not a schoolgirl to be so affected by a man.

'Miss Endacott, are you quite well?'

The sound of that deep voice, rich and smooth as chocolate, did nothing to calm her, but the thought of making a fool of herself in front of everyone stiffened her resolve. She raised her head and managed to respond with tolerable equanimity.

'Quite well, thank you, my lord. My thoughts were elsewhere.'

'Thinking of the long journey you are to undertake at the end of the week, no doubt,' said Mrs Bentinck, sitting on her other side.

Mary pulled herself together. She said gaily, 'Oh, do not let us talk about me, I would much rather be distracted from the sad inevitability of leaving my friends.'

'Randall, too, is leaving on Friday,' put in Harriett.

'Ah, to join Wellington's army, no doubt,' said Mr Bentinck. 'Do you sail from Dover, my lord?'

'Folkestone,' the earl replied. 'I have my own yacht there.'

'Really?' said Harriett. 'I thought you had sold it.'

'No. I sent it to Chatham to be refurbished.'

'I told you he would not have disposed of it,' declared Mr Graveney. 'The rich must have their playthings, eh, my boy?'

'It was used to carry some of our troops home from Corunna, was it not?' Mary wondered why she had felt it necessary to jump to the earl's defence, especially since it brought her to his attention once more.

'Yes, it was.'

'I think it was very good of you to join us this evening, my lord,' declared Mrs Bentinck, relieving Mary of the necessity of saying anything more. 'Mrs Graveney will have told you that our little gatherings tend to attract young men with rather revolutionary ideas.'

'Which is why we enjoy your parties so much,' cried Mr Graveney, waving his fork in the air. 'For the cut and thrust of the debate. Some of these youngsters have fire in their bellies, eh, Bentinck?'

'They do indeed,' replied their host, 'but most of them burn out as they grow up. One only has to look at Southey. Angry young rebel one day, tugging his forelock to the King the next.'

'I rather fear expediency cooled a great deal of his radicalism,' said Mary. 'A poet must support himself.'

'His principles must be in question,' put in Lord Randall. 'He could not otherwise relinquish them so easily.'

Mary shook her head. 'I do not agree. Sometimes we have to compromise if we are to make a living.'

'As you have done, Mary,' Harriett added.

Mary felt the earl's eyes upon her again and felt sure he was about to ask what compromises she had made, but before he could speak Mr Graveney introduced a new topic, which Mary took up with alacrity.

* * *

'Well now, that was not such a bad evening after all, was it?'

In the darkness of the carriage Randall could not see his sister's face, but he could hear the laughter in her voice.

'Some of those young men would benefit from a little army discipline,' he replied. 'That would put their idealism to flight.'

'But we need such men,' argued Graveney. 'Once these young fellows have formulated their ideas and matured a little, they will be the next to govern our great nation.'

'If we *have* a nation by then,' said Harriett. 'The reports all say that Bonaparte has returned stronger than ever.'

'That may be,' replied Randall. 'But this time he must face Wellington himself.'

'And do you seriously believe the duke will be able to beat him?'

Randall thought of the seasoned troops not yet returned from America, the untried soldiers already waiting for their first taste of action, to say nothing of their leaders; the impulsive Prince of Orange, the bickering factions of the Allied forces. His response indicated none of his concerns.

'Of course we shall beat him and this time it will be decisive.'

'And you must soon go off to join your men.'

Harriett clutched his arm. 'Promise me you will be careful, Randall.'

'I am always careful.'

'And you will take Grandfather's sword with you?'

'I never fight without it.'

He felt her relax. The sword was something of a lucky charm. Randall's father had shown no inclination to become a soldier and the old earl had left the sword to his grandson. Randall had worn it at every battle, coming unscathed through even the heaviest fighting. He was not superstitious, but he knew his family placed great store by the talisman. He had been fortunate so far, but he knew his luck could not last forever.

Randall gave a little inward shrug. If this was to be the end, he hoped he would live long enough to see Bonaparte defeated. As for the succession, he had brothers enough to carry on the line. Thank goodness he had no wife to weep for him.

A vision of Mary Endacott came into his mind, with her dusky curls and *retroussé* nose and those serious green eyes that could suddenly sparkle with merriment.

As if reading his thoughts Harriett said, 'I have invited the Bentincks to take tea with us on Wednesday. I doubt if Mr Bentinck will attend, but I hope Mary will come.'

'Oh, Bentinck will be there,' said Graveney

cheerfully. 'I told him I had acquired a copy of Hooke's *Micrographia* and he is mad to see it. I have no doubt that you, too, would like to inspect it, my lord?'

Randall agreed, but was uncomfortably aware that he was even more keen to see Mary Endacott again.

'Oh, fie on you, Theo, with your dusty books,' cried Hattie. 'I have something that will be much more diverting for Randall. If the rain holds off we will ride out together in the morning, Brother. You will like that, will you not?'

'My dear, Randall has been in the saddle most of the day,' her spouse protested mildly.

'But he is a soldier and used to it, aren't you, Justin? Surely you will oblige me by accompanying me tomorrow?'

'To be sure I will, Hattie. I should be delighted to see what changes have occurred here since my last visit.'

'Good. And I am lending my spare hack to Mary, who loves to ride. What a pleasant party we shall be.'

Even in the darkness there was no mistaking Hattie's self-satisfaction. Randall sat back in the corner of the carriage and cursed silently. His sister seemed set on matchmaking.

Chapter Two

Mary should not have been surprised when she looked out of her bedroom window the following morning and saw Lord Randall riding towards the house with his sister. He was staying at Somervil, so of course Hattie would want him to ride out with her. His horse had clearly been chosen for its strength and stamina rather than its appearance: a huge grey, so dappled that it looked positively dirty. However, she had to admit Lord Randall looked very good in the saddle. Her heart gave a little skip, but she quickly stifled the pleasurable anticipation before it could take hold. He was an earl, a member of an outmoded institution that bestowed power on the undeserving, and despite his attempts to be polite last evening, Lord Randall had made it very apparent he did not approve of her. His presence today was unlikely to add to her comfort.

Not that it mattered since she did not care a jot

for the man. She was looking forward to riding out with Hattie and, if Lord Randall was with them, she would not let it spoil her enjoyment.

Harriett had promised to bring her spare horse for Mary, but the spirited little black mare that the groom was leading exceeded expectations and was clearly far superior to the elderly hack Harriett was riding. Mary expressed her concern as soon as she came out of the house to meet them.

'No, no, I much prefer old Juno,' said Hattie. 'Besides, if you are only to ride out with me the once I would have you enjoy it.'

'I shall,' declared Mary, making herself comfortable in the saddle while the mare sidled and sidestepped playfully.

She was conscious of the earl's eyes upon her, but he did not look pleased. Perhaps he would have liked to ride out alone with Hattie. Mary was aware of a little spurt of irritation. If so, that was hardly her fault. She turned the mare and rode beside Hattie, resolutely keeping her gaze away from Lord Randall.

Harriett led the way to open ground where they could give the horses their heads. As they galloped across the springy turf the earl kept a little distance behind, although Mary was sure he could have outstripped them had he wished to. Even when they slowed to a walk he showed no inclination to join them. By the time they turned for home Mary was beginning to feel a little uncomfortable and she decided to speak out. As they slowed to pass through a gap in the hedge she turned to address him.

'I think you would rather have had your sister to yourself today, my lord.'

'Nonsense,' cried Harriett, overhearing. 'Justin is always taciturn. He has no social graces, do you, Brother?'

'One can enjoy riding without being obliged to chatter incessantly.'

'Of course, but a little conversation would not go amiss,' retorted Harriett. 'For instance, perhaps you could compliment Mary on her gown last night. I thought it was particularly fetching.'

'I never notice female attire.'

His crushing reply had no effect upon his sister, who continued blithely. 'You cannot have failed to notice how well she rides, so you could praise her for that.'

'Pray, Harriett, do not put me to the blush,' protested Mary, trying to laugh off her embarrassment.

'My sister is right. I am not one for female company.'

'A gross understatement,' declared Hattie warmly. 'If ever I have a new gown I have to prompt him to say what he thinks of it, and even then he is very likely to make some devastating comment, if he does not like it.'

'You cannot blame him for telling the truth,' Mary pointed out.

'Of course I can,' replied the earl's fond sister. 'He has been too long in the company of soldiers. There is not a romantic bone in his body. And he is shockingly bad at compliments.'

'I think Harriett is trying to say it is best to have no expectations where I am concerned, Miss Endacott.' Lord Randall replied gravely, but there was a smile lurking in his eyes and Mary chuckled.

'Thank you for warning me.'

'No,' went on Harriett with an exaggerated sigh. 'My brother is a confirmed bachelor.' Her eyes crinkled up as she added mischievously, 'But we live in hope.'

'Well, Mary, did you enjoy your ride today? It has certainly brought the colour to your cheeks.'

Mary smiled at Mrs Bentinck's remark when she entered the drawing room before dinner that evening and she replied quite truthfully that she had indeed enjoyed her outing.

'And how did you find the earl?' asked Mr Bentinck. 'Was he as cold and unsociable as last evening?'

'Every bit,' she agreed cheerfully. 'Apart from

one brief exchange he barely said a dozen words to me the whole time.'

They had not actually ridden together, he had made a point of keeping his distance for most of the ride, but she had been aware of his presence and had enjoyed knowing he was there. A little too much, if she was honest. The fact that they had hardly spoken to one another meant at least that there had been no chance for them to quarrel.

Mary was surprised and not a little shaken by the thought. Why should she not want to fall out with the earl, if they held opposing views? Heavens, could she be developing a *tendre* for him? She was far too old for that, surely? It was immature schoolgirls who became infatuated with a gentleman without any knowledge of his character, his thoughts or opinions, not sensible ladies of four-and-twenty. As Mary settled down to her dinner she had the uncomfortable suspicion that she was neither as mature nor as sensible as she had thought.

Randall and his sister returned to Somervil in silence. Hattie might have been tired from her ride, or anxious about the gathering rain clouds, but Randall suspected she was cross with him because he had not played the sociable gentleman she wished him to be. This was confirmed when they returned to the house and met Theo crossing the hall. He greeted them cheerfully.

'Ah, there you are, Harriett. Did you enjoy your ride, my love?'

'*I* did,' she replied. 'But I am going to tell Robbins to dose his master with Tincture of Spleenwort. Justin is decidedly liverish today.'

'I am decidedly *not*.'

Harriett rounded on him.

'You hardly said a word while we were out and you virtually ignored Mary. I was mortified.'

Randall ushered his indignant sister into the morning room. Theo followed and shut the door upon the wooden-faced servant in the hall.

'You deliberately set out to be odious!' fumed Harriett.

'No, I set out to enjoy the ride. It was never my intention to entertain anyone.'

'Mary is not anyone, Justin, she is my friend!'

'All the more reason not to raise false expectations, then.'

'There is very little chance of that,' snapped Harriet. 'She must think you quite the rudest man she has ever met.'

Randall frowned at her. 'My life is in the army, Harriett. Women—ladies—play no part in it and never shall. You should know better than to play matchmaker with me.'

'I was not,' she protested, not very convincingly. 'But I would have you be kind to Mary. It has not been easy, since her parents died, and although many would not approve, she is determined to earn her living in the best way she can.' His brows rose and Hattie said impulsively, 'Let me tell you about her?'

'No. Harriett, I have neither the patience nor the inclination to be kind to your charitable causes.' He paused and tried for a milder tone. 'I have deliberately not spoken of Miss Endacott to you, nor have I made any enquiries about her, because I know that should I do so, your immediate reaction would be to start planning a wedding. And in this instance you must know better than I that Miss Endacott would not be a suitable match.'

'She is no longer a part of our world, but her birth is perfectly respectable—'

'Enough!' Randall barked out the word and silence fell. He sighed, saying more gently, 'Hattie, I am off to Brussels to meet the greatest threat to this nation that we have ever faced. I have no time for dalliance.'

Theo touched his wife's arm, saying in his gentle way, 'Let him be, my love. Your brother is about to go to war, his mind will not be distracted by such frivolities.'

Randall was grateful for Theo's intervention, but his brother-in-law was not entirely correct. Randall *was* distracted by Mary Endacott. Uncomfortably so, which was why he had deliberately avoided her during their outing. There was no denying she rode well and looked extremely attractive on horseback. Her plain russet-coloured habit might be made of serviceable twill, but it did nothing to hide the curves of her body. He had been obliged to keep his eyes from her, and having spoken with her the previous evening he knew how easily she might draw him into conversation, so he had kept his distance for most of the ride.

Harriett was regarding him in reproachful silence and his conscience stirred. He would be leaving in a few days and did not wish to fall out with her.

He gave a wry smile. 'I behaved badly, Hattie, I admit it. Forgive me.'

She pursed her lips, not completely won over. Theo chuckled.

'I have never heard Randall make such a handsome admission before, my dear. You would be wise to accept it, I think.'

'Oh...oh, very well. But I hope you will be a little more courteous when the Bentincks come to drink tea with us.'

Randall said nothing, reluctant to commit himself, and when Harriett suggested they should change out of their muddied clothes he was glad to make his escape.

* * *

A night's reflection did nothing to restore Mary's peace of mind and after breaking her fast in her room she went off for a long walk, hoping to regain her equilibrium before facing her hosts. Her favoured route took her past Somervil, where she was in the habit of calling upon Harriett, but knowing that the earl was in residence she set off in the opposite direction, preferring to take the rocky path through the woods rather than risk running into him.

Her strong attraction to Lord Randall at their first meeting must have been due to the amount of wine she had consumed that night. She had not considered herself inebriated, but there was no doubt that Mr Bentinck's cellars were well stocked and the quality of the wines superb, so in all likelihood she had imbibed more than usual during the course of the evening. It was easily done, she knew, especially if one was anxious or distracted and there was no doubt that she *was* anxious, about her business, her finances and the long journey ahead of her. As for distraction, the presence of Lord Randall in the Bentincks' drawing room had certainly caught her attention.

It was not that she had thought him the best-looking man in the room; tall, lithe men with handsome faces bronzed by the sun had never attracted her before. She preferred intelligent, cultured men. Scholars. Indeed, she had always considered hawk-like features such as Lord Randall's to look a little predatory.

Nor was it his title—she despised the power that rank and wealth conferred upon a man, the inbred certainty that he might behave exactly as he wished, however badly. Perhaps the attraction was those blue eyes that seemed to burn into her. Or his deep, mellifluous voice. Whenever he spoke she was aware of its resonance and when he was addressing her it was as if he was running a feather over her skin. Even over deeply intimate places. Just the thought of it sent a delicious shiver running through her.

Perhaps she was becoming an old maid. She had observed how elderly ladies could turn positively skittish in the presence of a personable gentleman. They would simper and fawn over him in the most embarrassing way. Was that what was happening to her? She stopped, aghast at the thought. Good heavens, did she have so little self-respect that she was prepared to make a fool of herself over a handsome face? It must not be.

She pulled her pelisse a little closer and set off again, striding out purposefully along the track beside the stream. She would not allow herself to become such a figure of fun. She was an intelligent woman with more strength of character than that.

Anxiously she thought back over her ride yesterday. Thankfully she had done nothing, said nothing to show herself infatuated. Indeed, she had barely spoken to Lord Randall and when they had parted he had not rushed to help her dismount, but remained on his horse and at a distance, as if eager to get away. In fact, looking back, he had done nothing at all to win her good opinion.

'So the attraction is all on your part,' she told herself. 'And you would do well to nip it in the bud, since it can bring you nothing but trouble.'

She was so caught up in her thoughts that she barely noticed the discomfort she felt in walking until it became positively painful. Something was rubbing against her left foot with every step. Coming upon a fallen tree trunk on the edge of the water, she sat down to investigate. The cause of the pain was soon discovered, a piece of grit had lodged itself in her boot. It had not only worn a hole in her stocking but had rubbed away the soft skin at the side of her foot, which was bleeding and throbbing painfully. How she had come so far without noticing it was a mystery. She looked around to make sure she was alone then removed her ruined stocking and dipped her bleeding foot into the stream. She gasped a little as the cold water rushed over her inflamed skin but after the initial shock she found the cool stream very soothing.

While her foot was soaking she picked up her discarded footwear. The brown half-boots were almost new so she was relieved to find the soft kid bore only the slightest trace of blood on the inside. They were so comfortable she planned to wear them on the long journey home, so she was very thankful they were not ruined.

Mary pushed aside the skirts of her walking dress and began to dry her foot on one of her petticoats. It was then that she heard the unmistakable sounds of hoofbeats. Someone was approaching.

'Lord Randall!'

'Miss Endacott. Can I be of assistance?'

Mary's heart sank. Why did he have to come upon her when she was sitting with her dress pulled up over her knees? Her instinct was to shake her skirts down to cover her ankles, but after taking so much care to keep the blood from her gown it would be foolish to pretend there was nothing wrong.

'I have a cut on my foot,' she explained, trying to be calm, as if she was quite accustomed to exposing her leg to a gentleman. 'It is only a small cut, so please do not...'

Too late. He had jumped down from his horse and was coming over to her.

'Let me see it.'

'No! It is nothing, I assure you. You do not need to trouble yourself.'

He ignored her protests and dropped to his knees, taking her heel in his hand. Mary kept very still and concentrated upon her breathing, which had become very erratic.

She said, with as much dignity as she could muster, 'Thank you, my lord, but I do not wish to keep you from your ride. I am about to put on my boot—'

'Nonsense,' he said crisply. 'It is still bleeding and needs to be bound up. Allow me.'

He pulled a clean handkerchief from his pocket and shook it out. Mary wanted to protest, but somehow the words died. His touch was sure and gentle, and a pleasant lassitude stole over her as he quickly folded the handkerchief into a bandage and wrapped it around her foot.

'There, that should hold.' He jumped to his feet. 'However, your boot will not fit over it.'

'Oh.' Mary tried to drag her thoughts away from how disappointed she was that he was no longer cradling her ankle. 'Oh, well, I—'

The earl handed her the empty boot.

'I shall take you home on Pompey.'

Before she could protest he swept her up and placed her sideways on the pommel, then he himself scrambled up into the saddle. Mary felt herself blushing as he pulled her back against him.

'There,' he said. 'You are perfectly safe.'

Safe in the sense that his arms were either side

of her and she could not fall off, but she had never been so close to a man before, apart from her father, when she had been a little girl and he had pulled her up on to his knee. Now she felt the earl's hard thighs pressing against her. She sat bolt upright, clutching at her empty boot and fighting the temptation to lean back and rest her head against his coat. As they rode off she noted that her bloodied stocking was still lying beside the stream. She said nothing. It was ruined, so there was no point in going back for it.

It was strange, thought Mary. Everything seemed much more intense than when she had been walking this same path only minutes earlier. Then she had barely noticed the bluebells and wild garlic that carpeted the ground, now the sight and the smell of them filled her senses. The sun shone more brightly through the budding trees and the birdsong was even louder and more joyous. It made her think of spring, and poetry. And love. She pushed the thought aside. She despised such sentimentality.

The earl made no effort to converse, but neither did he squeeze or fondle her. She began to relax.

'I suppose I must thank you, sir, for rescuing me. It would have been a long walk back.'

'I would do the same for any lame creature. Although if it was Pompey who had lost a shoe I should be obliged to walk with him rather than ride.'

She said unsteadily, 'Are—are you comparing me to your *horse*, Lord Randall?'

'Pompey is very valuable, Miss Endacott.'

He sounded perfectly serious and she stole a glance up at him. He was staring ahead, his countenance sombre but she had the distinct feeling that he was laughing at her. As if aware of her regard he looked down and she saw the glimmer of a smile in the depths of his blue eyes, like a sudden hint of gold at the bottom of a deep pool.

She dragged her eyes away. It could not be. This was Lord Randall, the stern soldier, a man completely without humour, Hattie had said so. But that look unsettled her.

'If you put me down here, sir, there is a little gate in the palings that leads directly into the Bentincks' garden. I need not trouble you to take me any further.'

'It is no trouble, Miss Endacott. Pompey can easily take the extra weight, I assure you.'

Mary discovered that it was possible to want to laugh and to be angry with someone at the same time. She tried her firmest voice.

'I think I must insist, my lord.'

'But the gates are in sight. I shall deliver you to the door.'

Mary looked down. Pompey was a very big

horse and it was a long way to jump. That is, if the earl did not tighten his arms and prevent her from escaping.

She said angrily, 'Lord Randall, I find you odiously autocratic.'

'And I find you annoyingly independent.'

She put up her head.

'I am very proud of my independence,' she told him. 'I own my own house and my establishment is much sought after. It is patronised by some of the foremost names in the land.'

'I am sure it is. But none of that is going to make me put you down so you can hobble back to the Bentincks and risk doing more damage to your foot.'

She ground her teeth.

'I think it fortunate that you are a bachelor, sir. Your manners would not endear you to any woman.'

'Then we are in accord, Miss Endacott. That is the very reason I remain single.'

Mary was so surprised by his answer she could think of nothing to say. Thankfully they were almost at the door, where her cousin was waiting for them.

'I saw you from the drawing-room window,' Mrs Bentinck declared. 'What on earth has happened?'

'Miss Endacott has injured her foot.' The earl

dismounted and lifted Mary into his arms, depositing her neatly on the doorstep. 'Since she could not fit her boot over the bandage I brought her home. It is nothing to be anxious about, ma'am. Once the foot is bathed in salt water and a sticking plaster applied she will be able to walk on it again.'

'Yes, yes, of course.' Mrs Bentinck put her arm about Mary, saying in a distracted way, 'But Mrs Graveney invited us all to take tea with her this afternoon at Somervil House.'

'There is no reason why you and Mr Bentinck cannot come,' he replied. 'Although I am sure my sister will understand if Miss Endacott feels the need to lie upon her bed for the rest of the day.'

The earl gave them a brief nod and nimbly remounted his horse, riding off without a backward glance. Mary's hands clenched around the hapless boot and she longed to hurl it after his retreating form. As if she was such a weakling that she must needs take to her bed over such a trifle.

Randall resisted the urge to look back. He felt sure that Mary would be looking daggers at him. He felt a smile tugging at his mouth: what was it about the woman that made him want to tease her? He rarely teased anyone. It was childish, but Mary Endacott made him feel like a callow youth again. Perhaps it was her independence, her determination not to seek his good opinion. That was unusual—he was far more used to females using every trick they could to attract him. She was the only woman he had met who considered he was right to remain a bachelor, although she could not know the true reason he would never marry.

After watching his mother lose her bloom while the old earl amused himself with a succession of mistresses, as well as the women at Chalfont Magna, Randall was determined never to inflict such a life on any woman. He had grown up with the conviction that one should marry for love, though heaven knew where that sentiment originated. But how could he insist that his wife should love him when he could not guarantee to be faithful to her? Like father, like son. Had he not proved, years ago, how alike they were? No. he would remain a soldier. That was a life he understood, a life he could control.

Mary pulled a clean silk stocking carefully over the sticking plaster on her foot. It barely hurt at all now, but she had decided she would not go to Somervil that afternoon. She had preparations to make before her departure, she did not have time for such a frivolous occupation as tea drinking. Harriett would understand.

And you will not have to see Lord Randall again.

'All the better,' she said aloud.

It will demonstrate to the world that you are the weaker sex.

'It will demonstrate that I have the intelligence not to place myself in a position of danger.'

Danger? What danger can there be from a man who barely notices you?

She fluttered her hand, as if to bat away the unwelcome arguments that revolved in her head.

Lord Randall is no threat, and you will be leaving soon. There is no reason at all to avoid him. Unless you are afraid.

'Of course I am not afraid,' she told herself crossly.

But the thought rankled. Papa had brought her up to fear nothing and question everything. There was a logical explanation for all things, he had said. Face your demons and you will understand them. And Lord Randall could hardly be called a demon. Proud, yes. Autocratic, definitely, and used to being obeyed, but no demon.

She rose and shook out her skirts. She would go with the Bentincks this afternoon and prove to herself that there was nothing remotely dangerous in taking tea at Somervil House.

Harriett came forward as they were shown into the drawing room, saying cheerfully, 'I almost suggested we should put a table on the terrace, it is so warm. But, Mary, what is this Randall tells me, you have hurt your foot?'

'It is the veriest scratch,' she replied, 'As you see I am perfectly able to walk upon it.'

Mr Graveney and Lord Randall were standing together by the window and Mary dipped a curtsy to them both before choosing to sit down in a chair on the far side of the room. She had hoped that in his sister's house the earl might look a little less imposing, but no. His upright bearing and long-limbed figure were even more noticeable next to portly Mr Graveney. Just looking at the earl made her mouth go dry. He looked so solid and dependable, and Mary thought suddenly how comfortable it would be to have someone she could lean upon.

'That would be lovely, would it not, Mary?'

Mrs Bentinck was handing her a cup of tea.

'I beg your pardon,' she stammered. 'My thoughts were miles away.'

'Mrs Graveney was suggesting we should take a walk later, to see how they have landscaped the gardens.'

'Yes, an excellent idea,' Mary concurred. She really must concentrate.

'Unless you would rather sit here and rest your foot,' suggested Harriett. 'Randall could keep you company.'

'No, no, I am perfectly well, thank you,' Mary

replied hastily. 'And I would very much like to see your gardens before I leave.'

'Yes, they have turned out very well, I think,' said Mr Graveney. 'Although they are nothing to the grounds of Chalfont Abbey, Lord Randall's country seat.'

'I can take no credit for that. My military duties do not allow me much time at the Abbey, but my mother keeps everything in excellent order.'

Mr Bentinck turned to the earl.

'I trust, my lord, that you did not suffer overmuch from being thrust into the lion's den the other night?'

'Not at all, sir.'

Harriett laughed.

'My brother is being polite, Mr Bentinck. He thinks many of your guests would be improved by a spell in the military.'

'And so they would,' agreed Mrs Bentinck, chuckling. 'Or even if they had to work for their living, as poor Mary is obliged to do, and to suffer the indignity of being shunned in polite society by those who are only too willing to use her services. Is that not so, my dear?'

'Oh, it is not so bad, really.'

Randall saw the telltale blush stealing into Mary's cheek as she murmured her reply and was glad for her sake when Bentinck took the discussion in a different direction.

It was no wonder she should look embarrassed. He glanced at his sister; she was continuing to pour tea as if nothing was amiss at all. He felt his jaw set hard in disapproval. Graveney had led his sister too far down the path of radicalism for his liking, but he was a guest in the fellow's house, he could hardly voice his disapproval now.

When they had finished drinking their tea and the idea of a walk was again mooted he decided to make his excuses and withdraw. Unfortunately Hattie had other ideas.

'Oh, but you cannot disappear now, Randall. Theo wants to show Mr Bentinck the new book he has purchased, and since you saw it when you returned from your ride this morning you must escort us.' She took his arm. 'Come along, a little fresh air will soon put that gloomy look of yours to flight!'

Harriett shepherded the ladies into the hall, saying as they put on their bonnets, 'I intended to show Mary the gardens when she arrived last week, but the weather has been so inclement I have not yet done so. Do not worry, though, the new gravel paths will make it perfectly dry underfoot.'

The paths were indeed dry, but Randall soon discovered that they were not wide enough for them all to walk together. Harriett took Mrs

Bentinck's arm and moved ahead, leaving him no option but to walk beside Mary Endacott.

'I doubt this is how you intended to spend your afternoon,' she remarked. 'If you have business elsewhere I do not mind walking alone.'

'I am perfectly happy to escort you.' He held out his arm to her. 'Besides, to do anything else would incur my sister's wrath.'

She chuckled at that.

'I cannot imagine that would worry you over-much.'

'You were at school with Harriett, Miss Endacott. You know that she is not one to be gain-said. All the Latymors are strong-willed, except my youngest sister, Sarah. She is very biddable.'

'Overwhelmed by the rest of you, no doubt.'

'Very likely. She is certainly unlike her twin, Gideon. He is a hothead.'

They strolled on, mainly in silence, but occa-sionally stopping to admire the new plantings and statuary that had been installed in the gardens. Randall found himself relaxing and enjoying the afternoon sunshine. He glanced down at the si-lent figure beside him. Mary looked completely at ease and he thought how comfortable it was to have a woman on his arm who did not consider it necessary to be chattering all the time. She was just the right height, too, her head no higher than his shoulder. They passed the new rose garden with its arbour at the far end. He imagined sitting beside her on the bench when the roses were in bloom and filling the air with their heavy scent. She might rest her head on his shoulder then. And if the air should be a little chill he might put his arm around her and rest his cheek against those dusky curls…

Confound it, man, you need to stop this, now!

'I beg your pardon, my lord, did you say something?'

She turned her face up to him, delicate brows raised, green eyes enquiring. Randall felt a sudden impulse to pull her close and plant a kiss on those full, red lips. The rush of desire that fired his blood surprised him and he looked away quickly, clearing his throat as he sought for words.

'You are returning to your, ah, business very soon, I believe.'

'Yes, my lord. On Saturday.'

He kept his eyes fixed ahead, noting idly that they had fallen some way behind his sister and Mrs Bentinck.

'And will you be sorry to leave?'

'Of course. The Bentincks are not only relatives but very old friends and I allowed myself this short holiday after completing my trip to Cuckfield. My father left certain…affairs outstanding there when he died just over a year ago and I have now resolved them.' She added, after a brief pause, 'Debts, my lord.'

'Ah, I see.'

'I doubt it.'

'Is that why you are obliged to, er, earn your living, to pay off his debts?'

She surprised him by laughing at that.

'Not at all, I enjoy what I do, my lord. I hope you will not think me boastful if I say I have a talent for it. I am an independent woman, beholden to no one. In fact, I shall be glad to get back to work. I could not be happy with a life of idleness.'

'Nor I.'

'Then we are agreed upon something.' She smiled up at him, as if relieved at the thought.

A mood of recklessness swept through Randall.

'Why wait?'

'My lord?'

They had reached a crossing in the path and with his superior height Randall could see over the surrounding hedge. Harriett and her companion were now making their way back through the box garden and towards the house. He led Mary into the shrubbery.

'If you wish to *work*, as you call it, then you should do so.'

'I do not think I understand you, Lord Randall.'

She stopped and turned to look up at him, still smiling, but with a faint crease between her brows. Unable to resist he put his fingers beneath her chin, tilting it up as he lowered his head and kissed her.

Mary was so surprised she could not move. Then, as his mouth worked its magic, she did not wish to do so. When he put his arms around her she leaned into him, kissing him back as if it was the most natural thing in the world. As if she had been waiting her whole life for this moment.

This reaction shocked Mary almost as much as his kiss, and when he raised his head she made no attempt to free herself, but laid her head against his chest, listening to the thud, thud of his heart. She was dazed, unable to understand what had occurred. Lord Randall, the taciturn, unromantic, unsociable earl, had kissed her. *Her*: plain, sensible Mary Endacott!

'We have a couple of days before we must part,' he said, his mouth against her hair. 'We should make use of them. We must be discreet, of course. However free-thinking the Bentincks might be, I cannot allow my sister to know what is going on.'

Mary's thoughts were still in chaos, her body trembling with the shock of his kiss, but even so she was aware that his words did not make sense. She put her hands against his chest and pushed herself away until she could look up at him.

'What has this to do with my work?'

He was gazing down at her and there was no mistaking the look in his eyes, fierce desire that sent the hot blood racing through her limbs and made her aware of the ache pooling deep in her body, at the hinge of her thighs. If she had not been clutching at his coat she thought her legs might well have given way as that beautiful deep voice caressed her.

'Everything. Let us understand this from the outset; it has always been my objective never to raise false hopes in any woman's breast. I take my pleasures and I pay for them—and give pleasure in return, I hope.'

Those smooth, measured tones stroked her skin like velvet. She was in his arms, her lips were still burning with the memory of his mouth upon hers and at first she did not comprehend his words. But as their meaning filtered through the haze of well-being that his kiss had engendered, her euphoria began to ebb away.

'You, you wish us to be…' She swallowed. 'To be *lovers*?'

Could she do it? Suddenly elation was replaced by uncertainty. She had discussed the possibility with her radical friends, but only as a concept, a brave and radical step that would fly in the face of convention. And in all her thoughts and discussions, her ideal man was one she had known for a long time, a trusted friend and companion, not a soldier whom she had met only days ago.

'If that is the word you wish to put to it, yes,' said Randall. 'It will be business for you, but very lucrative, for I intend to be generous.'

Mary blinked. No endearments, no promises. The earl talked of business and suddenly his meaning became all too clear. She freed herself from his arms.

'You...you think I am a—that I—' Her hands went to her cheeks. 'You think I would *sell* myself for money?'

There was no mistaking the bewilderment in his eyes. It was clear that was exactly what he thought. Disappointment, bitter as gall, swept through her.

'Is that not the case?' he said. 'You told me you were in trade, spoke of your ladies, but perhaps since you are so successful you yourself no longer partake—'

'P-partake?' she stuttered. 'Oh, good heavens, this is dreadful!'

She turned away, taking a few agitated steps along the path before wheeling around again. 'I am an *educationalist*, Lord Randall. I run a school for young ladies!'

'What?'

If she had not been so overwrought, Lord Randall's surprise and consternation would have amused her, but she had never felt less like laughing in her life. In fact, she felt very much like weeping. Her hands crept to her cheeks again.

'I see how it came about,' she went on, almost to herself. 'The radical talk, the company Mr and Mrs Bentinck had invited to their house—'

'Not to mention your own teasing ways, madam,' he added in a tight voice. 'You said yourself you were trying to be outrageous.'

'Yes, I know I set out to tease you, but when I spoke of earning my living I never thought that you would assume—' She gasped. 'Good heavens, that is disgraceful! Did you suppose that the Bentincks, that *your own sister*, would continue to acknowledge me if that were the case?'

A dull colour had crept into his lean cheek, but whether it was anger or embarrassment she did not know.

He said, his tone harsh, his words clipped, 'Harriett warned me I would be shocked by the company. You yourself told me you did not believe in marriage.'

'And in an effort to prove yourself *unshockable* you thought the very worst of me. You are correct, I do not believe in marriage. I was brought up to believe in a free union of minds, of hearts. A union of *love*, my lord, not prostitution!'

He said stiffly. 'It was an error, but a reasonable one, given the circumstances.'

'The circumstances?'

'Of course,' he retorted. 'Your whole demeanour when you told me of your business, as if it were something quite shocking, and you made a point of informing me that you had no reputation. What else was I to think? Yes, quite reasonable, I would say.'

Mary gasped in outrage.

'Quite *unreasonable*, my lord.' Her lip curled. 'But you are an earl. Perhaps you are in the habit of propositioning any lady who takes your fancy?'

'Certainly not, but with your radical views you should appreciate my honesty. I would rather take my pleasures with a woman who understands there can be no possibility of marriage. I am no saint, Miss Endacott. There are many ladies of my own set, married ladies whose husbands go their own way and leave their wives to find pleasure elsewhere. I have enjoyed several liaisons of that sort in the past, but I make no secret of the fact that I consort with women of a more dubious reputation occasionally.'

'And you pay them well for the privilege. Contemptible.'

'Is it contemptible for two adults to enter into an agreement that gives them both satisfaction?' His eyes narrowed and for an instant she saw a glint of something dangerous in their depths. 'And

I assure you the ladies are *always* satisfied, Miss Endacott.'

Confusion fluttered in Mary's breast. Instead of begging her pardon he was boasting of his prowess and the worst thing was the way her body responded to his words, to that wicked light in his eyes. She wanted to throw herself into his arms, to beg him to kiss her again and show her just how satisfying his lovemaking could be.

She felt the rage boiling up inside her. How dared he do this to her? She was furious with him and with herself for allowing him to engender such emotional turmoil in her. Mary took a step away from him, saying in a voice that was not quite steady, 'Excuse me; we can have nothing more to say to one another.'

Fighting back angry tears, she hurried out of the shrubbery. The scrunch of footsteps behind her told her that the earl was following and she quickened her pace until she was almost running.

'Wait—Mary—Miss Endacott. Please!' He caught her arm, forcing her to stop. 'If you return to the house in such distress it will not go unnoticed. My sister would not rest until she had the truth from you.'

'I am not distressed,' she flung at him. 'I am furious!'

He pulled a handkerchief from his pocket and held it out.

She looked at it for a moment, wanting to consign it and its owner to Hades, but her eyes were wet and it would be difficult to remain dignified with a streaming nose. She took the proffered handkerchief and proceeded to dry her face.

The fine linen was freshly laundered, but mixed in with the clean smell of soap was a hint of spices, the same that had filled her senses while he was kissing her. Even now the memory of it made her ache with longing to be in his arms again. To repeat the experience. Heavens, how could she feel this way when he had treated her in such a fashion? Yet a tiny whisper of conscience could not be silenced. She had tried to shock him, but she had wanted him to think her a radical, not a, a...

'You have good reason to be angry,' he said quietly. 'I have offered you a gross insult and I would not blame you for wishing to make my abominable behaviour known to the world. It is no more than I deserve, but to do so would reflect badly upon others. Upon my sister and your cousin, and I do not think you would want that.'

'It was not only *your* behaviour that was at fault,' she muttered, incurably truthful. 'I have not acted with proper decorum and constraint, where you are concerned.'

She remembered when he had come upon her by the stream, her skirts pulled up around her knees. The image filled her mind, clear as a painting. Might he not think she had been deliberately leading him on?

'What did you do, apart from take pity on a stranger and introduce yourself to me at the Bentincks?'

So he had not misinterpreted their meeting by the stream. Alongside her relief another emotion bubbled up. Her legs from knee to toe had been on plain view. A young man had once praised her neat ankles and now she felt a tinge of disappointment that the earl had not even noticed them.

'No...' he shook his head '...I have repaid your kindness very ill, but I do not want to make a bad situation any worse by subjecting you to questions you would rather not answer and possibly causing a rift between Hattie and her friends.'

'Much as it pains me to admit it, you are right,' she said bitterly, 'I would not want anyone else to know of this.' She took a few deep breaths and said coldly, 'I am better now. Let us return to the house. We will forget this conversation ever took place, if you please.'

'As you wish.' He stepped aside. 'Shall we go?'

They set off, keeping a space between them, as befitted distant acquaintances.

I might have been his mistress. I might have shared his bed.

Mary buried the thought. A free union, without

marriage, to a man she truly loved and respected, that was something she might one day contemplate, but not a brief coupling with someone who was almost a stranger. She had not been prepared for how strong a lustful attraction could be. Her response to the feel of his lips on hers, the instinct to return his kiss, to mould herself to his body, that had shocked and surprised her, but Mary told herself now to put aside her distress and embarrassment. Such an experience would help her to be a better mentor to her pupils.

The gardens seemed to go on forever. Had they really walked so far? At last they reached the house. Lord Randall opened the door for Mary to enter. She dared not look up at him, but her eyes strayed to his body as she passed, remembering how she had laid her head against that superbly tailored coat, taken in the detail of each minute stitch, the fine embroidery on his waistcoat, the intricate folds of his neckcloth. The shameful thing was she wanted it all to happen again.

No, Mary, stop it!

'I am leaving the day after tomorrow,' he informed her, his steady voice indicating that his thoughts at least had moved on. 'I shall take my leave of Mr and Mrs Bentinck now, so there will be no need for us to see each other again.'

'None at all,' she replied. 'I shall make sure *both* your handkerchiefs are laundered and returned to you by then.' She preceded him into the drawing room. She kept her head up, hoping her face showed no signs of the turmoil within. Only a little longer and her ordeal would be over.

'So there you are. I vow I was about to send a search party into the shrubbery!' Harriett's knowing glance brought the colour flooding back to Mary's cheeks.

She is teasing. She cannot know anything.

'Quite unnecessary,' Lord Randall responded coolly and Mary felt a sudden urge to laugh. His tone held the merest hint of disapproval for his sister's levity, as if he was affronted she should even consider he might be dallying in the gardens. 'We stopped to admire the *rhododendron ponticum* on the west terrace.'

'Yes, yes, it has taken very well, has it not? I sent to Hackney for it, to Mr Loddiges's nursery.' Mr Graveney chattered on, delighted to discover the earl shared his interest in horticulture.

Mary took her seat beside Harriett, relieved that the conversation had moved on, although her mind was still too disordered for her to take part. She almost jumped when Harriett reached out and took her hand.

'It has been so good to see you again, Mary, are you sure it is necessary for you to leave on Saturday?'

'Imperative, I assure you,' she responded. 'My

assistants at the school are very good, but they write to tell me there is a great deal of activity in Brussels—'

Lord Randall cut in. 'I did not know your school was in Brussels.'

She managed to look him in the eye, albeit briefly.

'Because I did not mention it, my lord.'

'No.' The earl turned a frowning look upon his sister. 'Odd that Harriett should not mention it, either.'

'Oh, well, it slipped my mind, Brother, but it is a most fortuitous circumstance for you, Mary.'

Mary shook her head. 'I do not see…'

'While you were in the gardens we came up with the most perfect plan.' Harriett continued as if she had not spoken. 'Mrs Bentinck and I agreed that we should feel so much happier to know you were not making that long journey alone, Mary. So Randall shall escort you!'

Chapter Three

'No!'

'Impossible!' Randall's curt exclamation was as instant as Mary's faint denial. He glowered at his sister. 'Impossible,' he said again. 'I depart on Friday and will be travelling in haste.'

'No, how can that be so when you have two carriages with you?'

'But I shall be riding.'

'I am sure Mary will not object to being alone in your carriage.'

'But I do object,' put in Mary, her colour considerably heightened. 'I could not possibly impose upon Lord Randall.'

'Now it is not like you to be missish for the sake of it,' said Mr Bentinck. 'What could be better than to have his lordship escort you to Brussels? It means you will have to leave a day earlier, of course, but Mrs Graveney has already told us that the earl has his own private yacht at Folkestone.

So much more comfortable than taking the packet from Dover, what?'

'I do not want to give up my last day with you,' replied Mary firmly.

Randall glared at his sister, willing her not to continue with this farce. She ignored him.

'That will be a wrench, of course, Mary, but I am sure Mr and Mrs Bentinck would be much happier to know you have an escort.'

'I do not *need* an escort, Harriett, I am an independent woman.'

'Of course you are, but you are also a sensible one, and with Wellington gathering so many troops together you may find it difficult to get a passage from Dover, not to mention the trouble you might experience once you reach the Continent. And it is not as if Randall does not have room for you,' Harriett continued, breaching her brother's next line of defence. 'I saw the two carriages when they arrived; there is plenty of space for you and your baggage. Well, Justin, what do you say?'

Randall surveyed the assembled company. What could he say? To refuse Mary his escort would be extremely uncivil and against his own code of honour. That she was equally unhappy with the situation was evident. He managed a stiff bow.

'If Miss Endacott would accept a place in my carriage, I would be only too delighted to escort her to Brussels.'

* * *

Mary cast a fulminating glance at the earl. She had been hoping he would provide some incontestable excuse why he could not take her up. If she was to refuse his offer now her cousin would be sure to ask why, and Harriett, too, would not rest until she had uncovered the true reason.

Mr Graveney broke the tense silence with a little laugh.

'Poor Miss Endacott. It goes against the grain, I am sure, to be beholden to any man, does it not? And an earl, at that. I am sure you would much rather make your own way to Brussels.'

'I would indeed.'

'But my wife is quite right, my dear. With the current unrest in Europe you would be much safer travelling under escort and there could be none better than Lord Randall. We would all of us sleep easier in our beds to know you were with him.'

'It is best to give in,' said Harriett cheerfully. 'Remember the Laytmor motto, Mary, *semper laurifer.* We always succeed. You cannot hold out against us.'

Mary bit her lip. Did she have any choice?

'Miss Endacott,' Lord Randall addressed her. 'I appreciate that we have not long been acquainted and I am aware that our opinions are very different. However, they are right. There is danger for any young lady travelling alone. If you would honour me with your company for this journey, you will be treated with every respect and courtesy. You have my word on that.'

Mary knew he was referring to what had occurred in the gardens, he was telling her she could trust him. There was sincerity in his eyes, but more than that, there was understanding in their blue depths. She nodded.

'Then I accept your offer, my lord. Thank you.'

A sudden murmur went about the room, as if everyone had been holding their breath waiting for her answer. Harriett clapped her hands.

'Then it is settled. Randall shall take you with him, Mary. He travels with quite an entourage, you know—two carriages, his valet and groom—I am sure that it will be the most enjoyable journey you have ever undertaken.'

Harriett's words came back to Mary as she stepped into Lord Randall's elegant travelling chaise early on Friday morning. The carriage was well sprung, the seat and backrest thickly padded: physically she was assured of every comfort, she had no doubt, but after what had occurred, how could she be in the earl's company without feeling some constraint? Her only consolation was that Lord Randall was riding, so she was relieved the necessity of conversing with him.

They set off at a frantic pace, the stops were

short with barely time for Mary to drink the proffered coffee and nibble at a biscuit, but when the earl politely asked her if she would like more time she declined.

'I was warned you travel at breakneck speed, my lord,' she said as he accompanied her back to the carriage. 'I am prepared for a little discomfort.'

'I need to join my men as soon as possible. I have stayed too long in England.'

His cold tone vexed her and she retorted sharply, 'Then pray, sir, do not mind me. I shall not hold you up.'

'No, I do not intend that you shall.'

'I expect no quarter from you,' she told him bitterly.

'Then you will not be disappointed.'

Biting her lip, Mary climbed into the carriage without another word and the door was closed behind her. Insufferable man, he seemed determined to annoy her. But as she settled back in his luxurious carriage she realised that she might be angry with him, but at least she was no longer embarrassed in his company.

The carriage door was wrenched open again and Lord Randall's frame filled the opening.

'Miss Endacott, we have a long journey ahead of us. Neither of us wanted to be in this situation, but it will be best if we remain civil to one another.' His blue eyes bored into her and she felt compelled to respond.

'You are quite right, my lord.'

'I am not accustomed to looking out for anyone else when I travel. If there is anything you need during our journey, then you will tell me, if you please. I do not wish you to be uncomfortable.'

'Thank you, I will remember that.'

With a nod the earl closed the door again and Mary sank back against the squabs. His speech had surprised her. She did not doubt he was sincere and a little smile tugged at her mouth. How infuriating of him to offer her that olive branch just when she had made up her mind that he was insufferably high-handed.

They reached Folkestone in good time for dinner. The landlord of the inn did not blink an eye when Lord Randall announced he would require another bedchamber for Miss Endacott. If he thought it odd that a single lady should be travelling alone with the earl, without even a maid to give her countenance, he did not show it as he escorted them to a private parlour.

'No doubt, Miss Endacott, you will wish to rest and refresh yourself before we eat.' Lord Randall dragged off his gloves and took out his watch. 'Shall we say an hour?'

Mary inclined her head. 'That will be more than sufficient for me, sir.'

'Very well.' His cool, aristocratic gaze moved to the landlord, who bowed low.

'Dinner in an hour, my lord.'

Mary followed a serving maid to her bedchamber. Lord Randall had barely looked at her since handing her down from the carriage. It was possible he was embarrassed in her company, but she was beginning to suspect that this scant courtesy and abrupt manner was habitual. As soon as she was alone she washed her face and hands, then took out her hairbrush and began to brush out the tangles that a day's travel had introduced into her hair.

Well, he had warned her, she should not complain. And besides, what was there to complain of? He had told her she only had to speak out if there was anything she required to make her journey more comfortable. She had been brought up to believe herself the equal of any man, so why should she object if she received no special treatment from the earl while they were travelling?

Mary paused, the brush strokes slowing. Strange that Lord Randall should be so lacking in social graces, when his father had been such a libertine. Perhaps his years of soldiering had coarsened him. Immediately she rejected the idea. Lord Randall's manners were not coarse, it was merely that he did not flatter and cajole. She realised she did not mind his abrupt tone, in fact, she found it refreshing. Their walk in the gardens at Somervil had been perfectly amicable, until the moment he had made his disgraceful suggestion. Yet had she behaved much better? Had she not revelled in his kiss, in the feel of his arms about her?

A distant clock chimed, her hour was nearly up. Hurriedly, she re-pinned her hair. She would have to sit through dinner alone with the earl, and it would be very uncomfortable for them both if she showed embarrassment in his company. No, if he could cope with the situation, then so could she.

'How is your room?'

'Very comfortable, my lord, thank you.'

I can do this; we only have to remain polite to one another.

Mary walked to the table, which was already spread with a tempting array of dishes. The earl stood behind her, holding her chair. She could not see his face, but could feel his presence like a cloud hovering around her and she did not know if she preferred that or when he took his seat across the table and she was subject to his all-too-perceptive gaze. To avoid it, she surveyed the food on offer.

'Are we wise to eat dinner, my lord, if we are sailing at midnight?'

'Are you a poor sailor, Miss Endacott?'

At least he was not using her first name, even though the servants had departed. She tried to relax. He had given her his word he would treat her with respect.

'My experiences so far have been very good, but I have not yet been aboard ship during a storm.'

She raised her head, listening to the wind buffeting the windows. The earl merely shrugged.

'There is a light breeze blowing, nothing more serious. I spoke to my captain earlier and he is confident we will make a speedy crossing.' He held up one of the dishes. 'Come, try the chicken, it is excellent. And you will feel much better for a good meal, I promise you.'

Mary was not sure she believed him, but she took some chicken and added a little rice and vegetables from the selection before her.

The meal proceeded comfortably enough; they kept the conversation to unexceptional topics and Mary's anxiety eased. She was able to enjoy her meal and the wine that accompanied it, so that by the time the covers were removed and a small dish of sweetmeats placed upon the table she felt quite comfortable in the earl's company.

'You said experiences, Miss Endacott. Have you made many crossings?' he asked, pushing the little dish towards her.

'No, this will be my third.'

'And how long have you lived abroad?'

'About seven years. I joined my parents in Brussels when I left Miss Burchell's school.'

'But your family was originally from England?'

'Yes. Papa went abroad in the short-lived peace of Amiens. He had friends in Brussels, so he decided to settle there rather than in France.'

'Ah. His radical ideas drew unwelcome attention in this country, I suppose.'

Lord Randall's tone held no hint of condemnation and she answered with more frankness than she was wont to show to any but close friends.

'Yes. His support for the revolutionary government in France brought him a notoriety he did not deserve. He was outspoken, yes, he supported the new government and the redistribution of wealth, but when he realised that democracy, true democracy, was being crushed in a reign of terror he spoke out against it, just as vehemently. Alas, it was too late, his name was too closely associated with the revolution. It was very hard on Mama, especially after...'

'After what, Miss Endacott?'

She hesitated and forced herself to speak.

'My sister died that same year.'

'That must have been very hard for you.'

'It was.' She touched her napkin to her lips,

avoiding his eyes. That subject was too painful to dwell upon, even after all these years. 'My father had run up considerable debts, too, and the only way to avoid debtors' prison was to flee the country. He and Mama set up a girls' academy in Brussels, based upon the precepts of Mary Wollstonecraft, but it was not a success.' Talking of the school was safer ground. She even managed a wry smile. 'The *Bruxelloise* were no more progressive in their thinking than the English. Very few wanted to give their daughters an education that would rival or even surpass that of their sons, so Papa was obliged to abandon his high ideals and include more dancing and pianoforte lessons, at the expense of Latin and Greek. When I joined them I became a teacher at the school.'

'Really? But you could not have been more than a child yourself.'

'I was seventeen. Very well qualified to teach the younger ones, I assure you. Your sister was at the same school, my lord, you must be aware that Miss Burchell's establishment gave us an excellent education.'

'It gave Harriett a lot of dangerously progressive ideas,' he retorted.

Mary laughed. 'Teaching women to think for themselves is not dangerously progressive, Lord Randall.'

The look he gave her indicated that he disagreed.

'And you took over the school when your father died?'

'Yes. He had insisted I continue my studies when I joined him, so I was able to teach the older girls, too, by then.'

'When did he die?'

'Four years ago. My mother had passed on twelve months earlier, so I was alone. I took control—there was nothing else to be done. If I had sold the school there would not have been enough funds to support me for very long.'

'Could you not have considered marriage?'

Her brows went up. She was comfortable enough now in his presence to challenge him.

'You would advocate wedlock, when you will not contemplate it for yourself? That is rather hypocritical, my lord.'

'Not at all. I freely admit that marriages can be successful, if one is fortunate. Hattie and her husband, for example, are very happy together.'

'I am sure that is not merely a matter of chance, my lord. As with anything that is worth having, a happy marriage has to be worked at, by both parties.'

'I am sure you are right,' he conceded. He rested his elbows on the table and leaned forward. 'But if not wedlock, was there no man amongst your radical acquaintances who would support you?'

She shook her head.

'There has never been anyone for whom I have felt strongly enough to give up my independence.'

'No one? Not even for a, er, temporary liaison?'

'Do you mean have I had a lover?' She met his eye without flinching. 'Not one, Lord Randall.'

If she had expected to embarrass him into an apology, she did not succeed. He merely held her gaze.

'No. He would have to be a very special man to win you, Mary Endacott.'

The compliment was unexpected and her cheeks flamed. Quickly she looked away, concentrating on choosing another little treat from the dish of sweetmeats while he continued as if he had said nothing amiss.

'So you became a schoolmistress. It could not have been easy for a young lady on her own.'

'It was challenging, certainly, but I had been involved in running the school since I arrived in Brussels, so I knew what was required. I abandoned the last vestiges of the radical education Papa had envisaged for his pupils and concentrated upon providing an excellent education for young ladies of refinement. Besides English, of course, and arithmetic, we teach geography, natural history, French and Italian, dancing classes, singing, harp and pianoforte. I was obliged to include some religious instruction, although it went sadly against the grain, but I salve my conscience by also teaching Latin and Greek, natural philosophy and Classics to the older children.

'Word spread and the school began to grow, slowly. The Endacott Academy for Young Ladies is now one of the foremost establishments in Brussels, and not only for the *Bruxelloise*. I have a large number of English pupils, too.' She smiled. 'My father was not the only one whose financial situation made it expedient to leave England. However, I insist that fees are paid in advance.'

'I admire your spirit. It takes courage and determination to make a success of such a venture.'

'It was certainly hard work, but it is easier now. I have good staff working for me.' She smiled. 'What have I said? Why do you look at me in that way?'

'I beg your pardon. I was searching for a word to describe you.'

She sat back, raising her hands in mock alarm.

'Obstinate?' she asked him. 'Brazen? Infuriating?'

He shook his head. 'No. Indomitable.'

Shock rattled through Mary. Was the earl paying her another compliment? She looked down at the table, unable to trust her voice and in truth not knowing what to say. Just when she thought she could be comfortable in his company he rocked her off balance. She thought again of the Latymor motto. *Semper laurifer*. Hattie had said it meant *always succeed*. Mary preferred to translate it as *we never fail*. To surprise.

From the corner of her eye she saw Lord Randall take out his pocket watch.

'I have sent the carriages and the baggage on ahead to be loaded on to the yacht,' he said brusquely. 'We can walk to the harbour from here and since we have more than an hour before we need to board I suggest we go to bed.' When she recoiled he gave an impatient sigh. 'Not *together*, madam. You claim to be an intelligent woman, so please use that brain of yours.'

'I was, my lord. I was remembering what you proposed to me!'

'When I made you that offer I was under a misapprehension. Since then I have endeavoured to treat you with respect. But I am a soldier, Miss Endacott. I speak plainly and if that offends your sensibilities then I am sorry for it, but you'll get no soft words from me.'

'No,' she muttered, 'I am beginning to realise that.' She rose. 'But you are right, my lord. An hour's rest now will stand me in good stead for the crossing, since I may not be able to sleep once we are at sea.'

She left the room with her head held high, but

she had the uneasy suspicion that Lord Randall would consider she had flounced out. *Semper laurifer.* Never fail. To infuriate!

When they left the inn Mary was pleased to note that the wind had dropped a little and a good moon sailed high above them, bathing everything in a silvery light. The harbour was bustling with activity and noisy with boisterous male voices. She was glad of the earl's arm as they made their way along the quay to a sleek, tall-masted ship, its outline black against the night sky. Lord Randall guided her up the narrow gangplank to the deck, where the captain was waiting.

'Welcome aboard, sir. I have had a cabin prepared for the lady, as you instructed. Jack will show you the way now, miss, if you'd like to follow him.'

They had moved across to a large opening in the deck of the yacht and Mary stopped.

'Oh, I...' Her words trailed off as she saw the cabin boy disappear down the ladder-like steps into a dark void.

'Allow me.'

Before she could protest Lord Randall had scooped her up and thrown her across his shoulder. The action was so unexpected that words failed her. Keeping one arm wrapped about her thighs, he made his way one-handed down the steps. Her cheeks were scalding as he set her on her feet and she was thankful that it was too dark for the waiting cabin boy to see her embarrassment. She was thankful, too, that she could not see his face clearly in the dim lamplight. He might well have been smirking, but all she could make out was his hand coming up to tug at his forelock.

'This way, if you please, m'm.'

Mary hesitated. She wanted to rip up at the earl for his cavalier treatment of her, but he was already making his way back up on deck and she was obliged to swallow her indignation and follow Jack to her cabin.

It was small but surprisingly comfortable and as soon as she was alone she stretched herself out on the bunk while the heat of embarrassment faded. How dared he manhandle her in such a fashion, as if she was nothing more than a sack of wool? And he had carried her so effortlessly, as if she had weighed no more than a feather. She did not know when she had last felt so helpless. It had been most unpleasant, to be at the earl's mercy like that. If only he had given her some warning, some time to prepare herself.

The yacht was rocking gently. Mary turned over and cradled her cheek on her hand. He had not even offered her an apology. Really, the man was impossible. He had no manners, no finesse. No wonder he had to pay for his, his *pleasures* as he called them. Surely no woman would want his attentions. But here she found herself remembering the glint in his blue eyes, the way his rare smile had sent her heart racing, the way her senses reeled when he had kissed her. He might well be able to please a woman, if he were to exert himself…

'Miss Endacott! Miss! We will be arriving in Ostend very soon.'

The cabin boy's shouts penetrated Mary's dreams. She stretched, luxuriating in pleasantly sensuous feelings that still lingered until reality stepped in and she sat up quickly. Heavens, had she been dreaming of Lord Randall? She crossed her arms and hugged herself, trying to recall her dreams, but they had flown, leaving only the vague sense of well-being.

Pure foolishness. Mary turned up the lamp fixed to the wall and proceeded to tidy herself, ready to disembark. Her gown was sadly crumpled, but there was no help for that. She fastened her cloak about her shoulders, picked up her reticule and went out. Ascending the steep steps to the deck presented little problem. She gathered her skirts into one hand to climb up, thankful that there was no one to see her since everyone, including the earl, appeared to be on the deck.

It was growing light, the silvery moonlight replaced now by a uniform greyness of both sea and sky. Mary clutched her cloak tightly around her as the wind tried to whip it away. To the east she could make out the darker line of the coast. She could see two buildings on the skyline, one recognisable as a church tower, the other the Ostend lighthouse. As they drew nearer to the town they were joined by a number of other craft all heading for the port.

Amongst all the hustle and bustle on deck Mary saw the earl at the centre of a small group standing near the gunwale and she made her way towards him. The crew moved aside as she approached, and Randall drew her closer to the ship's rail.

'There is too much shipping for us to enter the harbour,' he explained. 'We shall be rowed ashore and make our way to the inn. It's the one with the sign of the ship; you can see it from here. We will have breakfast there while the crew offload the carriages.'

She looked over the rail. A small boat was bobbing alongside, the sailors resting on their oars while they waited for their passengers to join them. If she had considered the steps leading below deck to be steep, the rope ladder dangling down the side of the yacht looked to be vertical. Robbins was already descending and the ladder was shifting alarmingly with every step.

'Do not worry,' said Randall, reading her mind. 'I shall carry you.'

'Oh, no, not again!' She stepped away, but not quickly enough. She had put up her hand to tell him nay, but he merely grabbed it and pulled her close. In an instant he had thrown her over his shoulder again. She tried to kick, but he clamped one arm like a steel band around her thighs while the other pushed the voluminous folds of her cloak and skirts away from his face.

'It will be better for you if you stop fighting me and hold on,' he advised her as he threw one leg over the ship's rail.

He was right. There was nothing she could do now. Struggling would only result in them both being thrown into the water. She closed her eyes and clung to him, trying to ignore the dreadful swaying and lurching as Randall made the peril-ous descent. At last she was dumped unceremo-niously into the longboat and the earl sat down beside her. She was too full of mortification and anger to speak to him, and huddled beneath her cloak as the oarsmen rowed them towards the sandy beach. Even then her ordeal was not over. They were grounded several feet from dry land and the earl dragged off his boots and handed them to Robbins before jumping over the side. The water reached past his knees and silently he turned to Mary. One glance at his implacable face told her there was no going back. She allowed him to lift her out of the boat. At least this time she was in his arms and not over his shoulder like a sack. It was impossible not to slip her hands around his neck and try as she might she could not avoid breathing in his scent, an elusive hint of spices mixed with sweat and brandy and the salty tang of the sea. He strode through the water, his step never faltering despite the rolling waves that broke against his legs. She glanced up at his strong profile, the long nose, determined set of his jaw, his eyes fixed firmly ahead of him. There was no denying his was a commanding figure. If one was interested in such things, which of course she was not.

At last they were free of the water and he set her on her feet.

'There you are, Miss Endacott. And your shoes are quite dry.'

He still had his hands on her waist and was looking down at her, eyes glinting and a faint smile curving his sculpted lips. It sent her heartbeat skittering wildly, but did nothing for her temper. Did he think he could placate her with such pleasantries?

As soon as her legs would bear her weight she pushed herself away from him and marched off towards the inn.

* * *

What on earth was wrong with the damned woman now? Randall watched her stalk away, cloak flapping in the breeze and her dainty feet leaving a trail of footprints in the sand. Would she have preferred that he leave her to her own devices, to ruin her skirts by wading through the water?

'Here you are, Colonel.' Robbins was holding out a towel. 'I've a fresh pair of stockings for you in my pocket, too.'

Randall glanced again at Mary's retreating figure before sitting on a convenient barrel and taking the towel from his man. He would follow her to the inn once he had put on his boots. It would be better for everyone if their words—and he knew there would be words—were exchanged in private.

The inn was an expensive establishment and Randall wondered how Gaston would receive the small, soberly dressed Englishwoman who stormed in through the door. He had caught up with her sufficiently to hear the short explanation she gave the landlord of her presence there. It was delivered in excellent French and had Gaston bowing until his nose touched his knees. They were shown into a private parlour, where the landlord pointed out the meats, bread and little cakes he had placed on the table for milord as soon as he had seen that milord's vessel had arrived. He had also brought in his best wine for milord, and if there was anything else he required, or *mademoiselle*, they only had to tell him and it would be theirs.

Randall eased their voluble host out of the room and closed the door. Then he stood with his back against it, watching Mary. She had discarded her cloak and now paced about the room, dragging her gloves through her hands with sharp, agitated movements. There was a becoming blush on her cheek and her green eyes positively glittered with wrath. When she realised he was watching her she stopped and threw the hapless gloves on to a chair.

'How dare you treat me in that manner,' she declared angrily. 'Without so much as a by your leave—'

'Ladders and skirts are not a good combination, Miss Endacott.'

'I would prefer to make up my own mind about that. It was bad enough that you threw me over your shoulder to take me below deck last night, but to do the same thing here, with everyone watching—'

'Have ever tried climbing down the side of a ship?'

'No, but—'

'I did not carry you down for my own benefit, believe me.'

'I have never been so humiliated—'

'You would have been a lot more humiliated if you had attempted to descend by the ladder,' he retorted. 'The breeze would have whipped your skirts up around your—' He broke off, realising he could not use soldiers' language in front of her. 'Let us just say that the oarsmen would have enjoyed far more of you than was seemly. There was a hoist that you might have used, but in this wind the effect would have been the same. It would not have been just your garters on display, believe me.'

He watched with satisfaction as the meaning of his words hit her. The hectic flush on her cheek deepened and her eyes widened in horror.

'Just so,' he said grimly. 'The men would go wild if any doxy was to flash so much flesh at them, let alone a—' He turned away, trying to hide his final words in a cough. 'Beautiful woman.'

Had his wits gone a-begging? This was no time to be paying her compliments, however backhanded. Yet the memory of her in his arms haunted him and brought the heat pounding to his groin. He could still remember the moment her arms stole around his neck, a gentle touch, as if she was afraid to hold him too tightly. And the smell of her, that fresh, womanly smell. No cheap perfumed water for this lady, just a subtle, lemony scent from her hair as she nestled her head beneath his chin.

'I beg your pardon.'

She had turned away from him and her words were barely audible, but he heard the tremble in her voice. Something twisted inside of him at her distress. He wanted to go to her, to hold her and make the hurt go away. The thought disturbed him. He had never comforted anyone, even his sisters. As he wondered what to say Mary straightened her shoulders and turned back to face him.

'Your methods were unconventional, my lord, but I should have had a great deal more reason to blush if I had tried to make the descent in my skirts. I beg your pardon for ripping up at you. I have been struggling so long for independence that I have forgotten how to be gracious.'

He admired her courage in looking him in the eye and apologising.

If you were lovers you would take her to bed now.

Randall cleared his throat.

'Let us say no more about it.' He went to the side table and began to pour wine into two glasses. 'We should take a little refreshment before we continue our journey.'

'Yes, of course.' Her tone was light, matter of fact. 'I have had nothing to eat since last night.'

'And did you sleep at all on board?'

'Yes, very well, for the whole of the crossing.'
She came up to take a glass of wine, glancing up
at him shyly. 'I know you will want to be with
your men as soon as you can. I shall not delay
you.'

The angry glow had left her eyes; they were
now a soft green, the colour of an English hedge-
row in spring. He realised he would not object if
she delayed him, if he could sweep her up and
carry her off to bed. He wanted to bury his head in
her thick dark hair, or even between the thighs that
his arm had been wrapped around when she had
been thrown over his shoulder. Desire slammed
through him, heating his blood, and he moved
away from her, alarmed at his reaction. He had
thought himself beyond the age of such imagin-
ings. Women had no place in his life, beyond as a
pleasurable distraction. He went over to the window and gave his attention to the view.

'*You* may not delay me, but the lack of trans-
port might well do so. Those fools are trying to
offload my carriages now and making a hash of
it. I had best go out and see what they are about.'

Draining his glass, he grabbed his hat and went
out, relieved to have an excuse to leave Mary Endacott's disturbing presence.

Mary watched him go, then sank down on a
chair by the table. What she had read in Ran-

dall's eyes when he looked at her had shaken her
to the core and her legs felt decidedly weak. It
had been like looking into the hot blue flames of
a fire. She had seen in them the promise of untold
delights; delights she was sure were beyond her
experience. It was a look of burning desire. She
had seen it before, when they had been alone in
Harriett's garden, but then he had believed her to
be a—she swallowed convulsively—a woman of
experience. Perhaps men's eyes always gleamed
in that way when they looked at a pretty woman?
But she was *not* a pretty woman; she was sensible, respectable Miss Endacott, proprietress of an
academy for young ladies.

She sipped her wine. Lord Randall could not
help what he felt, of course. After all, he was a
man and she knew very well that men were prone
to strong carnal lusts, but what shook her was
her own reaction to his look. She had studied
Mary Wollstonecraft's teachings, read Mr Godwin's thoughts upon the nature of love and it had
all sounded so reasonable. A man and woman
would become well acquainted and fall in love.
They would enter into a union of mutual interests,
built on trust and respect without the need for the
blessings of any church. The only union she had
thought of when she saw that hot look in Randall's
eyes was a physical one. She had wanted to reach
out for him, to pull his head down and taste his

lips again, feel his body pressed against hers. Even now the thought of it made her grow hot and her muscles contracted deep inside.

Thank heavens he had gone out when he had, otherwise she was very much afraid she might have given in to her instincts and thrown herself at him.

'You must control yourself, Mary Endacott. Lord Randall has already told you the sort of women he allows into his life and you are not going to become one of those. Think of all you have to lose.'

Yes, think, she told herself sternly. Mr Godwin's idealistic doctrines might work for some, if they had independent means, but she only had her school to support her, and if she lost her reputation no one would entrust their daughters to her care. Randall might take her as his mistress for a while, but what then? What would she do when he had tired of her? She would have to find another protector, and then another, until she was too old and ugly to attract any man for more than a brief coupling in a dark alley.

She shuddered. That fate was too hideous to contemplate.

Chapter Four

By the time Lord Randall returned Mary was in control once more. She allowed him to hand her into the carriage and resolutely kept her eyes averted from him whenever his horse came alongside the window. She had developed an infatuation for the earl. She had seen it in some of her pupils, but never expected that she would be so foolish. It was based on nothing substantial—after all, what did she know of the man? They came from different worlds; their views were so dissimilar there could be no common ground. What she felt for him was pure lust and she would fight against it with every fibre of her being.

She was relieved that Lord Randall appeared to be working equally hard at fighting the attraction. When they made a brief halt to change horses he was distantly polite and when they stopped for the night nothing could have exceeded his attention to her comfort, even arranging for a maid to wait upon her and sleep in her room. If Mary's slumber was disturbed by dreams then she could hardly blame the earl for that.

'No, we shall go on very well,' she murmured to herself as she rose from her bed the next morning. 'By this evening I shall be back in the Rue Haute and I need never be troubled by Lord Randall again.'

On this encouraging thought she made her way downstairs. The inn was a small one, but the earl's largesse had persuaded the innkeeper to put aside a private parlour for them. When Mary entered she found the earl was already breaking his fast. For a moment she hesitated by the door. He had changed his civilian clothes for a dark blue uniform that hugged his lean, athletic figure. He looked even more severe and imposing than before. It also accentuated the blue of his eyes, she noted as she met his gaze. Her heart jumped to her throat and began to pound so heavily that she quickly looked away, trying to regain her composure.

'Good morning, Miss Endacott.'

Lord Randall rose and held her chair for her.

'Thank you, my lord. You expect to be in Brussels today, I think?'

'Yes.' He poured a cup of coffee for her before returning to his seat. 'I have told the baggage coach to go direct to the schoolhouse and drop off your trunk, but I want to stop off at Roosbos, where the Rogues, that is, my men are camped. There will be no need for you to get out of the carriage when we get there, in fact I must insist that you do not. If all is well there I shall then escort you to the Rue Haute.'

'There is no need for you to trouble yourself, sir. I am sure your coachman will find his way without you.'

'Undoubtedly, but I promised Harriett I would see you to your door and she would not forgive me if I did not do my duty.'

Mary did not argue. They both had their duties to perform. He had his artillery troop and she had her school to run. Once he had delivered her to the Rue Haute their paths need never cross again.

When they emerged from the inn some time later the rain was falling steadily from a leaden sky.

'Surely you do not mean to ride in this?' exclaimed Mary, stepping back into the passage. 'You will be soaked to the skin.'

'I have a good hat and a greatcoat.'

She sank her teeth into her lower lip and observed the downpour.

'Tell me truthfully, if I was not here would you use your carriage?'

'Yes, but—'

'Then you must do so, my lord.' She met his eyes, but fleetingly, so as not to blush. She did not want him to think she was being anything but sensible. 'I am sure we can endure each other's company for a few hours.' He understood her meaning, she was sure of it, and when he hesitated she added with a touch of humour, 'Your sister would not forgive *me* if I was the cause of your catching a fatal chill.'

The stern look fled and a muscle twitched at one corner of his mouth.

'I am not so weak,' he said, 'but neither am I so stubborn that I cannot see the sense of keeping dry.'

He gave instructions to his groom, handed Mary into the coach and jumped in behind her. He seemed to fill the coach and suddenly she wondered if her kind-hearted impulse had been so very sensible after all. He was so very big, so very male now that they were shut up together. Mary felt decidedly awkward as they rattled out of the inn yard and she sought for something to say to break the silence.

'I know your troop is known as Randall's Rogues, but are they so very bad, my lord?'

'Worse. A ragtag collection of the most ungovernable men in the army. Thieves, and villains, the lot of them. My company is their last chance; the alternative is transportation or the noose for most of them.'

'But you give them the opportunity to redeem themselves—that is very noble.'

His mouth twisted. 'There is nothing noble about it. They are all good artillerymen. As long as they obey me then they remain in my unit.'

'And the officers?' she asked him.

'Much the same. Villains or by-blows.'

Her brows went up. 'Surely you do not condemn a man because he has the misfortune to be a bastard?'

'Of course not, but circumstances can make or break a man. My soldiers are desperate fellows, all of them. They need desperate men to lead them. Together we make a formidable force.'

Mary sat back in her corner, watching him. She said quietly, 'You are very proud of them, I think.'

'Yes, I am.' His face softened a fraction before he recovered and added roughly, 'There is no room for sentiment in war, Miss Endacott. The Rogues are what they are and I would strongly advise you to stay away from them.'

Even their colonel?

The question hovered on her tongue but she did not utter it. She already knew the answer to that. Especially their colonel.

As the day wore on the rain eased and by the time they reached the woods at Roosbos the sun was shining. The coach turned off the highway and made its way along a track that bore signs of recent heavy traffic. Soon they reached the fields where the earl's artillery troop was camped. Mary gazed out at the chaotic jumble of tents, wagons and horses. In amongst them were the gun carriages, their heavy barrels gleaming in the sunlight. With a curt command to her to stay in the coach Lord Randall jumped out and strode across to the nearest camp fire. The men seated around it scrambled to their feet as he approached.

After her experiences on the yacht she did not attempt to disobey him, although she did let down the window glass so that she could see and hear better. The earl's commanding voice came clearly across to her.

'Sergeant, where is Major Flint?'

'Gone off to see Major Bartlett, sir. Shall I go fetch 'im?'

'No need, Hawkins. I shall be back later, once I have found my lodgings in Brussels.' He was interrupted by a sudden deep barking and a large shaggy dog came bounding towards him. Mary caught her breath, expecting the animal to launch itself at Randall in a ferocious attack.

'Sit!'

The command caused the animal to skid to a halt before the earl, where it remained, panting and looking up slavishly. Randall's next words were quietly spoken, but Mary noticed how his men stepped back nervously.

'What the devil is this animal doing here?'

'That's Dog, our new mascot, Colonel,' said one of the men cheerfully. 'Major Flint found 'im. He didn't seem to have no home so the major adopted him, so to speak.'

'Hmm.' The earl gazed down at the dog, who responded by putting back his ears and hanging out his tongue as he gazed up, hopeful of a soft word. He received only Randall's hand resting briefly on his shaggy black head. 'Very well. Make sure he doesn't get in the way.'

'Here comes Major Flint now, Colonel.'

The soldier's words were drowned out by the dog's ecstatic yelping as an officer came towards them. He was walking casually, as if in no hurry to meet his commanding officer. Mary's first thought was that he was as shaggy as the mascot. Her second, when he came up to the earl, was how alike they were.

His hair was a darker brown than Randall's and longer, but they were much the same height and build, and when he stood face-to-face with his colonel their profiles were strikingly similar. They spoke for some minutes before Randall came striding back to the carriage. Mary quickly sat back as the earl climbed in.

They began to move and when he made no attempt to speak she asked, as carelessly as she could, 'Is Major Flint a relative of yours, my lord?'

She did not miss the tightening of his jaw, the slight hesitation before he replied.

'He is my half-brother.'

'Ah, one of the...er...by-blows you mentioned.'

'Yes.'

His terse response suggested she should not say any more, but she was curious.

'You said there is no room for sentiment, my lord, so I take it Major Flint is a good officer?'

'Let us say I would rather have him on my side than against me.' When he found she was watching him he added impatiently, 'There is no love lost between us, madam, so pray do not be thinking there is any family feeling involved. Flint is just one of many bastards my father sired. He could not keep his hands off any woman, be it lady or laundry maid.'

'A typical nobleman, then.'

He turned to her, more haughty and aristocratic than ever, but at least his anger put to flight the bitter, brooding look.

'No, madam, *not* a typical nobleman.'

She met his furious gaze with a bland smile.

'I think it best to judge people as I find them rather than make assumptions, do not you, sir?'

For a moment she thought he might respond with a withering retort, then she saw his lips twitch.

'Is that aimed at me, because I made, er, assumptions about you?'

'If the cap fits, my lord.'

She heard him make a sound that was something between a curse and a growl.

'How you have come this far without being strangled, madam—'

She laughed at that.

'Never mind, Lord Randall. Another hour and you will be rid of me.'

It was late afternoon by the time they reached Brussels. As soon as the carriage drew up outside the schoolhouse Lord Randall jumped down to hand Mary out.

'Impressive,' he remarked, looking at the large building, set back a little from the street.

'Thank you. I am very proud of my school.'

'Do your pupils board here, too?'

'Most of them, although we do have a few day pupils, too.' She hesitated. 'I would invite you to take some refreshment with me, but…'

'Yes. I must find my own lodgings, then get back to Roosbos as soon as possible.'

Mary nodded.

'Goodbye, Lord Randall. And thank you.'

She held out her hand and he bowed over it, all very correct. He did not even squeeze her fingers before he released them and jumped back into the coach. She stood for a moment, watching the dusty equipage bowling away along the Rue Haute.

It was done, over. He was gone and there was no reason for them to meet again. She had no links with the military in Brussels and did not mix with the English families who had taken up residence in the city. They might send their daughters to her school, but they would not consider her their equal. Her social circle would be very different from the earl's.

No, she thought, straightening her shoulders, she would not see him again.

Randall sank back against the squabs and closed his eyes. It was over. He had done his duty and delivered Miss Endacott to her home and now he need never see the infuriating woman again. By the time the coach rolled up to his quarters in the Rue Ducale his attention was wholly given over to military affairs. There were several messages waiting for him, including one from Wellington that would have to be answered before he could return to Roosbos. He gave himself up to the life he knew best, that of a soldier, a commanding officer.

It was not until he retired to his bed that Randall thought of Mary Endacott and even then it was not through choice. He could not get the damned woman out of his mind. Tired as he was, as soon as he closed his eyes it was her image he saw, the shy smile lurking in her green eyes, the little tilt to her head when she was puzzled. Try as he might he could not banish it, and when at last sleep claimed him, his wayward dreams relived that shockingly rousing kiss they had shared. She trembled in his arms, leaned against him, returned his kiss just as she had done in the gardens at Somervil, but in his dreams it did not end there. In his dreams their kisses grew even more passionate and he lifted her into his arms, intent upon taking her to his bed, but as he swept her up she faded, vanished and he was left with nothing but an intolerable, aching regret.

Randall stirred in his bed. The first grey fingers of dawn were creeping into his room. He covered his eyes with one hand, aware of the vague dissatisfaction of an unfulfilled dream. With a groan he threw back the covers and swung himself off the bed. There was much to be done. Work would prevent him thinking of Mary Endacott. He had never yet allowed a woman to distract him from his duties. But throughout the morning Mary's image haunted him. When he left Wellington's quarters on the Rue Montagne du Parc a woman's laugh rang out. He looked around, expecting to see Mary and finding only a stranger.

'This is madness,' he told himself, hurrying away. 'I have a duty to my troop, to my country. I have no time for such distractions.'

But without quite knowing how, he found himself heading for the Rue Haute.

Mary's homecoming was greeted with pleasure by her staff. The school had run quite smoothly while she had been away, but some of the administration had had to wait for her return and there was plenty to be done, which helped to occupy her mind. She happily threw herself back into life at the school, but nevertheless, when Jacques, her manservant, came into the classroom late the following afternoon to tell her she had a visitor, she was more than a little disappointed when it was not the earl she found waiting in the little sitting room that doubled as her office.

'Bertrand, this is a surprise. How do you do?'

Dr Lebbeke bowed and held out a large bouquet of spring flowers to her.

'Very well, Mademoiselle Mary, I thank you. I knew you were expected home in the next few days and called to leave these to welcome your return.'

'How delightful, thank you.' She rang the bell

and sent for a vase and water to be fetched immediately.

'You made good time,' he observed, handing her the flowers.

'I set off a day earlier than I had originally intended.'

She wondered whether to tell him the reason for it, but her maid came in at that moment and she let it go.

'These are very beautiful, Bertrand, it was so kind of you to think of me.'

He stepped closer to the table where she was arranging the flowers in a blue and white vase.

'It is my pleasure, Mademoiselle Mary. Did you miss your friends in Brussels? I might hope that was the reason you hurried your return.'

His meaning was as clear as the ardent glow in his dark eyes. Bertrand Lebbeke had become a good friend to her over the last year and she knew he would like to be even more than that, but although he was good company and not unattractive, something had held her back from encouraging him. After meeting Lord Randall she knew now what was missing. She felt no spark, no attraction for him. Stifling a sigh, she moved away, wondering how best to respond.

'Bertrand, I—'

'Milord Randall, *mademoiselle*.'

Mary jumped as Jacques made the announcement and she felt the telltale blush rising to her cheeks.

'Lord Randall, good morning to you.'

She could manage no more. Her throat dried as he strode in, severely impressive in his dark blue uniform. He looked particularly forbidding as his eyes swept around the room and came to rest upon Bertrand. Mary coughed to clear whatever it was that blocked her throat.

'Do you know Dr Lebbeke, my lord? He is an invaluable support to me whenever there is illness in the school.'

'No, we have not met.' The earl inclined his head slightly in brief acknowledgement of the doctor before he placed his hat and gloves on the table. 'Since I only arrived in Brussels yesterday that is not surprising.'

'No indeed,' agreed Bertrand pleasantly, returning his bow.

'I came merely to see how you go on,' Lord Randall addressed himself to Mary. 'To ascertain that you were not too fatigued by the journey yesterday.'

Bertrand's dark brows went up and Mary hurried to explain.

'Lord Randall was kind enough to bring me from England in his own carriage. We met by chance in Sussex where I was staying with my cousins, the Bentincks. I was at school with his sister, you see.'

Be quiet, Mary, you sound quite hen-witted.

She knew she was gabbling and closed her lips firmly upon any further inane utterances, but her explanation appeared to satisfy Bertrand, who turned back to address the earl.

'You are with the Allied forces, my lord?'

'Yes. Artillery. And you are a doctor? I fear we may need your services in the coming months, although I wish it were not so.'

'I shall be ready,' Bertrand answered. 'I have some knowledge of war injuries. I was for ten years ship's surgeon with the French navy, until Bonaparte's abdication. I hope you will not hold that against me?'

'Your calling is to save lives, Bertrand, is it not?' said Mary quietly.

'It is, Mademoiselle Mary.' Bertrand smiled at her. 'Regardless of nationality.'

Mary returned his smile, aware that Randall's countenance had become even more stony. He walked to the window and stood there, silently staring out. It was like being in a room with two dogs who would start snarling at one another any moment.

She said quickly, 'Will you not sit down, sirs? I was about to send for refreshments.'

'Mais non, merci,' said Bertrand. 'You are very

kind, but I have the appointment that will not wait and must take my leave.' He saluted her fingers, bowed to Lord Randall and was gone.

'Full of Gallic charm,' remarked the earl drily.

'He is from Flanders, my lord, he is not French.'

'That is not my concern. What is he to you?'

She blinked, and was tempted to throw his words back at him, to tell him it was not his concern.

'A friend.' She sounded a little too defiant and tried to soften her tone as she continued. 'Pray sit down, my lord, and I will ring—'

'No, do not trouble yourself, I cannot stay. I am to dine tonight at the Hôtel de la Paix with the other artillery officers.'

'Then I thank you for taking the trouble to call.'

'It was nothing. I should like to call again.'

It sounded very much like an order. Common sense told her to prevaricate. She had plenty of excuses, she was very busy, it would not be seemly—

'I should like that.'

You are playing with fire, my girl.

She knew it, but it was too late to retract. Or was it? She wondered for a moment if Randall had heard her, for he made no sign. Then he nodded.

'Thank you.'

He moved towards the door, and as he collected his hat and gloves from the table he reached out and flicked one of the colourful blooms that Bertrand had brought for her.

'This is not my way, Mary,' he said. 'I have no charming manners; you will get no false compliments from me. I will not bring you flowers. It is best you know that, from the start.'

He gave her a curt nod and was gone.

Mary blinked. The start of what?

She shivered and crossed her arms, as if to ward off a sudden chill. She should never have invited him to call again. He would undoubtedly think it signified she was ready to accept a *carte blanche*. It meant nothing of the sort, of course, as any gentleman should know. But Randall was not a gentleman. He was an earl.

With a sigh Mary dropped her head in her hands. Could she blame him for thinking she would welcome his attentions? He had misjudged her from the start and her innate honesty compelled her to admit that it was not entirely his fault. She had teased him, led him to believe she was far more worldly-wise than was proper for a single lady. She had conversed with him more freely and openly than was proper, too, but for some inscrutable reason she found him so easy to talk to. She sighed. If that was the case then it should be a simple matter to write to him and explain that she had changed her mind, that it would be best if he did not call.

No, it would be easier to hold her hand in the candle's flame than to tell him they must not meet again. Mary closed her eyes—dear heaven, had she learned nothing from her sister's experience? Poor, deluded, heartbroken Jane, who had trusted a nobleman and paid the ultimate price.

She hugged herself even tighter, then, taking a long, resolute breath, she straightened and drew herself up. She would give orders that if Lord Randall should call he was not to be admitted. A clean break. Mary turned and walked back to her desk. It would not take long for them both to forget that they had ever met.

'Your pardon, milord. Mademoiselle Endacott is not at home.'

The manservant's English accent was well-nigh impeccable, but that was not surprising, thought Randall bitterly, since the fellow had repeated the phrase to him several times. It was the third call he had made in as many days and each time the response was the same.

'Do you wish to leave your card, milord?'

'No, not this time.' Randall stepped back from the door. 'I shall not call again.'

He walked away. Mary was avoiding him; he could not blind himself to the truth any longer. Indeed, he was not even sure why he had called so often. What had he hoped to achieve by pursuing the acquaintance of a woman who was too respectable to be his mistress and to whom he could offer nothing else? It was strange, but he was continually drawn back to the Rue Haute, as if Mary was a siren, calling to him.

That was ridiculous, of course. She was a respectable lady, even if he had at first misread the signals. But he had not misread the look in her eyes. There was a connection between them, tangible as a cord. She wanted him quite as much as he desired her, he would stake his life on it, yet he knew how the world would judge her if she succumbed to his advances. She needed to maintain her reputation if her school was to continue. He could neither bed her nor wed her, so why had he called at the schoolhouse?

The question haunted him and he was not sure of the answer. He wanted to see her again, to talk to her, argue with her. To hear her laugh.

'For God's sake, pull yourself together, man,' he muttered as he made his way back to the Rue Ducale. 'She's a woman you met barely two weeks ago. Surely you can forget her, especially now, when there is so much to be done.'

But as he went about his business over the next few days, he found himself thinking of her in the quiet moments, wanting to tell her about his troop, to share with her the frustrations of his day as well as the comic moments, such as how the unkempt and decidedly shaggy stray that had attached itself to the company had come to be known as Bennington Dog. One of the men had let slip that the animal was named after the preposterous Colonel Bennington Ffog, laughing stock of Brussels, with his foppish moustache and breeches so tight he couldn't get them on without greasing his legs.

It had been as much as Randall could do to keep a straight face when the story had come to him, but it would not do to show disrespect to a fellow officer, especially when that officer was in command of his brother Gideon's cavalry regiment. But he could have told Mary. She would appreciate it and perhaps her eyes would shine with that mischievous twinkle he had surprised there upon occasion. He could share such moments and trust her to keep his confidence. Not that he would ever need to do so now. She had shown all too clearly that their acquaintance was at an end.

Chapter Five

'You are very quiet today, Mademoiselle Mary.'

'I beg your pardon.' Mary smiled up at her companion. 'Did you say something, Bertrand?'

They were walking in the park, but every time she saw an officer in blue uniform she was reminded of Randall, and could not stop herself wondering about him, what he was doing, if he was thinking of her.

She had heard nothing of him for two weeks. She had told Jacques to deny him, should Lord Randall come calling, so she could hardly blame the earl for that, but he continued to invade her thoughts. She had learned to keep him at bay during the waking hours by throwing herself into her work, but at night, when she had blown out her candle and was trying to sleep he would creep, nay stride, into her dreams and disturb her rest.

'I thought you would be happy,' remarked Bertrand, 'I have stolen you away from your pupils for an hour, from your work. *Mais*, alas, I do not appear to have your attention.'

'I beg your pardon,' she said again. 'I was thinking of what would be best to do for my school.' She comforted her conscience with the sop that this was not a complete lie. 'I know there are rumours that the Allies will carry the war into France, but it is by no means certain. Some parents have taken away their children already, others are preparing to do so, but some will be left in my care because their parents are abroad and I must be ready to remove them from Brussels, if it becomes necessary.'

'I urged you to leave here weeks ago.' He shook his head at her, saying with mock severity, 'You are too independent, Mary.'

'Now why do you say that, Bertrand, when you know I have taken your advice and secured a house in Antwerp? When the time comes I shall remove there with my staff and pupils. My quandary now is when to go, if at all. It is commonly believed that Napoleon will not come here.'

'One can never rely upon Bonaparte doing what is expected of him. He will seize his chance and when he does he will move very quickly. It would be better if you were not in Brussels when he strikes.'

'I know that.' She squeezed his arm. 'Thank you, Bertrand, but I do not think you need to worry. I shall make my plans and prepare my staff and pupils. We will be ready to quit the city at a moment's notice. Yet while the duke thinks it safe to remain then I shall do so.'

'Ah, this Wellington. You place great faith in him, I think.'

'I do.'

'And his officers too, perhaps. Such as your friend Lord Randall?'

Mary shook her head.

'I have only seen him once since I returned to Brussels, the day you called, do you remember?'

'How could I forget? I thought then I had a competitor the most serious.'

She forced herself to laugh at that.

'What nonsense you speak, Bertrand.'

'Because I am fearful of a rival for your affections?'

She released his arm and stopped, saying in a tone of mild rebuke, 'Bertrand, you know we agreed not to speak of that. I value your friendship, but there can be nothing more.'

'Can there not?' He was looking down at her, smiling, and she had to admit that he was very handsome with his black hair and dark eyes, and until she had gone to England she had thought that, perhaps, one day she might agree to be more than friends, but now she knew that could never be. She felt nothing more than a mild liking when she was with him. He did not stir her; she did not feel as if a sack full of butterflies had been opened in her stomach whenever he looked at her. Not like a certain artillery officer, just the thought of whom set her blood pounding and created such an ache of longing inside that she wanted to burst into tears.

So she shook her head, saying sadly, 'I am afraid not, Bertrand. Please let us not speak of it again.'

He sighed.

'Eh bien.' Bertrand pulled her hand on to his arm and they began to walk on. 'But we are friends, *non*?'

'Mais oui,' she replied. 'Always, I hope.'

'Then I shall invite you to take a day out with me on Monday next. There is to be a grand cavalry review near Grammont.'

'Oh, but I cannot, Bertrand, I have too much work to do—'

'You are not so busy, you have told me so yourself, and now you say that many of your pupils, they have gone home. Your excellent teachers are quite capable of running your school without you for a day.'

'When you put it like that I do not seem to have any choice.'

'Exactement. It is settled, then. I shall bring my cabriolet to collect you Monday morning.'

* * *

The day of the Grammont review dawned bright and sunny and Mary found herself looking forward to it. Bertrand collected her punctually and they made good time, arriving before noon at the flat plain on the banks of the River Dender. It was a perfect arena for showing off the massed troops, who were even then assembling. Mary had to admit the lines of hussars and heavy dragoons made a colourful spectacle against the dark backdrop of the woods. Gazing out across the plain, Mary realised they had been misinformed, for amongst the ranks of cavalry were batteries of horse artillery, the men scrubbing and polishing everything, including their horses, ready for inspection.

Many civilians had driven out from Brussels and they were gathering on a slight rise which would give them a good view of the review. As Bertrand drove the cabriolet to join them Mary spotted a dashing cavalry officer riding beside a lady in a pale blue habit. They made a striking picture, both mounted on pure white horses, but it was not the elegant image they presented that made Mary's breath catch in her throat. The man was not Randall, she knew that, he was not quite so tall, yet something about the officer's posture, the way he sat his horse, his hawk-like profile made her think of the earl. It must be Randall's younger brother, Gideon Latymor. Harriett had told her he was a cavalry officer. But the lady— the resemblance between them was too great, she could only be his twin sister.

She glanced around nervously, wondering if the earl was present. Did he know Lady Sarah was in Brussels? That would not please him; he would want his sister safely out of the way, if there was a battle coming. But even so Randall would want to speak to Sarah today, and if he came this way he could hardly fail to see her, Mary, sitting with Bertrand in an open carriage. She quickly shifted her parasol, shielding herself from the handsome young couple and hoping, if the earl did appear, that her presence would go unnoticed.

'We have some time before the review begins, I think,' said Bertrand. 'Would you like to get down and, what is it you English say—pull out your legs?'

His question diverted Mary. Her eyes danced and she replied with a laugh in her voice.

'Yes, Bertrand, thank you, I would very much like to stretch my legs.'

She allowed him to help her down. The couple on their matching horses had ridden off to join a party of cavalry officers some distance away, but Mary decided it would still be wise to walk in the opposite direction, where they were less likely to bump into Randall.

The scene spread out on the plain before them was one of bustling preparation. Men ran about, riders cantered to and fro, the artillery pieces were being pushed and pulled into position and polished until they gleamed. She could not be sure, but she thought she recognised Randall's troop in their dark blue uniforms, the officers with a red sash about their waists. Bertrand asked her if she wanted to take a closer look at the artillery and she quickly declined.

'That is, unless you wish to do so?' she asked him, aware that her reason for avoiding the guns was perfectly selfish. However, she could not be sorry when he shook his head.

'I have seen the damage these machines of war can do. They hold no fascination for me.'

'No, of course. They look very peaceful now, but when they are unleashed upon an enemy…' she shuddered '…I do not like to think of it.'

'Then do not. We are here to enjoy the spectacle they make, and to take from it some comfort. The duke is clearly setting out to show that his army is far superior to Bonaparte's.'

They had reached the far end of the ridge and turned to retrace their steps.

'What will you do?' Mary asked him. 'If war comes will you stay in Brussels?'

'But of course.' For a moment his cheerful insouciance disappeared. 'My services will be in great demand, whichever side wins.'

Mary did not know what to say to this and they walked on in silence. They had almost reached Bertrand's cabriolet when Mary recognised the big horse trotting towards them. And its rider in his dress uniform, a dark blue coat with gold lace and scarlet facings. His long legs were encased in pantaloons so white they made his dappled grey horse look even grubbier than usual.

She told herself sternly that she did not believe in war and disapproved of the military, yet she could not stop the flutter of admiration when she looked at Randall—he looked quite magnificent. Nor could she prevent the breathlessness that afflicted her and made her incapable of speaking as the earl drew rein in front of them. Thankfully Bertrand was not so tongue-tied.

'Lord Randall, *bonjour.*'

'Dr Lebbeke.'

A quick peep at his face was all Mary allowed herself. Beneath the shade of his cocked hat his countenance was as inscrutable as ever, but when she looked away she could feel his blue eyes on her. He would see the colour in her cheek, note her ragged breathing and he would draw his own conclusions.

And they would be correct. She fluttered her

fan, mortified to think she was so transparent where Randall was concerned.

Bertrand was speaking and she tried hard to concentrate.

'Your artillery troop is here, today, milord, the infamous Randall's Rogues?'

'Yes, Doctor, they—' The earl was interrupted by sounds of a commotion coming from the nearby carriages. 'What the devil is that?'

'It is coming from the barouche over there,' observed Mary, pointing. 'Perhaps someone is ill. Bertrand, do you think you should—?'

'*Mais oui.* I will see what I can do.'

'A lady has collapsed, I think,' said Mary, watching him dash across to the barouche.

'By heaven, that's Blanchards's carriage,' exclaimed Randall. 'It must be Augusta.'

He jumped down and would have rushed off, but Mary caught his arm.

'Wait! Let Bertrand see your sister first. He is a doctor, after all.'

'Yes, of course.'

He looped the reins over his arm and they made their way towards the carriage. A crowd was already gathered about the barouche, where Bertrand was attending Lady Blanchards while her husband was giving orders for the hood to be raised. It was clear Lord Randall was anxious to know what was happening and Mary offered to hold Pompey while he spoke to his brother-in-law. The earl was back a few minutes later.

'It appears Augusta has had a touch too much sun, nothing more serious. When she swooned Blanchards panicked and set up a hue and cry, foolish fellow.'

'Pray do not be so hard upon him,' protested Mary, half-laughing. 'He was concerned for his wife.'

'No reason to set everyone in uproar just because Gussie fainted off. A few moments' consideration would have told him it was only a trifle.'

'Not everyone can apply such cold logic to a situation,' she retorted.

'You think me cold, Miss Endacott?' When she did not reply he shrugged. 'I have already explained to you I am a soldier, I am trained not to make a fuss over such a trifle.'

'But she is your sister!'

'What has that to say to anything? She is not in any danger, and besides your doctor is looking after her.'

'He is not *my* doctor.' Mary closed her lips together firmly, wondering why she had been so eager to stress the point.

'Yet you are on first-name terms.'

'We are good friends,' she replied coldly. 'Nothing more.'

She hunched a shoulder and stared towards the

Blanchards's carriage, hoping Bertrand would return soon and she could leave this disconcerting man.

'I did not expect to see you today,' said the earl. 'I take it you did not know I should be here?'

She did not even think of prevaricating.

'No, I did not.' She looked over her shoulder at the colourful ranks of horses and men that covered the vast plain. 'I am surprised your Rogues were allowed to take part, if all you say of them is true.'

'Oh, it is true, Miss Endacott. I had to threaten them with the rope's end to get them into in any shape to be presented to the duke and his entourage.'

'Even the officers?'

'*Especially* the officers.'

She laughed. 'And your mascot? That shaggy hound I saw at Roosbos?'

'He is here, but tied to a gun carriage. He is far too undisciplined to let loose. He might well attack Blücher. Or, even worse, Wellington.'

'Heaven forbid!'

'That *would* cause an uproar. He should not be here at all, of course, but it seems the animal is greatly attached to Major Flint and makes a great fuss if they are separated. At least being a dog one can tie him up to keep him out of harm's way.'

She noted the edge to his voice as he uttered these last words.

'Would you prefer that the civilians had stayed out of harm's way, too, my lord?'

'Not you,' he said quickly. 'No. It is my sister. My *sisters*,' he corrected himself. He waved towards the carriage. 'To my mind they would be safer in England. It was only when I arrived here that I learned Blanchards had brought Gussie and Sarah to Brussels. They were in Paris when news of Bonaparte's escape from Elba became known. I advised my mother to write and summon them home, but to no avail.'

'It is fashionable to be in Brussels, Lord Randall. It is where everyone of importance is gathered.'

'They should be in London, especially now. I have just learned that Gussie is increasing.'

'I am sure they will leave, should it be necessary.'

'And what of you?' he asked her. 'Will you quit Brussels?'

She nodded. 'I have made plans to take my school to Antwerp.'

'That is very wise.'

They were standing side by side and Mary kept her eyes fixed upon the barouche, where Lady Blanchards was now shaded by the hood.

'My school is everything to me,' she said. 'It is all I have.'

And it is the reason I cannot throw my cap over the windmill for you.

A high, anxious voice interrupted her thoughts.

'Justin! What is it, why is everyone gathered about Gussie's carriage?'

The young lady in the blue riding habit was trotting towards them, but now she was followed by a different cavalry officer, a florid-faced colonel with black pomaded curls and a startlingly black moustache, every bit as dark and glossy as the horse he was riding. The earl's mount sidled restlessly and Randall put one hand up to smooth its grey nose.

'Our sister is feeling a little faint, Sarah,' he replied. 'No need for you to fly into a pelter. It is nothing serious and there is a doctor with her now.'

So Mary was right, she was Randall's younger sister, Lady Sarah Latymor. Mary took the opportunity to study her. She was much fairer than Randall, but had the Latymor nose and the same blue eyes, which Mary realised now were studying her with unfeigned interest.

'And who is this, Justin?'

Randall performed the introductions and Mary saw the speculation deepen in Lady Sarah's eyes when he explained that they had travelled to Brussels together. Lady Sarah's companion brought his horse a little closer and subjected Mary to what she thought was a predatory smile.

'On your private yacht, eh?' he said. 'That was dashed good of you, Randall. We must do our bit to please the ladies, what?'

The earl did not reply to this sally, but said coolly, 'Miss Endacott, let me present Colonel Bennington Ffog.'

'My brother's commanding officer,' murmured Lady Sarah, as the colonel flourished a bow over the horse's neck and almost came unseated when the animal sidled and sidestepped nervously. She glanced again towards the carriage. 'If there is nothing to be done here for the moment, I think, Colonel, that we should be getting back. Your men will be wondering what has become of you.'

'No, no, fair lady,' the colonel disclaimed gallantly. 'I am entirely at your disposal.'

'Oh, that is so kind of you, when I know you are so busy,' murmured Lady Sarah, with a sweet, vague smile.

Mary glanced at Randall and was not surprised to see that his lips had thinned and he was watching this display stony-faced.

'But I cannot keep you from your duties, Colonel,' continued Lady Sarah. 'How mortifying it would be if the duke should arrive and your men were not in position. I will ride back with you now and have another word with Gideon, if I may, then I shall return here to look after my sister.'

'She is meant to be looking after *you*.'

Lady Sarah responded to Randall's interjection with a bland smile. 'Gussie knows I shall come to no harm while I am riding Castor. And when I return, perhaps there will be time for you to take me to see your artillery—'

'*No!*'

Randall's forceful refusal brought the eyes of both ladies upon him, but it was Colonel Bennington Ffog who replied.

'No, no, Lady Sarah, I wouldn't recommend that at all. Dashed unpleasant fellows, all of 'em. They ain't called rogues for nothing, believe me. Why, I've even had their insolence directed towards me. Dregs of the earth they are, ma'am.'

'Not so much dregs, more the scrapings of the privy,' added Randall with grim humour. 'But the colonel is right; they are not fit company for any lady. I would not only advise you to keep your distance, I would go so far as to positively *forbid* you to go near them.'

'Well, you are too late,' retorted Lady Sarah. 'Gideon and I have already spoken to some of them and if you are going to be so disagreeable I shall go back to Gideon now. *He* does not scold and bully me at every opportunity. But do not worry, I shall return once the review starts to look after poor Gussie. Good day, Miss Endacott. I hope we shall meet again.'

Mary gave a little curtsy. 'It is unlikely, my

lady. I rarely have time to leave my school. Today was an exception.'

Lady Sarah's look was decidedly sceptical. She glanced from Mary to Randall and back again, but without another word she turned and cantered away, Colonel Bennington Ffog following in her wake.

'That girl has been given far too much of her own way,' growled the earl.

'She is a young woman and, like a bird about to fly the nest, she is trying out her wings,' said Mary. 'It must be difficult for you, my lord, being head of such a family when your military duties keep you from home so much.'

'I have had little to do with my siblings,' he admitted. 'My mother has always managed things at Chalfont, while I pursued my army career. Until now it has worked very well.'

'You mean you have handed down your dictates and they have all followed them.'

'Not at all. I am not such an autocrat as you think me, madam.' There was the briefest hesitation before he said slowly, 'Perhaps I should have taken more interest in them all.'

'There is still time, sir. When this war is over.'

'If I survive.'

A shiver ran down Mary's spine at his words, uttered in such a matter-of-fact tone. Instinctively she put up her hand, as if to push away the thought. To distract herself, she turned back towards the barouche.

'I wonder how much longer Bert—Dr Lebbeke—will be?'

'Why would you not see me?'

The earl's question was not unexpected. It had hovered between them from the moment he had come up to her, but it did not make responding to it any easier.

'You. I.' Mary stopped, gathering her wits, which had an unfortunate tendency to desert her when the earl was present. *'It...'* she tried again. 'It frightens me.'

'My indomitable Mary. I did not think you frightened of anything. Even Bonaparte.'

'Well, you are wrong. And I am *not* your Mary!'

She felt his hand on her elbow, the briefest touch, but it sent a prickle of anticipation skittering over her skin.

'I would not have you frightened of me.'

Her heart clenched painfully. It was not the earl who frightened her. It was her own feelings. She desired him, so much that it was like a physical pain. She tried to concentrate upon the events in the carriage, glad that something was happening at last. Bertrand was climbing down. He was smiling, so it must be good news. As she watched

him approach, Randall's deep voice murmured
in her ear.

'I shall call on you tomorrow. We will talk
then.'

There was no time to reply. Bertrand was addressing the earl.

'Your sister was feeling the effects of the heat,
my lord. She is a little better now, but she must
stay out of the sun for the rest of the day. I advised
Lord Blanchards to take her back to Brussels, but
she will stay for the review.'

'The devil she will,' retorted Randall. 'I
will talk to her; perhaps if I add my voice to
Blanchards's we might persuade her.'

'You will not do it, my lord,' said Bertrand.
'She is determined to see the duke.'

'Is she, by God,' exclaimed Randall furiously.

Mary touched his arm. 'Speak to her, my lord,
and express your concern. She will appreciate
that, I am sure, even if she will not leave. Then
go back to your men and prepare for the review.
Show your sisters and His Grace the Duke of Wellington that Randall's Rogues are a troop to be
reckoned with.'

He hesitated for a moment, frowning, before
he strode off to speak to his sister.

'*Bon*, Mademoiselle Mary. A stirring little
speech.'

'Was I too patronising, Bertrand?' Mary asked anxiously as she watched Randall remonstrating with his sister.

'Not at all. But you clearly have the earl's interests at heart.'

Mary felt her spirits sinking. Was it so obvious? She heard cheering and looked up. A colourful cavalcade was approaching.

'It is the duke and his guests,' observed Bertrand. 'Come, let us return quickly to our carriage. We shall be able to see everything from there.'

He helped her on to the seat and they watched Wellington and his cortège moving past the troops gathered for inspection. Despite the number of distinguished officers surrounding the duke, Mary's eyes followed one dark-coated colonel on his grey horse and while she watched him, her mind went over all he had said to her, every word, every gesture. He had said he would call. Would he do so? She must tell Jacques to once more deny him, just in case.

'Well, Mademoiselle Mary, have you seen enough?'

Bertrand's words recalled her wandering attention. The duke was at the far end of the impromptu parade ground now. The review was almost at an end.

'They will all be dismissed soon and everyone

will be trying to get away,' he continued. 'If we leave now we shall be ahead of the crush.'

'Then by all means let us go now,' agreed Mary, consciously avoiding taking a last look at Lord Randall. 'It has been a most interesting day, Bertrand, thank you.' She added impulsively, 'I feel I should repay your kindness—will you join us for dinner this evening?'

'Us?'

'Well, of course, my teachers will be there. It would be improper for me to dine alone with you.'

'Did you dine alone when you travelled from England with Earl Randall?'

'Yes, but that was different.'

'It was?'

She sucked in a breath. It was very different, but she dared not tell him in what way.

'Lord Randall escorted me here to please his sister. She was concerned at my travelling back to Brussels alone. The earl was very reluctant to bring me with him, I assure you.' A faint smile bubbled up when she remembered their arguments. But there had been very pleasant moments on the journey, too. She shook off the memories and looked Bertrand in the eye. 'It is not the earl I am inviting to dine at the Rue Haute tonight, Bertrand. It is you. Now, what do you say?'

'I say I would like that very much, *mademoiselle*. Thank you.'

* * *

Randall followed the duke and his entourage as they made their way through the colourful ranks, but his mind was distracted. What had possessed him to tell Mary he would call again? Better to let this obsession die now. There could never be anything between them. Even if he had not set his face against marriage the head of the noble house of Latymor could not ally himself to a mere schoolteacher, especially one whose father had been such a prominent supporter of revolution. And Mary did not welcome his attentions, he knew that. It would be better to leave well alone.

He followed the inspection party with impatience, but at last his duty was done and he rode back to have a quick word with his officers. He glanced across to the colourful crowd of spectators. As soon as he had finished here he would ride over to Mary and put her mind at rest. He would not call upon her. But even as he dismissed his men an aide came galloping up.

'Lord Uxbridge requests that you join him for dinner this evening, my lord.'

'I am already aware of that. I shall be there.'

'His lordship would like you to accompany him now, sir, if you will,' said the aide, adding in a colourless voice, 'He requires your presence to escort his distinguished guests to Ninove, my lord.'

'He requires my title, you mean.'

The aide kept his gaze fixed somewhere over Randall's shoulder.

'His lordship cannot talk to them all at the same time, my lord.'

There was no getting out of it. With a nod of assent he turned to follow the aide. As he cantered past the spectators he looked along the lines, seeking Lebbeke's carriage, but it had gone.

Chapter Six

The teachers at the Endacott Academy for Young
Ladies were all very accomplished and Mary was
rarely needed in the classroom, although she did
continue her father's habit of teaching the brighter
pupils Latin and Greek. She had lessons sched-
uled for the following morning and used this as
an excuse not to tarry over her dinner with Bertrand. She was also adamant that she would not
alter her timetable because Lord Randall had said
he would call. She informed Jacques that her lessons were not to be interrupted, and did not know
whether to be relieved or disappointed when she
returned to her sitting room in the afternoon to
find that there had been no callers.

She decided to deal with the small pile of mail
on her desk, which was mostly from anxious parents. With the growing unrest many had already
removed their daughters from her school and she
would soon be obliged to let two of her teachers

go. The others would accompany the remaining children to Antwerp, where they would stay until it was safe to return to Brussels. What would happen then, and what she would do, was impossible to say. If the French were victorious she would lose the daughters of the English families and she did not have enough local children on her books to make the schoolhouse on the Rue Haute viable.

She rubbed her temples. She could cut her costs, move to smaller premises, but for now she must wait and see what happened. She was not the only person whose livelihood depended upon the outcome of a battle.

The sounds of an arrival caught her attention and drove all other considerations from her mind. Randall. Her heart began hammering so hard she could hear the drumming in her ears. He had come. Mary rose and took a few hasty steps into the centre of the room. She would not see him. Yes she would, but only to tell him that he must not call again. No, safer to have Jacques say she was not at home.

That decision was taken out of her hands. She heard a hasty step crossing the hall, there was a peremptory knock and the earl came in. He closed the door behind him and stood for a moment, stripping off his gloves. He was frowning, his eyes hard, mouth straight and firm. Was it only yesterday that she had spoken to him? It seemed a lifetime ago. But much as she wanted to keep him here, to talk to him, he must go. He was dangerous, he threatened to destroy her peace of mind and her livelihood. As the earl threw his hat and gloves on to her desk Mary took a deep breath.

'Lord Randall, I—'

She got no further. He crossed the room in two strides and took her in his arms.

All Mary's good intentions disappeared. She raised her face to his and accepted his kiss, clinging to him and returning it passionately. His mouth was hard on hers and her lips parted to allow his tongue to enter, exploring and teasing, drawing a primitive response from her. Instinctively she leaned closer, excited by the hard, aroused body pressed against hers. She was on fire, from her head to the very tips of her toes she burned with desire for him. She drove her hands through his hair, tangling her fingers in its silky softness, wanting to cling on to him, to hold him close forever.

He began to cover her face with kisses and she breathed in the familiar scent of him, the combination of soap and spices and something very masculine that was all his own and deeply exciting. She sighed as his lips left hers and trailed down the length of her neck in a series of butterfly-soft kisses that sent a shiver tingling through her whole body. Her breasts felt swollen, they pushed against the bodice of her gown, straining to be free, to feel his caresses. She shuddered, shocked, frightened, exhilarated by what was happening to her.

'I could not stay away,' he murmured between kisses. 'You haunt my thoughts. I had to see you.'

'Oh, Randall, I have missed you so.'

Hearing her own words, whispered against his cheek, brought Mary back to reality. With a sob of regret she pushed her hands against his chest and held him away, just a little. It was torture to keep the distance between them when all she wanted to do was to cling tightly to him.

'Please let me go.' His arms dropped and she stepped back, out of reach, praying her legs would not give way beneath her. 'It will not do, my lord. I had decided I would tell you so today.'

His laugh was short and unsteady.

'And *I* had come to say goodbye, until I walked in and you were standing there.' He ran his fingers through his hair. 'Then all my resolutions flew out of the window.'

Mary turned away. It would be easier if she was not looking at him. She took out her handkerchief to wipe her eyes. Tears were a sign of weakness. She despised them. One good, deep breath and she was sufficiently in control to speak.

'This is merely a, a carnal attraction, my lord. I have considered very carefully and I know there can be nothing more to it. Our social spheres are too far apart.'

'I cannot agree with you there. Your birth is as good as mine.'

'You are a nobleman, although there is nothing noble about the class you represent. I despise it wholeheartedly.' The silence that met her words pressed upon her, insisting on an explanation. 'I mentioned that I had a sister, Jane. She fell in love with a younger son of a marquess, a so-called noble family. He courted her assiduously, but he convinced Jane to keep their attachment secret. Jane understood his arguments, that our parents' radical views would set them against him. It was true, my father would not have looked favourably upon the match, but he was not a tyrant and would not have stood out against an honest suitor. Instead this, this *noble* man persuaded Jane to run away with him to Tonbridge. He promised to marry her, but after a month his passion cooled. He abandoned Jane, leaving her penniless. Thankfully, my father was not one to disown his daughter, whatever she had done. When she wrote to tell him of her plight he fetched her home immediately.

'She was in a sorry state, and very unhappy. My father went looking for the scoundrel but he was abroad. On his honeymoon. His promises had all been lies, he had been betrothed even when he was courting my sister.'

'What happened to her?'

'She never recovered. Once she knew there was no hope she threw herself in the Thames.' She turned to face him, seeing not Randall but the ignoble class he represented. 'I was just thirteen years old when I lost my beloved sister. The shock of it almost destroyed my family. Is it any wonder that I hold you and your kind in such contempt? But that need not matter to you. After all I am the daughter of a man who openly proposed the abolition of all such forms of privilege. So you see we have nothing in common.'

She waited in silence for his reply, wondering if he would express outrage at the events she had described, perhaps even apologise for the faults of his class. She studied his lean face, remembered the moments of companionship they had shared and a faint hope, fragile as a snowflake, suggested he might see a way through the barriers between them, although she had spent fruitless hours trying to do so. His harsh, unsmiling countenance was not encouraging.

'You are right, our worlds are too far apart,' he said at last. 'I have told myself as much a dozen times these last few days.'

The leaden weight inside her grew even heavier.

This was the end. They would not meet again. She was surprised how much the thought hurt her.

She said bleakly, 'We are agreed then. There is no hope for us.' Treacherous tears were welling up and she did not want him to see them. She said, while she could still command her voice, 'You had best go now, my lord. I have nothing to offer you.'

She closed her eyes, willing him to go before she collapsed, a sobbing, distraught wreck, on to the sofa.

'We could be friends.'

'I beg your pardon?' Her eyes flew open.

Had she misheard him? His eyes were still burning with deep blue fire, but he spoke quite steadily.

'Let us be friends, if we cannot be anything else to each other. Merely soldier and school-teacher, enjoying a brief companionship.'

Her hand crept to her cheek. 'My lord, I do not think I—'

He turned away from her and began to pace the room, his brow furrowed.

'It can only be for the short time that I remain in Brussels. This peace can only last a few weeks more. If the worst happens and Bonaparte comes to us, you will be leaving for Antwerp. If the duke decides to take the fight to France then I shall be gone.' He stopped before her. 'This is new to me, Mary. I have never felt like this in my life before, about anyone. I would be glad, when I am not engaged upon my duties, to have your company. It need not be alone,' he added, as if thinking it through. 'You may provide yourself with a chaperone—or a maid, to be with you at all times. I would not wish to damage your reputation. I merely wish for your company.'

She stared at him.

'Friends?'

'Why not?' His mouth twisted and the ghost of a smile glinted in his eyes. 'It is quite a radical idea, I think.'

Now he was teasing her. But it could work. The heavy cloud on her spirits lifted, just a little.

'You would ask nothing of me save my company?'

'That is correct.'

It was Mary's turn to walk about the room, her fingers pressed to her temples. A little laugh shook her.

'You continue to surprise me, Lord Randall. At almost our first meeting you suggest I should be your mistress and now you declare that you wish us to be *friends*?'

'Yes, since there cannot be anything else between us. War is coming, Mary. Everything will change. There is very little time and I want to spend some of it with you.' He shrugged. 'Perhaps friends is all we ever could be, given what lies between us. I am a hard man, Mary, you know I lack the social graces to make a woman happy.'

'I do not believe that. Despite your rank you have good qualities,' she admitted.

'But you do not know me very well. My sisters will tell you it is true. I do not back down, I do not apologise. My intransigence would hurt you, in the end, if we were lovers. As friends you may fare better at my hands. Unlike your poor sister you would be able to walk away and your reputation would not be damaged.' He added quietly, 'I am not ready to say goodbye to you, Mary Endacott.'

This is madness.

She stopped her pacing. 'Nor I you, Lord Randall.'

'Then let us try it. After all, what have we to lose?'

Only my sanity.

'Why, nothing, my lord.' She held out her hand. 'Cry friends with me, then.'

He clasped her fingers. The bolt of heat shot up her arm, desire curled deep inside her, but she ignored it. Friends or nothing.

Half a loaf.

Randall stared into the green eyes that looked up at him so uncertainly. What had it cost her to tell him about her sister? She had wanted him to understand. His proud, indomitable Mary. He wanted her so badly he was prepared to go to any lengths to see her, even if it meant acting like a eunuch. They said familiarity bred contempt. He only hoped that by spending more time with Mary this obsession might burn itself out. For now it was making itself felt most uncomfortably in his groin. He released her hand and turned away before she could see that he thought of her as anything but a friend.

'Very well,' he said briskly. 'Will you ride out with me tomorrow, Miss Endacott?'

'I—yes, thank you.'

'Do you have a horse here?

She nodded. 'My gelding, Marron, is in the stables nearby. He is an indulgence, I cannot ride as often as I would like, and they keep him exercised for me.'

'I will call for you in the morning. I have business to attend to, but it should not take more than a few minutes. I merely need to confirm orders with some fellow officers who are billeted in a small château outside the city. Once that is done we could ride in the woods, they are particularly fine in that area. Do you have a groom to accompany you?'

'No, but—'

'Then I shall arrange for my man to come with us, for propriety's sake.'

Mary could do no more than mutter her thanks, dazed by this sudden change in the earl's demeanour. He remained just long enough to agree a time to call, then took his leave, departing with no more than a nod in her direction. As if he had come on a business call. As if that searing kiss had never happened.

Mary walked back to her desk and sat down. She picked up her pen, dipped it in the ink and looked at the half-written letter on her desk. Then she carefully laid the pen back down again. How could he change so quickly from passionate lover to cool acquaintance? Her own head was still spinning with the events of the past half hour. That kiss had told her she had not imagined the attraction between them, so how could they meet as mere friends? Was it possible? Randall certainly seemed to think so. She closed her eyes and shook her head, a rueful smile playing on her lips. He had told her he was not the man to woo her with pretty words or little gifts and she expected none, but his latest proposal was almost as shocking as his first.

Mary picked up her pen again and tried to force her mind back to the response she should be making to this particular parent. Friends. To be in Randall's company and deny the fierce longing that enveloped her at the very thought of him.

Could she do it? Of course she could. It was a most sensible solution. If they were chaperoned there could be no impropriety. She would have his company without risking her reputation or her livelihood. The alternative was never to see the earl again, and although that parting must happen eventually, it could be put off, at least for the moment.

The following morning dawned bright and clear and Mary was waiting with her horse on the Rue Haute when Lord Randall came riding up. His man, Robbins, was trotting behind him, his wooden countenance giving nothing away. Mary was already in the saddle, preferring to use the mounting block than to have the earl throw her up. It would be easier to maintain the friendly camaraderie if he did not actually touch her.

The road out of Brussels was busy, not only with the usual city traffic but also with military personnel. Mary was soon uncomfortably aware that she was exposing herself to gossip by riding out, even with a servant in attendance. Almost everyone they passed was a military man and the majority acquainted with the earl. They saluted or greeted him, but it was Mary that they regarded with varying degrees of amusement, surprise or sheer curiosity.

'Oh, this was not wise at all,' she exclaimed,

her cheeks flushed from the stares of the latest group of officers to pass them. 'This will set the whole of Brussels talking.'

'Does that matter? You are doing nothing improper.'

His haughty indifference made her smile.

'I had not thought of it yesterday, my lord, but it occurs to me that you are not in the habit of being accompanied by a lady.'

'No, that will of course cause some comment, but it will soon die down.'

His lack of concern went some way to reassuring her, but Mary did not relax until they had left the crowded highways and were following a track through the woods with no one else in sight. When they reached the pretty château that was Randall's destination Mary realised how quickly the time had gone by. They had been too busy talking to notice the miles passing. A laugh bubbled up inside her when she remembered Randall describing himself as a man who disliked incessant chatter.

Randall ordered Mary to remain at the end of the drive with Robbins while he conducted his business.

'It would not hurt your master to be a little more civil when he is making his requests,' she remarked to Robbins, when the earl had ridden off.

'Lord Randall is accustomed to command,

ma'am. 'Tis his way, and to my mind he's too old to change now.'

Mary bit her lip. What she saw in the rude, autocratic peer she could not think. Yet when he came cantering back towards her a few minutes later, the sight of his proud, upright figure made her heart skip a beat. She had heard Lord Randall described as cold and aloof. She had thought so herself, at their first meeting, but she had soon learned to take note of the tiny changes to his countenance that made it less inscrutable: the lines at the side of his mouth that deepened when he was withholding a smile, the way his eyes changed to a warmer shade of blue when he was cheerful. She recognised those signs now and her own tension eased.

'Well, my lord, is your business done?'

'It is. I am now at your disposal. Shall we ride through the woods?'

He led the way to a nearby valley and they plunged down between the trees until they reached a small rushing stream that babbled and chattered over its rocky bed.

'Oh, how charming!'

'We could walk a little way, if you wish.'

He dismounted and came across to help her down. She hesitated for a moment before dropping into his outstretched arms. She felt the dizzying excitement of his touch and had to concentrate not to clutch at him as he set her on the ground. They left the horses with Robbins and set off along the path, walking very close, but taking care never to touch. She could not help remembering their last encounter in the woods in England, when he had put her before him on his horse, held her close against him. Even now the thought of it sent a little shiver of pleasure running through her. It was a memory she would treasure, since it could not be repeated. She sighed.

'I hope I am not keeping you from any vital schoolroom duties,' said the earl.

'Not at all. With everything being so uncertain many of my pupils have left, so I have more staff than I require at the moment, although they do not all come to Antwerp with me.'

'Your plans to move the school there are in place?'

'Yes. Now we await events.'

'I think you should consider going very soon.' She stopped.

'Oh? Have you heard something?'

He shook his head. 'We thought there would be no engagement here—excuse me, but all I can say is that I would have you safe out of the way.' When she looked up at him he gave a self-conscious cough. 'Well, no, I would keep you with me, if I could, but you must think of your charges.'

'I shall do so, my lord.'

'Can we not be less formal when we are alone?'

'But we are not alone, my lord.' She glanced back at Robbins, following behind them leading their horses.

'Do not tease me, Mary.'

'I must tease you, if I am not to fall into a green-and-yellow melancholy over this horrid war.'

'It will be over soon enough.'

His cool tone flayed her nerves. When it was over he would be gone.

'And do you think that is any consolation?' She sank her teeth into her bottom lip. 'I beg your pardon. We agreed, did we not? We will enjoy each other's company for the little time you have left in Brussels.'

'We did.' They strolled on in silence until he spoke again, the words coming with difficulty. 'I think it will be very hard for me to leave you, Mary.'

And I you.

She summed up a smile, determined that she would not be the weak one.

'We come from very different worlds, Randall. Those worlds have tilted a little and brought us together, but they will right themselves again. We will say goodbye and go on as we did before.'

'Of course.' Randall spoke with more confidence than he felt. The looming conflict would be bloody and brutal. There was no certainty that he would survive, but if he should do so he was not at all sure that he wanted to go on as before. He was not sure he would ever want to say goodbye to Mary Endacott. He wanted her in his bed, that was true, but what he felt for her was more than that. He liked her company and when they were apart he was constantly wondering where she was, what she was doing. She said their worlds were too different, but were they? If so, surely they could not be so easy together, they could not find so much to discuss.

He stole a glance at her, studying her solemn profile, the shapely figure, enhanced by her olive-green walking dress. It was tailored to hug her waist and it accentuated the rounded swell of her breasts. He imagined the thrill of slowly unbuttoning the bodice of her gown. She would tremble as his fingers pushed aside the fine cotton chemise to reveal the soft, plump flesh beneath. How he wanted her! His arms ached to hold her but he had resolved they would be nothing more than friends, and he was too much a man of honour to go back on that. Yet he could not resist holding out his arm.

'In the meantime, we should enjoy our time together, should we not?'

Her fingers slid tentatively on to his sleeve. He covered them with his free hand and they fluttered a little, like a trapped bird. Their steps slowed and her eyes lifted to his face, a little shy, a little anxious, but there was no doubting the invitation in them. She *wanted* him to seize the moment.

'Ahem.' Robbins's voice floated down to them through the trees. 'The path looks a trifle rocky up ahead, my lord. P'raps it'd be best for you to come back to the main track now.'

Mary was still looking up at him, but the warm glow in her eyes had changed to amusement. She was equally aware of what might have happened, if Robbins had not been present. But she was not disheartened. His indomitable Mary! The dark lashes swept down, veiling her eyes and she said in her matter-of-fact way, 'Your man is quite right, Randall. We have gone far enough today, I think.'

Mary rode back beside the earl, enjoying his company, his conversation. She could not deny the ache of longing inside, but it was subdued, under control. If this was all that heaven allowed them she would be content, knowing from the look in Randall's eyes that he felt it, too.

When they reached the Rue Haute she drew rein and reached out her hand to him.

'Thank you, my lord. I enjoyed that, more than I thought possible.'

He caught her fingers.

'There is a recital at the Great Concert Rooms

tomorrow evening. If I am free, would you like to come with me?'

'I should, very much. But you must not be afraid to tell me, if your duty calls you away.'

He smiled and she felt the fine spiderweb of attraction growing stronger, binding her to him.

'Be assured I will do that. Until tomorrow then, Miss Endacott.'

Mary looked out her newest evening gown for the concert, an apricot silk with a small train. It was trimmed with dark green ribbons and there was a matching shawl, should the evening turn chilly. She had occasionally attended concerts before, but then she had slipped in almost unnoticed. Now, as she walked into the room on Randall's arm Mary was aware of the surprised stares of many of the patrons.

'We are attracting no little attention,' she murmured as Randall guided her to her seat.

'Take no notice. They will soon become used to seeing us together.'

There were very few people in the audience that Mary knew, so she decided to ignore the curious stares of the strangers and settled down to enjoy the recital, which comprised a selection of Italian love songs, performed by a celebrated opera singer. She was soon lost in the music and delighted when she discovered that Randall, too, was enjoying it.

* * *

'You did not come here merely because you thought I should like it?' she ventured, when the concert was over.

'That would be a very unselfish gesture, Miss Endacott, and you know I am not given to those.'

'I do indeed,' she replied, laughter bubbling inside her. 'But I thought you a plain soldier.'

'A soldier, yes, but an educated one.'

'So I see.'

They had emerged from the concert rooms and now stood at the entrance where the crowds were milling around.

'It will take an age for my carriage to find its way through this crush,' remarked the earl.

'We could walk,' suggested Mary, throwing her shawl about her shoulders. 'It is a fine night.'

'Would you mind?'

She smiled. 'Not at all. It is not far and would probably be quicker than waiting for your carriage.'

'Very well, then.' He took her arm and guided her through the throng. 'Did you really enjoy the music?' he asked, when they had reached the relative quiet of the darkened street.

'Very much, thank you for inviting me.'

'And you understood the Italian: I am impressed.'

'My father insisted I should be proficient, so that I could teach it to our pupils.'

'Was that part of the radical education he envisaged for young ladies?'

'No, no, languages are generally considered useful. My father wanted girls to learn philosophy and politics and, oh, anything that would fit them for their place in the world.'

'But it would not necessarily fit them for marriage,' observed Randall. He hesitated. 'What place was your sister expected to fill in the world?' He added swiftly, 'I hope it does not grieve you to discuss her.'

'Not as much as it did,' she admitted. 'I think it helped to tell you about Jane. It is not something I have shared with anyone before. My sister...' She paused, waiting for the familiar pain, but it had lessened considerably. 'At seventeen Jane had given little thought to her future. But she was always romantic.' She sighed. 'I think it was inevitable that she would fall in love.'

'It was unfortunate that it should be with a scoundrel.'

'Yes. If he had been an honest man Papa would have resigned himself to the marriage.'

'Even though he did not approve of the institution?'

'Even so. After all he himself had married to

protect his family, but he continued to fight for what he believed in, a more democratic society.'

'And the abolition of titles such as mine.'

Mary chuckled. 'My father believed that people should be rewarded for their talents, not their birth. He would certainly not have approved of your title. However, he *would* have approved of the artillery, where rank is dependent upon merit.'

'I am relieved to hear it. Your father would not completely disapprove of me.'

'I did not think that would matter to you.'

'It doesn't, but it matters to me what *you* think.'

Mary caught her breath at the change of tone, the earnestness of his words. Suddenly their easy companionship was gone. There was no frivolous response she could give him and she noted with relief the black outline of the schoolhouse looming up.

'I should like to know,' he said as they turned in through the gate. 'I would like you to tell me truthfully what you think of me.'

Mary swallowed.

'I think,' she said carefully, 'I think that you are too serious. You have been a soldier too long, Randall. You face death without a qualm, but, in some way, you are afraid to live.'

He was silent as they made their way to her front door and she wondered if she had offended him. She stopped and turned to him, saying impulsively,

'Randall, I am sorry—'

'Do not be.' He was looking down at her; she could feel his gaze although he was no more than a solid black outline against the night. 'Perhaps you are right. I chose a military life, it has been a series of battles and engagements and I have never looked beyond the next campaign. I have never wanted to contemplate any other life.' He sighed. 'Is it too late to change, do you think?'

'It is never too late to change, Randall.'

She whispered the words and was not sure if he had heard her.

He took her hands. 'Thank you, my friend, for your honesty. You must help me to live in the little time we have left together.'

'I will, my lord, if I can.'

He squeezed her fingers, waiting only until the door was opened before striding away into the darkness, leaving Mary to enter the house, keeping her face averted from the light so Jacques would not see that her cheeks were wet with tears.

Chapter Seven

May became June and Mary's ordered life was turned upside down. She arranged her days so that she could be free to join the earl at a moment's notice. She left the teaching of pupils to her staff and any matters requiring her attention were dealt with as quickly as possible each morning. The earl's duties kept him busy most days, but as soon as he returned to his lodgings he would dash off a note and she would be waiting for him when he came to take her to the theatre, a concert or a private recital, or on a fine evening merely to stroll in the park. Afterwards he would escort her to her door and take punctilious leave of her with no more than a kiss of her fingers.

It was a bittersweet time. Mary lived for Randall's visits, even though they were never alone and conducted themselves with rigid propriety. Every word, every look left her longing for more, but it was not to be and she would rather have his company than not. Her only comfort was that Randall felt the same, she knew it from the warmth she surprised in his eyes at times, the weight of his hands when he helped her with her cloak, resting on her shoulders a moment longer than necessary.

Although Mary felt incomplete when Randall was not with her, she did not idle away the rest of her day gazing out of the window, or daydreaming about him. She scorned such foolishness. Instead she filled her time helping out in the classrooms, reading the newspapers and making preparations to remove her staff and pupils to Antwerp. If there was nothing else to do she would pick up her embroidery, and if her stitches slipped every time she heard a knock on the door, it was not to be wondered at. All of Brussels was nervous now, buzzing with rumour and conjecture about the future.

There were other callers, of course, the most surprising of whom was Lady Sarah Latymor, who came several times to see Mary. She told her that her sister, Lady Blanchards, was increasing and could not accompany her about the city. Mary was duly sympathetic, but when Sarah suggested they should chaperone one another Mary was obliged to tell her that it was not possible.

'I do not think your brother would approve of you being here, Lady Sarah.'

'How can he object, when you and he are such good friends?'

Mary wondered how best to reply.

She said at last, 'You are a lady; I have to earn my living.'

'Oh, fiddle,' declared Lady Sarah. 'No one cares about that any more. Your birth is respectable, is it not?'

'Well, yes, but—'

'Then there can be nothing wrong with our being friends.'

'I do not think Lord Randall would agree.'

Sarah refused to believe it and went away promising to call again. Mary could only hope that Randall would not find her there. It was one thing for the earl to befriend a schoolmistress, quite another for him to allow his sister to do so.

Bertrand Lebbeke also called upon her, suggesting they might see a play, take a carriage ride, or even that she should join him for dinner with friends. Mary gently declined every one of his invitations. She was relieved when he accepted her refusals with a Gallic shrug but once, when he took his leave, he stopped at the door.

'Did you enjoy the concert last night?' When her eyes flew to his face he gave a rueful little smile. 'I saw you coming out of the Grand Concert Rooms, but you did not see me, you had eyes only for your companion.'

'L-Lord Randall managed to get tickets. It was a concert of Mr Haydn's music and extremely popular.'

'And you were extremely grateful to him, *non*?'

'Lord Randall is a friend, Bertrand, as you are.'

There was a hint of sadness in the look he gave her.

'You are trying to be kind, *ma chère*, but I think I know the truth, even if you are not yet ready to admit it.'

His words stayed with her, nagging at her conscience, and when a message came from Lord Randall to say he would take her to the play that evening she sent a note back to say she would meet him at the theatre.

He was waiting for her at the entrance, his height and bearing making him easy to spot. His shrewd gaze bored into her when she came up to him.

'Why this sudden independence, Mary, has something upset you?'

'Why, no, I thought I would save you the trouble of coming to collect me.'

'It would have been no trouble, my dear.'

She took his arm and accompanied him to their seats. Bertrand's comment made her more aware of her situation. She put up her chin. They were doing nothing wrong, Randall's attentions to her were perfectly proper, as an escort he could not be faulted, and if the warm look in his eyes set her heart thudding, and the merest touch of their hands made her spine tingle, no one could see that.

Besides it was all about to end.

'I received a letter this morning,' she said brightly. 'The house in Antwerp is ready for us. We leave on Monday. I have spent the day packing and very nearly did not accept your invitation this evening.'

'I should be sad to think you would leave Brussels without seeing me.'

Her mask slipped a little.

'I could never do that.'

'So this is to be our last outing together.'

'We have one more day,' she said, trying not to sound too eager. 'Tomorrow is Sunday. We take the girls to church in the morning, but after that I shall be at home. Perhaps you would come and take tea with me, or perhaps we might walk in the park, if the weather is fine.'

He shook his head. 'I shall be at Roosbos all day.' She tried to hide her disappointment, but he sensed it and took her hand. 'There are rumours that we shall see action soon. I have to make sure our preparations are complete. Otherwise—'

She squeezed his arm. It was reassuringly solid,

muscular. She could feel its power even through the thin silk of her gloves and his woollen sleeve. 'You have your duty, my lord. I would not keep you from that.'

'Thank you.'

The hot blue flame that lit his eyes was her reward, even as the misery of knowing they must part grew within her, like an inexorably rising tide. She pinned on her brightest smile.

'So after this we must say goodbye. I hope it is a good play.'

And with that she settled back in her chair to try and enjoy her last few hours in his company.

They sat side by side, watching the play, but Mary was all too conscious of him beside her, his thigh so close to hers, only a few thin layers of cloth between them and when, in the shadowy gloom of the auditorium, his hand sought hers she felt faint with longing to throw herself into his arms, to be so much more than a friend.

'What did you think of the farce?' asked Randall when the performance was ended.

They were waiting in the foyer for his carriage to come to the door. The crowded chamber was brightly lit and Mary kept her smile in place, knowing that speculative eyes would be upon them.

'It was very good.'

'Liar,' he said, without heat. 'I do not think you laughed once.'

'My thoughts were elsewhere.'

'Would you like to tell me?'

'No.'

'Ah. I understand.' He briefly touched her fingers as they rested on his sleeve.

That was the trouble, she thought miserably. They understood each other so well. At times there was no need for words. If only—

'Lord Randall!'

A shrill voice accosted them and Mary saw a matron in a fashionable bronze gown bearing down on them, the ostrich feathers in her turban nodding wildly.

'Lady Morrisey.' Randall's greeting was polite, if unenthusiastic.

'Sir Timothy told me you were in Brussels.'

The lady chattered on, her inquisitive eyes constantly darting from Randall to Mary and her conversation so pointed that the earl had no choice but to make the introduction.

'Miss Endacott, how do you do. Have you been in Brussels long?'

'About eight years, ma'am. I live here.' She added, a touch of defiance in her voice, 'I run an academy for young ladies.'

'Ah, that explains why I do not know the name, I have no daughters.' Lady Morrisey gave a trill of affected laughter and turned her attention back to the earl. 'I am off to meet Sir Timothy now, at the Appletons. He is not one for the theatre, you know, and much prefers to enjoy himself at cards, so he has gone directly to their little party. Are you going, my lord?'

'No, ma'am, I have already made my apologies.'

'Oh, but you could retract, I am sure. Why do you not bring Miss Endacott with you? There could be no objection, I am sure. There are so many officers in Brussels now that our parties are always in need of more ladies! Do say you will come, my lord. Sir Timothy would be pleased to see you again, and the Appletons' gatherings are always such lively affairs.'

Randall looked down at Mary. 'It is still early, would you like to go?'

Mary assented. A few more hours in Lord Randall's company, even if they were never alone, was better than the alternative, to return to the Rue Haute and her lonely bed. It was there, in the dark reaches of the night, that she would allow the truth to close in upon her and she would soak her pillow with tears of longing for a man who could never be more than a friend.

The Appletons had rented a house near the park and their rooms were overflowing by the time

Randall and Mary arrived. There was a predomi-
nance of uniforms and the earl was greeted on all
sides by his acquaintances and by fellow officers.
This was his world, Mary knew no one, but it was
not by chance that Mrs Appleton had become an
acclaimed society hostess. When Randall joined
a group of officers the lady drew Mary away to
introduce her to some of her other guests.

Mary was no shy débutante, she had been in
the world long enough to be at ease in company
and she could converse on a wide range of sub-
jects. Randall was occupied elsewhere and not by
the flicker of an eyelid would she betray that she
would rather be at his side than discussing the latest fashions with an overdressed matron and her
two giggling daughters.

It was inevitable, with so many officers present,
that the conversation would turn to the forthcoming battle, and speculation was rife as to how soon
they would be in action. Randall was caught up in
such a discussion, but all the while he kept an eye
on Mary as she made her way around the room.
His heart swelled as he watched her. She carried
herself with confidence, laughed and chatted as
easily with a crusty old brigadier as she did with a
shy young girl who looked as if this was her first
society party. She was much more at home than
he was at this sort of gathering.

She would make a good wife.

He stifled the thought. Soldiers were better off without wives. And libertines should never marry.

When the group dispersed he made his way across the room to where Mary was standing. He scooped two glasses of wine from a passing waiter and handed one to her.

'Here, Mary, I hope you have not been too uncomfortable without me. I did not mean to abandon you.'

She shook her head at him.

'I am perfectly content, my lord, everyone is very kind.'

'Truly?' He looked at her closely. 'We have never before been in company like this; it has given rise to speculation.'

She sipped the wine, her green eyes twinkling.

'There has always been gossip, my lord. And if there is any speculation about us, they are all too polite to raise the matter in my hearing.'

Randall grimaced. His fellow officers had not been so circumspect with him this evening. They had looked at him askance when he had introduced her, and when she had moved off they had been frankly sceptical of his explanation that Miss Endacott was no more than an acquaintance. He had ignored the sly glances and curtailed the lewd jokes with a haughty stare, but it irked him that they should immediately assume the worst of her, merely because she was a schoolmistress.

'I should not have brought you here,' he muttered.

But if he had not, then they would have driven back to the Rue Haute and he would have been obliged to leave her at the door, when what he wanted to do was to sweep her off to bed and make love to her. By heaven, it was becoming more and more difficult not to do so. The touch of her hand sent the heat hammering through his body once more, but it did recall his wandering thoughts.

'I am glad we came,' she was saying, smiling up at him in a way that made him want to kiss her. 'We are friends, are we not? I would not like to think that you are ashamed of me.'

'Ashamed? Confound it, Mary, you are as good as any woman here, and better than many of them. I wish I could—'

She put up her hand to stop him and for an instant he saw something cloud her eyes, like a shadow of pain, but when she spoke her voice was calm and light.

'We are agreed, are we not? Friendship is all we can offer each other. Pray, Randall, let us not spoil our last evening. Off you go. Enjoy talking with your fellow officers and leave me to amuse myself.'

* * *

Mary sent him away. He would never know how much it cost her to speak and act so cheerfully. It took all her will power not to cling to his arm and keep him by her side. She watched him walk away, noting his straight back, his broad shoulders, his noble bearing. She loved everything about him.

A sudden chill ran through her, like ice in her blood. Love? Is that what she felt for this abrupt, disdainful soldier? No, no, it could not be. Attraction, yes, and lust. Liking even, but nothing more. Yet when she remembered how low, how empty she felt when he was not with her, she wondered if perhaps she was deceiving herself. Mary quickly stifled all such disquieting thoughts, fixed her smile in place and turned her attention to the lady who was even now addressing her.

And so the evening went on. Mary and Randall went their separate ways around the crowded room, talking, smiling, joining little groups to listen to opinions and sometimes give their own. Occasionally they would meet then cheerfully move on, as if they truly were the friends they claimed to be. Mary did her part, holding up her head proudly as she explained to the ladies that she ran her own school, moving away from those who clearly thought she had no place in their gathering and conversing with those who were more liberal-minded. One part of her—the business side—realised that such contacts might prove useful to her school in the future.

That cold, bleak future without Randall.

It was well after midnight and Mary was growing tired. She was wondering how much longer the evening would continue, whether she might seek out Randall and suggest she should make her own way home when she heard her name.

'Miss Endacott, ain't it?'

A cavalry officer was standing behind her. There was something familiar about his carefully windswept hair and black moustache. She had seen him at the review, but that day his cheeks had not been quite so red, despite the sun and the heat. He was bowing low, affording her an excellent view of his black pomaded curls.

'Colonel Bennington Ffog, at your service, ma'am. Delighted to see that Randall has brought you into company at last.'

'Yes, thank you.' She could think of nothing more to say to this, but the colonel appeared not to need any encouragement. He put his hand under her elbow and guided her through the crowd.

'Always a dashed crush, these affairs, what? I believe you are a schoolteacher, ma'am.'

'Yes, I own an academy.'

'An academy, eh?'

'Yes. For young ladies.'

'No young men?' His eyes gleamed in a way that made her feel uncomfortable. 'By Jove, I would enjoy being a pupil in your class, ma'am. I can see why Randall is so enamoured.'

'I'm afraid I do not understand you, Colonel.'

'Discipline,' he replied with a grin that was very close to a leer. 'I have no doubt you keep our stiff-necked earl in line, what?'

She bridled at that. 'Colonel, I—'

Somehow he had manoeuvred her into an alcove and when she stepped away from him she found her back against a wall. To her dismay she realised she was out of sight of the crowded room.

'Oh, yes,' he continued, 'I would like to try a little of your discipline, Miss Endacott. A taste of your whip across my buttocks. Feel 'em.' He moved closer, trapping her against the wall as he grabbed her hand and pulled it around him and on to his backside.

'Let me go!'

'All in good time.' She turned her head as his mouth came towards her and she felt his lips against her cheek. 'Just a little kiss first.'

Mary struggled to free herself, but he was too strong, his body pressing against her, holding her prisoner. He smelled of brandy and hair oil and some sweet, sickly perfume that made her retch.

She felt his hands on her shoulders, pushing aside the silk gown while his wet mouth pressed kisses on her neck. She shuddered with revulsion. Why did no one come to her aid? There were dozens of people, she could hear them, laughing and talking. Surely one of them would step into the alcove? She tried to look past the colonel, but his body hid everything from her sight. He was pressing closer, his knee moving between her thighs.

Mary took a deep breath and was about to scream when Randall's voice cut through the air like a whiplash.

'What the devil do you think you are doing?'

She was free, she could breathe again. Bennington Ffog had been yanked away from her by Randall's hand on his collar. The earl subjected him to a furious glare.

'You had best apologise to the lady. Immediately.'

The icy fury in his tone made Mary wince. Her legs felt so weak that she dare not move away from the wall, but she managed to pull her gown back on to her shoulders with hands that trembled.

'Now, now, Randall, be reasonable. If you will bring your—'

'My what?'

The earl's voice was dangerously quiet and the colonel backed away.

'It, it appears I have made a mistake, then.' The

colonel ran his hands nervously over his body, straightening his uniform, his eyes never leaving Randall's stony face. 'I beg your pardon—'

'To the lady, Bennington Ffog. I will not accept your apology, and if she will not, then I swear you will meet me for this.'

The colonel's cheeks, flushed before, now turned beetroot. He swallowed, drew himself up and turned to Mary. She almost heard his heels click together as he bowed.

'Madam, my sincere apologies. It seems I mistook the matter.'

Mary's hands pressed against the wall as she looked at the two men before her. Randall's blue eyes blazed. There was murder in his face. If she said the wrong thing now he would challenge Bennington Ffog to a duel and heaven knew what repercussions that would have.

'I fear you have indulged in too much wine this evening, Colonel,' she spoke coldly, relieved that her voice was not shaking as much as the rest of her. 'I am willing to overlook your behaviour, this one time.'

His relief was almost comical, if Mary had felt at all like laughing.

'You are very good.' He bowed again.

'She is,' growled Randall. 'And more forgiving than I would be. You had best leave now, sir, before I take you to task for your impudence.'

Without another word the colonel walked off. Mary could hear the laughing chatter in the main reception, but she and Randall were alone in the alcove, screened from the crowds, and the air was taut as a bow string.

'Did he hurt you?' he asked at last.

She shook her head, not daring yet to move away from the wall that supported her.

'No. I am a little shocked. I did not expect—'

'You should not have been subjected to such gross impertinence.' The angry light in his eyes faded, replaced by concern. 'You are very pale; shall I fetch you a glass of wine?'

'No, no, thank you. I think I should like to go home.'

'Of course. Can you walk?'

'Yes, if you give me your arm. I refuse to have you carry me out of here over your shoulder, my lord.'

He relaxed slightly, as if this little show of spirit reassured him.

'Then let us go now.'

Their progress through the crowds was painfully slow, but Mary knew it would not do to hurry away. That would only arouse the conjecture they had so far managed to avoid.

'I cannot think that no one noticed what happened,' she remarked once they were in the earl's carriage and bowling through the dark streets towards the Rue Haute.

'No one could see you in that alcove.'

'So how did you know where to find me?'

'I have been watching you all evening. When I saw Bennington Ffog leading you away I followed, but it was slow work to do so without drawing attention to myself. I was obliged to stop and talk to goodness knows how many people on the way. I only wish I had got there sooner.'

Mary pulled her cloak a little closer around her.

'I am only thankful you arrived when you did.'

There was silence, then she heard Randall draw a breath.

'You should not have had to suffer that fellow's insults.'

'It is not your fault.'

'But it is.' He turned and pulled her into his arms. Gratefully she rested her head on his chest and felt the rapid thud of his heart against her cheek. 'I should have taken better care of you.'

She closed her eyes, feeling safe and comfortable at last.

'It does not matter now.'

'But it does. I wish—' He broke off as the carriage came to a stand. 'You are home.'

Reluctantly she pushed herself upright and allowed him to help her out of the carriage.

He said urgently, 'Let me come in. There is something I must explain to you.'

She hesitated. She felt drained, exhausted, but the thought of keeping him with her for a little longer was too strong to resist.

'Very well.'

He dismissed the driver and accompanied her to the door.

'I will walk back,' he told her as a sleepy maid-servant let them in.

Mary nodded and led him into the hall.

'Therese, light the candles in my sitting room, if you please.'

Randall followed Mary to the darkened room, where they waited silently until the maid had put a taper to every available candle. Mary removed her cloak and laid it carefully across a chair. He watched her strip off her gloves and put them down, her hands shaking a little. The shutters were already closed but the maid checked the catch, then hovered uncertainly by the window, reluctant to leave her mistress.

'Go to bed, Therese, I will see to everything.'

'But the door, *m'amselle*...?'

'I am quite capable of seeing the colonel out, Therese. Go to bed.'

'She is concerned for your reputation,' he remarked as the door closed behind the servant.

'After this evening I do not think I have any reputation left.'

'Bennington Ffog will not mention tonight's fracas, I will make sure of that.'

'Thank you, but it hardly matters now. I shall be leaving Brussels on Monday.' She glanced at the clock. It was gone midnight. 'Tomorrow.'

Randall was silent. He had said he would explain, but he had not thought how hard it would be. He took a turn about the room, coming to a stand by the table, where he stared down at the cheerful arrangement of fresh flowers.

'Are these from your doctor?'

'They are from Bertrand Lebbeke, yes.'

'You should marry him.'

He heard her sudden intake of breath. 'How can you say that?'

'Because I *cannot* marry you.' He closed his eyes, but the orange-and-yellow blooms had burned themselves on to his eyelids, taunting him with their sunshine colours.

'I have never asked that of you, Randall.'

'But I want you to know why. You already know that my father was a libertine, a womanizer. He fathered bastards wherever he went and made my mother's life a misery.' He paused, reliving the painful memory when, as a young boy, he had found his mother weeping over his father's peccadilloes. A tremor of repugnance ran though him; such a frivolous word to describe the old earl's philandering, his disregard for anyone or anything save his own pleasures. Had he been faithful to his wife in the early days of their marriage, or had she only ever been a brood mare, necessary for the continuation of the family name? It was the only time he had seen his mother cry. She had always been careful to hide her distress from her family but it was constantly there, in her eyes. He said now, 'I decided a long time ago that I could never marry, that I would never inflict such a future on any woman.'

'What makes you think you are like your father?'

'Suffice to say I know it,' he replied shortly. 'I have kept clear of the marriage mart. Oh, I know many women would marry me for my fortune and the title, but I do not want a loveless marriage. And yet the idea that a woman might care for me, love me, and I should treat her as my father used my mother—I could never do that. So I have done my best to avoid raising hopes where they cannot be fulfilled. I have consorted only with women who know it is mere dalliance. Married women or those who make their living by selling their favours.'

She was looking at him, hands clasped tightly before her. Her eyes were glowing, a deep sea green in the candlelight, shadowed with unhappiness.

'That does not mean you are a libertine, Randall.'

Did she want him to spell it out for her, that early episode that had shown him all too clearly that he was like his father? Even now he could not do it. He waved aside her arguments.

'Mine is not a constant nature. It is true, I have not looked at another woman since the day I met you, but we have only known each other a matter of weeks. What if I were to marry you—who is to say that in a few more months, a year, even, I won't tire of you?'

'That is a risk everyone takes when they marry.'

He shook his head.

'I am my father's son, Mary. His philandering broke my mother's heart, I watched it happen. I will not risk doing the same thing to you.'

The silence hung between them. Mary's hands were clasped so tightly they hurt, but she was glad of the pain, it helped her to concentrate.

'I am fortunate, then, that I do not ask you to do so,' she said. 'You know my views on marriage and we do not share that *commonality of intellectual interests* which would make a union acceptable to me.'

Was that true? Mary thought of the time they

had spent together. There had been no lack of conversation, but what it was they had found to discuss she had no idea.

'So we must say goodbye,' she continued, her voice unnaturally calm. 'There is no future for us once the war is over. I shall go to Antwerp, and by the time it is safe to return...'

'I shall be gone.'

Or dead.

She thrust aside the thought.

'We knew from the start it could not last, my lord.' She turned away from him, determined not to weaken. Pride came to her aid. The stubborn pride that had helped her to make her school such a success. 'I want to thank you for...for the pleasure your company has given me. And for your forbearance. There may be a little gossip about us, but by the time I return the fashionable set will have moved on and I shall be able to resume my business here as if we had never met.'

'Mary, I—'

'No!' She turned back to face him. She felt as brittle as fine glass. One wrong word and she would shatter. 'I am honoured by your confidences, my lord, and I shall not make this more difficult for you than it already is. Let us part now, as friends, with no hard feelings on either side.'

He looked at her, his blue eyes challenging. She knew then that if he took her in his arms they would neither of them be able to let go. Her head went up a little as she held out her hand to him.

'Goodbye, Lord Randall.'

The steady tick, tick of the clock was all she could hear. It seemed to go on for an eternity before he came forward to take her hand. She kept her fingers straight, not giving in to the urge to cling to him. His lips brushed her skin and she forced herself not to tremble.

'Goodbye, Mary. Bless you, my—'

He bit off the last word, turned and was gone. She listened to his footsteps as he crossed the hall, heard the outer door close with a thud, then silence.

It was over.

Chapter Eight

Randall rode to Roosbos early the following morning. Sunday. The bells were ringing, summoning the faithful to church as he left Brussels. He knew Mary would accompany her Protestant pupils to the court chapel for the service and he had to steel himself not to wheel Pompey about and detour there in the hope of seeing her. The past few weeks had been amongst the happiest, but the most frustrating of his life.

Never before had he put himself out for any woman as he had done for Mary Endacott, not even his sisters, and he was aware that by escorting her so publicly around Brussels he had aroused speculation. For Lord Randall, that confirmed bachelor, to take an interest in any single lady was bound to give rise to talk. He had made one mistake early in his career and since then his affairs had always been conducted out of the public eye. They were always brief, mutually satisfying, he hoped, and without any commitment on either side. He had also made sure the lady was well rewarded at the end of the liaison.

His friendship with Mary Endacott was very different. She asked for nothing save his company and it surprised him how much he enjoyed hers. He had quickly learned to recognise the little signs that gave away the emotion beneath her cool exterior, the way her eyes would light up with sudden humour, for instance. He soon discovered that very often he shared her amusement. She taught him to laugh, to appreciate the ridiculous. But she could be serious, too. Their very different upbringing gave them much to discuss and debate, but they always found some common ground that would bring them even closer. He liked the way her brow would crease when she considered some knotty problem or formulated an argument, and when a subject touched a raw nerve she would sink her teeth into her bottom lip as she struggled to contain her emotions.

He had seen her do so last night, when he had explained why he could not offer her marriage. She had used no tears or arguments to persuade him. Instead she had agreed, tried to make it easier for him to leave her, and in so doing the bonds between them had become even stronger. It had been as much as he could do to walk away. She was a completely new experience for him and he had not wanted to leave her, but there was no alternative. They had agreed the limits of their involvement from the start, neither of them could give more than friendship, and even then it could only be for a short time. But being friends with Mary Endacott had been a tortuous delight.

By the time he had known her a week the mere sight of her had set his temperature soaring. He was enchanted by the vision she presented with her creamy skin and dusky curls, and having held her in his arms, and carried her over his shoulder on more than one occasion he was well aware of the delectable figure hidden beneath her clothes. She liked to dress neat as a pin, but he had seen her ruffled, for example that very first time when he had kissed her and she had looked up at him, a hectic flush on her cheeks and eyes flashing with indignation, but also with the recognition of the connection between them. Since then he had kissed her only once, but he had often dreamed of it, and in his dreams he pulled the pins from her thick curls and watched that dark cloud of hair fall around her shoulders. She was not voluptuous, but neither was she thin; he judged that one gently rounded breast would fill up his hand. The thought aroused him and he shifted uncomfortably in the saddle.

'Thank God there is a battle coming,' he muttered as he rode into the camp. 'That will concentrate my mind very well. And by the time it is over Mary Endacott will be but a faded memory.'

He pushed aside the nagging whisper in his brain that told him it would not be that easy to forget her.

He spent the whole day at Roosbos, and if the officers thought him more curt and demanding than usual they knew better than to mention it. By the time he returned to Brussels the daylight was fading and after a solitary supper he fell into bed and a dreamless sleep of exhaustion. But Mary was there in his thoughts again the following morning. She would be on her way to Antwerp by now. They had said their goodbyes, but while he wrote letters, issued orders and concentrated upon his duties, her presence haunted him, like a ghost at his shoulder.

An officers' dinner at the Hôtel d'Angleterre occupied him for the evening, but when it was over he left the others drinking into the early hours of the morning while he set off for his lodgings in the Rue Ducale. However, his restless feet took him in the opposite direction. There could be no harm in it, he told himself as he walked through the dark streets towards the Rue Haute. Mary and her school had left, he merely wanted to assure himself that her property was intact, although when he asked himself what could have occurred in the few hours since she and her staff had quit Brussels he was unable to answer.

He should turn back. He had a meeting with Wellington in the morning and needed some sleep, but having come thus far he would at least walk to the school and take a look. The building came into sight, a solid square of black against the night sky. Randall stopped and stared at it, feeling a huge sigh welling up in him. She was gone and he would have to forget her.

He was just turning away when something caught his eye. A flicker of light through the cracks in the shutters. He stopped. There it was again, coming from Mary's sitting room. Common sense told him she would have left a caretaker at the house, but it could be an intruder. He could not walk away without ascertaining the truth. Quickly he strode to the door and banged upon it.

There was no sound from within. His hand went to the dress sword at his side. He would be a fool to investigate alone. Better to return in the morning when it was light. He was about to turn away when he heard the scrape of a bolt and the door opened a crack.

'Mary! What the devil—! What has happened? Have you delayed your departure?'

Shaking her head, she stepped back to allow him in.

'No, everyone went today, as planned.'

'And you stayed?' The leap of pleasure was instantly replaced by concern. 'You are here alone?'

'No, of course not. Therese has gone to Antwerp with the teachers, but she will return tomorrow. Jacques remains here to look after the schoolhouse, but he has gone to bed. He is very deaf and will not have heard your knock.'

'Then what the devil do you mean by opening the door?' he demanded angrily. 'I might have been anyone!'

The lighted candle she carried showed the twinkling gleam in her eyes.

'I glanced out of the window first to see who was hammering on my door at midnight, my lord. Your outline was unmistakable.'

His lips twitched, he could not keep the bubble of happiness inside him any longer.

'Mary, you are incorrigible!' He pulled her into his arms and kissed her, his heart leaping when he felt the tremor run through her, but she pushed him aside, protesting.

'My lord, be careful, or I shall spill wax over your uniform.'

'Damn my uniform,' he growled, but he released her, only retaining her hand. 'Is there somewhere we can talk?'

* * *

Mary led him into the sitting room, where only two days ago they had said their last goodbyes. Her heart was thudding so hard that it made her hand shake and she put the candle down on the desk as soon as she was able. As she turned back to him he pulled her into his arms again. They kissed; a long and deeply satisfying embrace that made her forget the tearing heartbreak of the past few days. She slipped her arms around his neck.

'I could not leave,' she whispered, when at last he raised his head. She rested her cheek against his coat, breathing in the dear, familiar smell of him, mingled now with the faint aroma of brandy and cigars. 'When the time came I could not quit Brussels, knowing that you were still here.'

'Mary—'

She raised her hand and put her fingers against his lips.

'Do you remember, you said that everything will change when war comes? I could not bear the thought of it happening without seeing you again, without feeling your arms around me.' She cupped his face in her hands, saying quickly, before she lost her nerve, 'I want you to make me your mistress, Randall. I want you to take me to your bed.'

He looked down at her, his eyes dark as the night sky in the dim light. Then he lowered his head and took her mouth. Her lips parted and she felt his tongue burn her, disordering her senses, and she responded hungrily. With something between a growl and a groan he picked her up.

'You shall have your wish, Mary. I cannot resist you any longer, I shall take you to bed this instant.'

'But there is no light on the stairs,' she protested, laughing in spite of the passion that raged within her. The look he gave her sent that passion soaring even higher and the laughter caught in her throat, leaving her breathless.

'You will have to carry the candlestick,' he muttered. 'Can you do so without spilling wax all over us?'

Giggling like schoolchildren, they made their way through the dark hallway and up the stairs, Mary directing Randall to her room.

When he set her on her feet she stood before him, feeling suddenly shy. Gently he took the candelabra from her hand and put it on a chest of drawers, then he turned and placed his hands on her shoulders.

'Are you sure you want this, Mary? There can be no going back.'

She knew it. She was risking everything for a brief spell of happiness that she might regret for the rest of her life. She smiled up at him. Tonight at least she had no doubts.

'I am very sure, Randall.'

He kissed her again, gently this time, while his hands worked loose the ties of her bodice. She did not question how he came to be so adept at undressing her or his familiarity with female clothing; instead she gave herself up to savouring every moment. His hands caressed her skin as her gown fell silently to the floor at her feet. He turned her around and began to unlace her stays. He laid a trail of feathery kisses across her neck and shoulders while his fingers pulled out the ribbons. As the constriction around her body lessened so desire flowered, filling her. At last she stood before him clad only in her stockings and chemise. She had never felt so vulnerable yet so alive. As he turned her back to face him she glanced up and found him smiling down at her, allaying her fears. He gathered up the soft lawn shift and drew it over her head, then he pulled her into his arms. The cloth of his coat was rough against her bare skin and suddenly she wanted him to be naked, too. She wanted to feel his skin against hers. She fumbled with the buttons of his coat even as he swept her up and carried her to the bed.

The covers were cold on her back but her body was already burning with desire. He eluded her arms and she watched him hastily shed his own clothes. The dim light of the single candle gleamed on his broad shoulders and across his chest with its shield of dark hair. Her throat dried, she ached to touch him and silently she reached out as he lay down beside her.

He pulled her into his arms and kissed her, long and deep. His tongue tangled with hers in a slow, sensual dance that sent little arrows of desire through her whole body. His hand slid down to caress her hip, but instead of slipping over the soft mound of her behind and pulling her close she felt it moving over her belly and sliding down to the apex of her thighs. She gasped as his fingers slipped inside her, slow and gentle. Her limbs began to relax, to soften beneath his caresses, but at the same time the pooling desire deep inside was growing steadily.

She sighed when he stopped. He pulled away, just enough to look at her. His face was no more than a shadow against the gloom.

'This is your first time, Mary,' he said, gently brushing the hair from her face. 'I do not want to frighten you.'

She reached up and cupped his cheek. 'I am not frightened, Randall. I want this. Truly.'

He kissed her again. She felt him hard and aroused, pressed against her body and her kisses increased in fervour. Instinct took over, she wanted him inside her and she allowed her body's movements to tell him so. He shifted above her and she responded, lifting her hips, offering herself, hot, moist and ready. Gently he slid inside her. When she flinched he paused, but her arms tightened.

She whispered quickly, 'Don't stop, Randall, don't stop now!'

He began to move, each time pushing a little deeper. She gave a little moan of pure pleasure. The pain had been small and momentary. Now she relished the sensation of having him inside her, those wickedly slow, sensuous strokes causing her body to contract. His mouth sought hers again, his tongue mimicking the actions taking place lower down in her body. He was moving quicker and she was aware of the excitement growing as he thrust into her, up to the hilt, and suddenly she was no longer in control. Her head went back and she cried out, clinging to him as her body rocked and pulsed with an energy all of its own, but even before the last tremors had faded he pulled away and she felt the warm wetness of him on her skin.

'Randall? I—'

He stopped her mouth with a kiss. 'I should not have entered you at all, but I could not resist you. But I will not make you pregnant, if I can avoid it.'

'Oh.' She hugged him against her, blinking away the sudden tears that moistened her eyes. His forbearance touched her and she pushed away the tiny pinprick of sadness at the necessity of it.

For a while they lay together, wrapped in each others' arms. Then Randall stirred.

'Are you happy?' he whispered, kissing her ear.

'Very.' It was true. She had never felt so at peace. 'Is that why my married friends have that satisfied look?'

He laughed softly and she felt its reverberations against her body.

'Possibly.' He nuzzled her neck. 'But we are not done yet.'

'Oh, I think I am,' she sighed and as he began to kiss her neck she put a hand against him. 'No, Randall, I cannot.'

'You can. You may have forgotten that we have not yet removed your stockings.'

She shivered delightedly as he ran one hand down her body, teasing her breast, caressing her hip, slipping over the sensitive join of her thigh and down to her knee. He pulled loose the garter and when he sat up she reached for him again, but he gently pushed her back. She lay still, enveloped in a pleasurable torpor and watched as he lifted her leg and began to roll down her stocking, kissing each inch of bare flesh as he uncovered it. Her body tingled, every inch of her felt alive from her head to the tips of the toes he was now laying bare to his kisses.

Her eyes devoured him, the flickering candlelight imparting a golden sheen to his skin and throwing into relief the taut, muscled lines of his body. He reminded her of the drawings she had

seen of classical statues, studies in grace and controlled strength. Randall was all that and so much
more. He was living flesh and blood and he was
hers, at least for tonight.

He transferred his attention to her other leg,
slowly untying and discarding her garter before
rolling down the stocking and kissing the exposed
flesh with infinite care until she was completely
naked. She should be nervous, this was all so new,
she had never exposed herself to any man like
this. Instead she felt a glorious sense of freedom
and power.

Randall was giving all his attention to her foot,
caressing the ankle, lifting it on to his shoulder before his fingers made their way back to the knee.
His hands were followed by his mouth, which
trailed lightly, teasingly along the sensitive, tingling skin. Slowly he inched onwards, smoothing
over her inner thigh, his fingers gently moving
towards the moist opening and she gasped to
feel those same fingers enter her warm core. Her
senses were still reeling from their first lovemaking and she gave herself up to the pleasure of his
touch.

Excitement rippled through her, so much so that
when she felt him withdraw her muscles tightened
as if to hold him within her, but a moment after
his fingers left her he was kissing her, his tongue
replacing those deft fingers and wreaking even

more havoc on her body. She responded by lifting her hips towards him, offering herself up to the pleasure of it. One hand slid over her breast, the touch of his fingers sending a thrilling shiver running through her, connecting directly with the pleasurable sensations he was creating with his mouth. Mary pressed her hands down on the bed on either side, clutching at the covers, unable to prevent a moan escaping her at the almost unbearable delight he was inflicting upon her. She wanted him to stop, to go on, she felt dizzy with excitement, losing control again.

'Randall!' She gripped his shoulders and tried to push him away, but his hands slid around her buttocks, holding her firmly while he continued to work his magic. Her body bucked and pulsed as he licked and suckled at her innermost core. She was shaken by intense waves of pleasure, one after the other. They rippled through her body, stronger, higher until she crested with a scream, and then she was falling, falling, as if in a dead faint, but she was not afraid, because Randall was holding her.

The soft grey light of dawn crept into the room around the edge of the drapes that curtained the window. Mary saw it and closed her eyes again. She had dreamed of this moment, of lying in Randall's arms. It was no longer a dream. He had taken her again in the early hours and she felt a little sore, her thighs ached slightly, but she was aware of a wonderful sense of well-being. She did not want to move, to disturb him but even as the thought occurred his arms tightened around her and he pulled her close to kiss her cheek.

'Good morning, Miss Endacott.'

She chuckled and snuggled closer. 'Good morning, Lord Randall.'

He kissed her again then raised himself on one elbow and smiled down at her.

'How are you this morning, no regrets?'

'None.' She felt the smile begin inside her and it was impossible to stop. 'I feel wonderful.'

His laugh was more carefree than she had ever heard it. He bent his head to plant a kiss on the tip of her nose.

'I am glad.' He rolled away.

'You are going?'

'I must. Brussels will be waking up soon and it will not do for me to be seen leaving a lady's house.'

She pulled the covers over herself, suddenly aware of the morning chill on her naked skin.

'Am I still a lady, after what we have done?'

He came back to the bed, his blue eyes glowing hot when he looked at her. 'You will always be a lady, Mary Endacott.'

She smiled, warmed by his words. It was not

true, of course, but she decided not to contradict him.

'If we are circumspect, it should still be possible to protect your reputation,' he said as he dressed. 'And yet I want to show you to the whole world. The Richmonds are holding a ball on Thursday. I will make sure you are invited.'

'I do not think so.' She sat up. 'A schoolteacher at a duchess's ball and invited at Lord Randall's behest? That would cause tongues to wag!'

'Very well.' He had finished dressing and now knelt on the bed for one last kiss. 'Then I shall not go. I shall come here instead.'

The kiss was a long one, but at last Randall dragged himself away.

'I must leave,' he said, smiling at her. 'The longer I stay the more chance there is of being seen.'

'You will return tonight?' she asked him, as he made his way to the door. She said impulsively, 'Come and dine with me, I have to go to the market to buy some food, I will buy extra.'

'Oh, and who will cook it?'

'I shall. I am quite capable, you know.'

'I do not doubt it. But what of your servants, what about the gossip?'

'Jacques has been with my family since he was a boy and Therese is devoted to me. They can be trusted to say nothing.'

'Very well, until tonight.'

When Randall had gone Mary slipped out of bed and ran to the window, from where she could watch him stride off down the deserted street. She remembered his warning, there could be no going back now, but she had no regrets. Not yet.

That evening she cooked for Randall. The servants had been given the evening off so he sat in the kitchen and watched her, and when the food was ready instead of carrying it to the dining room they ate at the big kitchen table, sitting side by side on the wooden bench and feeding each other with small mouthfuls from the delicious ragout she had prepared. Afterwards he took her to bed and made love to her. In the darkness he could feel the desire unfurling within her again, she became soft and pliant beneath his caresses. He was hard and aroused as his head moved to her breasts, where he took first one hard nub in his mouth and then the other, his tongue circling and stroking. She moaned softly, firing his desire to a fever pitch and when his hand slid through the triangle of dark curls at the apex of her thighs she gave a little gasp of delight. He cupped her, feeling her hips lifting as she offered herself to him. She was hot and slick and he slid into her easily, struggling to hold back as she tightened around him, her body stroking him. It took every last ounce of will-power to bring her passion to a head without losing control, but he succeeded, spilling himself harmlessly on the soft skin of her belly.

As he settled Mary in his arms and drifted off to sleep, Randall found himself wishing he might stay with her forever. He wanted her at his side for the rest of his life, to be his companion, his lover. The mother of his children.

He wanted to marry her.

The revelation unnerved him: she had turned his world upside down and he was no longer in control.

Mary stirred sleepily as he left her bed and began to dress in the half-light.

'Must you go?'

'My staying is like to ruin you.'

She watched him pull on his trousers.

'Most probably I am ruined already.'

'Do not say that.'

'Why not?' She sat up, pulling the sheet up to cover her nakedness 'I knew the risk I was running when I decided to remain in Brussels. Do not think I blame you for it.'

'But I blame myself.' He had picked up his shirt but now he cast it aside and sat on the edge of the bed. He took her by the shoulders. 'Mary, I know we discussed it, that you wanted this as much as I, but what you told me of your sister—'

She put her fingers to his lips, smiling lovingly into his face.

'I am not Jane and you have never deceived me. I know we must part and I am prepared for that.'

Randall shook his head.

'This is madness, Mary. We have let our passions run away with us.'

'Not quite.' She tried to speak lightly. 'You have behaved most responsibly by me.'

He did not smile. 'Not responsibly enough. I should have resisted.'

Even in the gloom Randall saw the pain flare in her eyes and he quickly drew her into his arms.

'Ah, love, I did not mean to hurt you.' She trembled against him and he dropped a kiss on to her curls, disordered from sleep and their lovemaking. 'These past weeks have been the happiest of my life.'

'But you would rather they had not happened.'

'No!' He let her go and turned away, saying in a low voice, 'You mean more to me than life itself, Mary, but we should stop now, before I hurt you.'

'You won't hurt me, Randall.'

'Not yet, perhaps, but I will, Mary. Given time what I feel for you will fade and I shall play you false.'

'You cannot know that.'

'I can, because it has happened before.' His hands gripped the edge of the bed on either side of him and he stared out of the window at the breaking dawn. He needed to explain.

'I was a young captain, spending my leave at Latymor House in London. It was one of the few times my parents were there together. They had decided it was time I should marry and arranged a match for me with one of Viscount Loxton's daughters.' He gave a little grunt of disgust. '*Any* of his daughters, I could take my pick of 'em, they were all for sale to the highest bidder. I shied away from that. I had the notion that I should marry for love.' He paused, letting his mind travel back to those heady days. He had been such a callow youth. 'Then I met the contessa. Teresa Carlotta di Rimini. She was a widow, beautiful, dark and exotic. I could not resist her. Within the week we became lovers.' He rubbed a hand over his eyes. 'I thought it was love and asked her to marry me. I promised to quit the military because she did not wish to follow the drum. I thought I was the luckiest dog alive. Then one day I called upon her unexpectedly and found another man in her bed.'

He heard Mary's soft gasp, felt her sympathy, but he could not stop now. She deserved to know everything.

'He was not the only one. I discovered she had been sharing her favours with several other men in London, including my father.'

'Oh, Randall!'

'I ended it as quickly as possible and paid handsomely for her silence. She had threatened to sue for breach of promise and what defence could I offer? I could not have all the sordid details dragged through the courts.

'My father...' Randall's lip curled '...my father laughed. He thought it a good joke. He told me I was most definitely his son. *"Do not worry,"* he said to me. *"Latymors are not made to be faithful. In a year from now you will have forgotten her."* And do you know the worst part of it? He was right. I had a succession of brief, heady affairs and soon realised I felt nothing for the contessa. Nor has my interest in any woman since lasted more than a few months. So you see, Mary, I cannot promise fidelity, I am incapable of a lasting passion. It has never worried me. I made up my mind I would never marry, never ask any woman to suffer as my mother has done.'

Mary listened in silence, her heart going out to him. She put her hand on his bare shoulder, aware of the faint roughness of the scars beneath her fingers.

'You were a young man then, Justin, little more than a boy.'

'That does not excuse my behaviour.'

'You fell in love with an experienced older woman who treated you shamefully. It is no wonder if you went a little wild. The fact that since then you have never allowed yourself to trifle with a respectable woman, that you have done your best to avoid raising false hopes, is not the behaviour of a philanderer.' Her hands slid over his shoulders and she pressed her naked form against his bare back, willing him to take comfort from her. 'You are not your father, Randall.'

'You are being very kind.'

'Kind!' She sat back, pulling at him until he turned to face her. 'I am telling you what I see. If you were truly a libertine, do you think you would be telling me all this? You would take your pleasures and leave me to suffer any consequences. Instead of that you wish to leave me, when we might have a few more days together.' She cupped his face in her hands and stared up into his sombre, brooding face. 'Is that what you want, Randall?'

His hands slid up her arms until they were resting on her shoulders.

'You know it isn't.'

She dropped her head to one side and rubbed her cheek against the back of his hand.

'Then come back to me when you can. I want to see as much as possible of you, until war comes.'

Randall felt his blood stirring again and fought to keep his calm.

'Don't, Mary. How can I do what is right when

you bewitch me like this? We are playing with fire, my dear, but this world is very unjust, and it is you who will suffer if we are found out.'

'I know it. We are agreed that marriage is out of the question and I am prepared to take the risk.'

His heart went out to her, his brave, indomitable Mary, who looked tousled and vulnerable and lovely in the cold morning light.

'You could lose your livelihood.'

'I shall manage.'

'I could make over an allowance—'

'No!' She pushed him away, her eyes suddenly fierce. 'I am willing to be your mistress, my lord, not your wife or your whore.' As always when she was angry, she addressed him formally, as if emphasising the difference she perceived in their stations. 'You insult me, sir.'

'That was not my intention.'

'Then let us talk no more of it.' The light of battle died from her eyes. She said wistfully, 'Shall I see you tonight?'

'I do not think that will be possible. Wellington is holding one of his suppers and I must attend. It will be very late when it is finished. Too late for me to call upon you.'

'I should not mind that.'

'But I should.' He kissed her. 'You take too many chances for me, Mary.'

She wound her arms about his neck.

'You are worth the risk,' she whispered. 'I believe in you, Randall.'

It was agony to leave her, but he managed it and made his way back to the Rue Ducale through the near empty streets. Telling Mary about the past had cleansed him and his mind was now full of her image, lying amongst the tumbled sheets, her hair a dark lustrous cloud against the pillows and a glow in her eyes that made him feel like a king. He had never felt so complete, yet he still wanted more, he could not wait to see her again. Mayhap he could send his apologies to the duke and spend the evening with Mary after all. He shook his head, knowing it was impossible and cursing himself for a fool, but a smile was bubbling up inside and his heart was singing as he returned to his lodgings to prepare for the day.

It was past midnight when Randall returned to the Rue Ducale and he was dog-tired. The news was not good; there were reports of the French moving towards the border. He must see Mary in the morning and persuade her to leave Brussels. The thought depressed him. At first he had tried to tell himself that it need not be the end, that he could send for her later, when the danger had passed, but in his heart he knew it would not work. Despite her protestations that she did not believe in marriage, if they entered into any other union the world would see her as his mistress. What would she do? She was not one for a life of idleness, but she would not be able to continue running her school. She would be shunned by his family and polite society, forced to live in the shadowy world of the *demi-monde* or the camp followers. The shame of it would kill her.

No, it would be best if they parted now, while it was still possible that he could leave her with her reputation intact.

It should not be difficult. He had known many women in the past and never felt more than a moment's regret at leaving any of them, but as he ran up the stairs to his apartment, some inner voice told him that leaving Mary would be different.

Robbins was waiting for him, a look of profound gloom and disapprobation on his rugged features.

'You have a visitor, my lord,' he announced in a voice of doom. 'She's waiting for you in your sitting room.'

'She?'

Robbins nodded. 'I tried to reason with her, my lord, but it was no good. Determined, she was.' He added as an afterthought, 'She did come veiled, though.'

Randall barely heard him. In two strides he had crossed the passage and opened the door to his sitting room. Mary was there, composedly reading a book. He should scold her and send her away, but he could not. It was as if he had conjured her by his wishful thinking.

'You should not be here,' he said, although he knew his eyes would give the lie to his words.

She rose and held out her hands to him.

'Jacques heard today in the market that the French are coming. Is it true?'

A ragged laugh escaped him. 'It would appear that gossip travels faster than the duke's spies.'

'But is it so?'

'I fear it is.' He took her outstretched hands and squeezed them. 'It is time; you must leave Brussels, Mary.'

'Not yet. I shall remain here as long as your fashionable ladies. You will not be rid of me as easily as that, my lord.'

At the sight of her smile, the soft glow in her eyes, his tiredness left him. All considerations of restraint disappeared. He swept her into his arms and kissed her before carrying her through into the adjoining bedroom.

Their coupling was as heady and overwhelming as ever. Her touch inflamed him as he covered her soft skin with kisses. He burned to bury himself deep within her, but forced himself to go slowly, determined to put her pleasure first. She moved restlessly beneath him but he refused to hurry, keeping himself under control until he had taken her to the edge of frenzy and only when she tipped over the edge did he allow himself to finish.

They lay together in the darkness, sated, complete. When the night air began to cool their skin they slipped between the bedcovers and fell asleep, waking with the dawn, still wrapped in each others' arms.

When Mary awoke she was aware of two things. One, that it was daylight and Randall was still with her. The other, that she was not in her own bed. She was at Randall's lodgings. She had arrived there after dark, heavily veiled. His man had recognised her and had not sent her away, although what he thought of such forward behaviour she dreaded to think. Instead she considered Randall's reaction. He had been surprised to see her, but pleased, too. She stretched and pressed herself a little closer to his naked body. He was sleeping, snoring gently, the soft sound like the quiet growl of some sleeping beast. A tiger, mayhap, certainly something dangerous.

She slipped her leg over his thigh, revelling in the feel of skin on skin. He shifted his position and she felt him, aroused and hard against her.

Such warmth, such closeness, how would she ever live without it? How would she ever live without Randall? The soft snoring stopped. He was awake now. His arms tightened around her and she felt the rough stubble of his cheek against her skin as he sought her lips. She pushed the unwelcome thoughts away as she gave herself up to his kiss.

An hour later they were still in bed, listening to the sounds of the city coming in through the open window.

'Thank goodness I have a veil,' she murmured as she lay beside him, her head resting on his chest.

'Robbins shall order a carriage to take you home.'

'And shall I see you there this evening, my lord?'

'Unfortunately not. The duke is insisting his officers attend the ball tonight.' Her disappointment must have shown in her face for he hugged her, adding, 'It is an order and I am obliged to obey it.'

'Perhaps the duke is trying to reassure everyone that there is no need for alarm.'

'Perhaps.'

'Will you be able to come to the Rue Haute afterwards?'

'I do not know.'

His hesitation was brief, but it was enough. She

clung to him, suddenly knowing that this would be the last time she would see him. She knew a moment of terror, or weakness, and could not stop the words from bursting out of her.

'Oh, Randall, I wish you did not have to fight, I would give anything to have you safe away from here!'

'I am a soldier, Mary. Fighting is what I do.'

'Of course.' She forced a smile, ashamed of her outburst. 'I would not have you other than you are.'

Her bravery was rewarded with a kiss, but much as she would have liked it to go on forever she broke it off.

'It is growing late, my lord. We must get dressed.'

'Always so sensible, Mary.'

'Would you rather I clung to you, weeping?' She slipped off the bed and began to collect up her clothes.

They dressed quickly and in silence, each wrapped in their own thoughts. Mary used the small mirror on the wall to brush out her curls and re-pin them. Her eyes strayed to Randall's reflection and their eyes met.

He cleared his throat. She had learned it was a sign that he was ill at ease.

'Mary, when this is over, do you think you could put aside your radical principles and live with me?' She froze and he continued, a note of apology in his voice. 'As my wife, I mean. It would have to be marriage, I'm afraid. I have responsibilities that I cannot shuffle off and I want you with me at Chalfont. Could you take that risk with me? And it is a risk, you know I have never proved faithful to a woman yet, but with you I think I could do it. So what do you say, do you think you could bear to be my countess despite your principles, could you bring yourself to marry me?'

Her hairbrush fell from her nerveless fingers and she turned towards him, staring.

She said slowly, 'I would not ask that of you, my lord.'

'I know, but it is the only solution I can think of since I cannot live without you. It would mean compromise, I know, but I would not expect you to give up everything that you believe in. You would be taking the fight to the enemy, so to speak.' For a moment his eyes glinted with laughter before they grew serious again. 'I do not want to lose you, Mary. I am very much afraid that I love you.'

Her vision blurred and she blinked rapidly.

'Oh, Randall!'

'You are crying,' he said, frowning. 'I did not mean to make you unhappy.'

She gave a shaky laugh.

'I am not unhappy. Knowing you love me has made me the happiest woman in the world.'

'And do you think, perhaps, that you might be able to love me?'

'I do.' She went into his arms, turning her face up for his kiss. 'Oh, Randall, I love you so much.'

'*Can* you love me?' he asked at last. His hand cradled her cheek as he wiped away her tears with his thumb. 'I am not adept at soft phrases or kindly gestures.'

'You told me as much from the beginning,' she said, smiling mistily up at him. 'I love you even more because of it.'

'Then you will marry me?'

With terrifying clarity she knew there was nothing she wanted to do more, but something held her back, some inexplicable feeling that if she agreed, if she went against all the teachings of her childhood, she would be punished.

'Ask me again, when the battle is over.'

'Say yes now and I will write to my mother, then if anything should happen to me—'

Quickly she put her fingers against his lips.

'Do not say such things. I am very much afraid that if I accept your proposal now some vengeful deity will take you away from me.'

Randall laughed and shook his head. 'My men will tell you I have a charmed life, or a charmed sword.' He nodded to where his uniform was hanging from a peg on the wall. 'You see the sword hanging up there? It is my dress sword, worn for occasions such as the ball tonight. In here is another sword.' He walked over to the large trunk pushed against the wall and lifted the lid. 'This one is a much older weapon. You can see how the decoration has lost its glitter and the scabbard is worn and faded with use. It belonged to my grandfather. He wore it at every engagement and I have done the same, it has always seen us through safely. It is the Latymor Luck.' He closed the lid and turned to her. 'Does that reassure you?'

She shook her head. 'I cannot believe you would put so much store in a superstition, my love, it is not like you.'

Randall wondered for a moment if he should answer truthfully, but he wanted to drive the anxious look from her eyes, so he said confidently, 'The Latymor sword is different: I would not think of going into battle without it.' One glossy ringlet was lying on her shoulder and he picked it up. It curled around his finger, reminding him of the way she had wound herself around his heart. A foolish analogy. By heaven, he was becoming quite sentimental, but for once he did not care. He lifted the curl to his lips. 'Go and finish putting up your hair, my love, you look as if you have been ravished.'

His words dispelled the shadow from her eyes and the twinkle returned. They sparkled at him, emerald green.

'That is just what has happened to me.'

She looked so adorable he could not resist another kiss, then reluctantly he let her go. A clock somewhere chimed the hour. Nine o'clock. Robbins would be pacing up and down, waiting to shave him. Let him wait. He would not rush Mary out of his rooms. He might never see her again.

Chapter Nine

At last Mary was ready to leave. She had delayed as long as she could, savouring those final moments with Randall, knowing it could be the last time they were together until after—she drew in a stiffening breath. She must be strong. He had enough to concern him without worrying about her, too.

She had only to put on her cloak and bonnet, but before she did so she went into his arms for one final kiss. She wanted to beg him not to leave her, not to fight, but she knew he would never neglect his duty so she must be brave, show him that she could be a good soldier's wife.

'Goodbye, my love.' She touched his cheek, the dark stubble rough beneath her fingers. He covered her hand with his own and pulled it down to his mouth, pressing a kiss into the palm.

'Never goodbye, Mary. If you have to leave

Brussels before I return, go to Antwerp and I will find you there.'

'Of course.'

What if we are overrun by the French? What if we have to quit the country?

What if you do not survive?

The questions ran around in her head, but she dared not voice any of them. Instead she said calmly, 'Will you ask Robbins to call a carriage for me?'

He went out to find his servant and she put on her cloak and bonnet. By the time he came back she was shrouded from head to foot, the heavy veil pulled down over her face so that Randall should not see the tears on her cheeks. When he reached out for her she resisted.

'No, please, do not touch me.'

She took his hands and squeezed them, knowing that if he came any closer, if he took her in his arms again, her bravery would desert her and she would break down in tears.

Randall stood by the window and watched the carriage drive off, carrying Mary back to the Rue Haute. She was gone and heaven only knew when they would meet again. He felt as if she had taken his heart with her and left a gaping, aching void. He turned away. There was no time to dwell on his feelings. There was work to do. Striding to the door, he called impatiently for Robbins to bring his shaving water.

The morning was well advanced when Randall rode out to Roosbos. As he trotted into the camp he was struck by the air of calm tranquillity. Men were sitting around camp fires or lounging at their ease against the gun carriages, enjoying the sunshine. They needed to be ready: from the reports he had heard in Brussels he knew it would not be long before they were called to action. He sought out Flint, eyeing the dishevelled officer with disfavour. He knew before he gave the order what Flint's reaction would be. He saw the look of horror on the major's face even before he had finished speaking.

'Many officers would give a month's pay for an invitation to the duchess's ball,' he barked, when Flint had made it perfectly clear that he would rather not attend.

'Then let Major Bartlett go,' suggested Flint, his tone only a hair's breadth away from insolence. 'Or better still, Sheffield. He's less of a rogue than the rest of us.'

'If you think I would let Bartlett anywhere near the ladies then your wits have gone begging,' retorted Randall. 'And as for Sheffield…'

He paused. Major Sheffield was more of a soldier and less of a rogue than the others and that was the problem. He had not yet stamped his authority on his men and Randall could not risk taking him away from them at this vital juncture.

'No,' he said now, fixing Flint with a stare that would make lesser officers back away. 'I need you there. Get yourself cleaned up and try, just try, to look like a gentleman for a change.'

'I don't see—'

'You will smarten yourself up—that's an order,' roared Randall. 'The duke may not be a stickler, but I'm damned if I'll have you bringing my command into disrepute!'

'Yes. Sir.'

Those blue eyes, so very like his own, glared back at Randall. Damn his father for littering the country with his bastards. Having his half-brother in his troop was a constant reminder of the old man's philandering. It brought back all Randall's doubts about marriage and he felt a sudden chill, a fear of failing Mary.

'By heaven, I will not disappoint her,' he muttered.

'Colonel?'

He realised Flint was still standing there and he dismissed him with a growl. By God, he was getting too old for this.

Randall rode back to Brussels, pushing Pompey to a gallop wherever he could, as if he could

outrun thoughts of Mary. He must concentrate
on the coming fray, it would not be long now. He
had sent a message to Bennington Ffog, asking
him to release Gideon for dinner that evening.
Randall had seen little of his brother while they
had been in Brussels and he thought he should
spend some time with the boy, especially with a
battle looming.

When he walked into his lodgings on the Rue
Ducale his first question was whether there had
been a reply.

'Yes, my lord, Major Latymor will be dining
with you: he sent a messenger with the news, not
half an hour ago.'

'Thank you, Robbins. I suppose it must be the
dress uniform tonight.'

'Yes, indeed, my lord. I have it all ready for
you.'

Randall stifled a sigh and went through to the
bedroom with his man close on his heels. It was
not that he disliked his uniform, just the pomp
that wearing it entailed. To be paraded around the
ballroom like some sort of trophy—he thought
of Flint's disgust at being asked to make himself respectable this evening: perhaps he and his
half-brother were more alike than he was prepared to admit.

* * *

Randall was just wondering whether to put dinner back when Gideon came in, apologising, but not very sincerely, for being late.

'You are off to the Richmonds' afterwards?' he ended, taking in Randall's uniform, complete with an impressive number of medals. 'I was not lucky enough to get an invitation, hence my undress this evening.' Gideon indicated the ankle-length frock coat which he now shrugged off and threw carelessly over a chair.

'Luck, do you call it?' said Randall, handing him a glass of wine. 'I would as soon not be going.'

'It is your title,' replied Gideon sagely. 'The duchess wants all the nobility she can muster in her rooms tonight.'

Randall held his peace: his young brother was prowling restlessly about the room, nervous, unsure of himself and Randall had no wish to sound conceited by admitting that Wellington himself had commanded his attendance.

They sat down to dinner, Randall doing his best to show an interest in the conversation and putting aside the thought that he would much rather be dining with Mary Endacott. He found his brother's stories a trifle tedious, relating the tricks and pranks that he and his fellow cavalry officers had indulged in over the past few weeks. Randall tried to be generous. They were little more than boys, after all, and Gideon would not be the only one who had not yet been tested in combat. There was a brittleness about him, a bravado which Randall had seen many times in young men before they went into their first battle.

By the time the covers had been removed and the brandy put on the table Gideon was looking a little flushed, his blue eyes over-bright. Randall poured them one glass each, then deliberately put the stopper back in the decanter and pushed it out of reach.

'Have you seen Sarah today?' he asked casually.

'Aye, we went riding this morning.'

'She and Gussie should have left for Antwerp by now.'

'Well, they haven't gone,' replied Gideon, unconcerned. 'You worry too much, Justin.'

'I thought you said I did not interest myself enough with my family.'

'Aye, well that's as may be, but Sarah and I are of age now, you know. You need not concern yourself over Sarah, I never do.'

Randall's frown deepened.

'Perhaps it would be better if you did.'

'She will go in the morning, I am sure, but she has an invitation to the ball tonight.'

'The devil she has!' Randall sat back in his chair and tried to curb his irritation. 'You might not think it, the pair of you, but I do have your best interests at heart.'

'I doubt that,' retorted Gideon bitterly. 'Why, you would not even buy me a commission.'

Randall's brows went up.

'You never asked it of me.'

'No, because I knew what it would have been if I had done so! You would have told me to wait a few more months, and by heaven if I had done that then I should have missed all the fun of Brussels.'

'Fun? Confound it, Gideon, isn't it enough that there are two of our family already caught up in this war?'

'You count that mongrel Flint as family?' Gideon's lip curled. 'God knows why you advanced his career.'

'Because he is a good officer who looks after his men,' snapped Randall. 'Something you have yet to learn.'

With a curse Gideon threw himself out of his chair.

'It is always the same,' he said bitterly, 'No one can do anything but you! Well, I have had enough. I have escaped from under your thumb, Justin, and I mean to distinguish myself in this campaign.'

Randall regarded him in silence. It would be useless, inflammatory even, to remind Gideon that he had never been under his thumb. Perhaps it would have been better if he had taken more responsibility for his siblings, instead of leaving their upbringing to Mama, but she had always said that looking after the children was her only solace and after the hell his father had put her though, with his insatiable appetite for women, he had not the heart to interfere.

He watched Gideon for a few moments. The boy was prowling up and down the room like a caged animal. At last he said quietly, 'It is merely that I would rather you were safe back in Chalfont Magna.'

'No! It is *you* who should be at the Abbey, looking after your interests. Mama cannot be expected to run your affairs forever, you know.'

'I do know it, but it gives Mama an interest. Besides, we have an excellent steward and the present arrangement has worked very well for years.'

Randall wondered if he should tell Gideon that he intended to go back after this engagement. But it was never wise to think too far ahead. He might not survive, and if that was the case, Gideon was the next in line. And if Gideon should fall? Well, there were the younger twins, but they were still at school and his mother would have to hold the reins for a few more years yet.

He said, as much to reassure himself as Gideon, 'I am not needed at Chalfont.'

'Oh, aren't you?' Gideon retorted. 'Do you know what our people think, Justin? They think you are just like Father.'

'What nonsense. They know nothing about me.'

'Aye, and that's the trouble! Everyone thinks the reason you stay away from Chalfont Magna is that if you did your whoring there you would be wenching with your own kin.' Gideon glared at him. 'You should quit the artillery, Randall. You are the sixth earl, your place is at the Abbey, not here. And if I had my way I would see that you were forced to go back and take up your responsibilities!'

Randall jumped to his feet. 'Why, you—!'

'My lord.'

Robbins's entrance prevented Randall from replying. His man told him that one of the duke's aides was downstairs and wanted a word. Randall excused himself, glad to leave the room before he said something rash. He had been close to losing his temper and uttering a blistering set-down to the insolent cub, and he really did not wish to do that, not tonight. Besides, on one point Gideon was right. He had left the running of the Abbey and the estates for too long in the hands of others.

When Randall returned, Gideon had put on his frock coat and was ready to leave. He was standing very stiff and regarded Randall with a defiant look.

'Let us not part on a sour note.' Randall put out his hand. 'You are quite right, I should be thinking of settling down and leaving this business to younger fellows like yourself.' He smiled. 'I have no doubt you will acquit yourself well, Brother.'

Gideon's eyes slid away from his, but he reached out and gripped Randall's hand for a moment.

'Yes, that is—thank you.'

'Goodnight, Gideon, and I wish you success. Truly.'

He thought for a moment that Gideon would speak again, but he only nodded and quickly left the room. Randall listened to his footsteps dying away on the stairs, then with a shrug he called for Robbins to bring his hat and gloves and made his way to the Rue de la Blanchisserie and the Richmonds' ball.

Mary did not enjoy her solitary dinner. When she had left Randall the streets had been busy with soldiers and wagons. There could be no doubting that the army was on the move. And yet the fashionable English would continue with their merrymaking. She thought of Randall attending the ball in all his military splendour. He would look magnificent, she was sure, but no more so than when he stood before her in the bedroom, quite naked, his lean body strong as whipcord, the muscled contours accentuated by the gleaming candlelight. She pushed away her plate. She would go to bed and try to get some sleep ready for her departure to Antwerp in the morning.

She was in her sitting room, trying to compose a short note to Randall when Lady Sarah Latymor was announced.

'No, no, do not get up,' cried her visitor, flying across the room and waving her hand in a peremptory manner. 'We are such friends now we do not need to stand on ceremony. I have come to invite you to the ball.'

'I beg your pardon?'

Mary's eyes moved to Jacques, who had followed Lady Sarah into the room. He put a large box down upon a chair before retiring and closing the door upon them.

'The Duchess of Richmond's ball,' said Sarah. 'My sister is indisposed and cannot go with me. I have told her I have found a perfectly respectable chaperon. That is *you*, Miss Mary Endacott.'

Mary stared in astonishment at her guest's smiling face.

'I hardly think that will satisfy her. Why, I do not know her.'

'Well, she knows that you are a great friend of Harriett's and she has seen you with Justin, too.'

Mary felt her cheeks grow hot, but thankfully she was not obliged to reply, for Lady Sarah was continuing blithely.

'It would be such a shame to waste the invitation.'

'Surely you can go alone?' Mary saw the shadow cross Sarah's face and her eyes narrowed. 'Is there some reason why you should not do so?'

'Oh, well, Justin does not know I am still in town.' She pouted. 'He almost *ordered* Blanchards to take Gussie and me out of Brussels immediately, but if the duke has told Lady Richmond· that she should hold her ball, there cannot be any immediate danger, can there? So Gussie said we may stay a little longer. She was eager to go tonight, but unfortunately her interesting state has made her very unwell and she is quite prostrate, poor darling. And so I thought you could come with me instead.'

In spite of herself, Mary's lips twitched. 'You need a little moral support.'

'Do you not want to go?'

Mary hesitated. She had not wanted to go and be pointed out as Randall's mistress, or snubbed because she was not one of the fashionable set, but to attend the ball with Lady Sarah would be an altogether different matter. And the thought of seeing Randall once more was very tempting. Sarah gave a little laugh and clapped her hands.

'I can see by your face that you do wish to go. Come along, Mary, the carriage is outside, waiting to take us there.'

Mary rose and shook her head, spreading her hands to indicate her sober gown.

'I cannot go. I am not dressed for a ball, and it is nearly ten o'clock.'

'Oh, no one arrives at these affairs early. Mary, do not be difficult.'

'I am not being difficult, but—'

Lady Sarah overrode Mary's flustered denials by saying triumphantly, 'And if you are going to tell me you have nothing suitable for a ball, I have brought you one of my gowns! It is only a muslin, so you need not think it is anything very special. There can be no objection to your wearing it.'

Mary stared at the box that Sarah was holding out to her. Common sense told her to refuse, to send Lady Sarah away, but she could not resist carrying the box to the table and opening it.

'Oh.' She lifted out the gown and held it up. It was fashioned from the finest cream muslin, gossamer-thin and embroidered with tiny white flowers. 'Oh, it is quite exquisite.'

'I have never worn it,' said Sarah carelessly, 'it is too short for me, but it should fit you beautifully.'

Mary stared at the pale confection and thought ruefully that it was far too virginal for her now.

However, the thought of seeing Randall once more had taken hold. She smiled.

'Give me ten minutes!'

Slightly more than ten minutes later she was back in the sitting room, shyly asking Lady Sarah's opinion. Recalling the Rogues' uniform, she had added a dark red sash to the gown and threaded a matching ribbon through her curls. Another ribbon fixed her only ornament, a small cameo, around her neck and her finest Norwich shawl completed the ensemble.

Lady Sarah clapped her hands delightedly.

'You look very elegant, Mary! Randall will be so enchanted he will quite forget to scold me.'

'Let us hope so,' murmured Mary as her companion took her arm and led her out to the waiting carriage.

The house the Duke of Richmond had hired for his family was in the less fashionable lower town, but the lights blazed and even at this advanced hour a number of carriages were drawing up. Mary was relieved to think they would not be the last to arrive. She accompanied Lady Sarah into the ballroom where dancing was already in progress. The ladies were arrayed in all their finery and the majority of the men were in uniform, providing a glittering, colourful spectacle. She spotted Randall immediately, catching her breath when she saw his tall, upright figure resplendent in his long-tailed dress coat, the dark blue embellished with gold lacing and scarlet facings. As if aware of her glance he turned and met her eyes. The smile that lit his face put to flight any remaining doubts she'd had about attending. Lady Sarah was swept away by a crowd of laughing cavalry officers and Mary made her way towards the earl, as if there was some string between them, drawing her in. He took her hand and bowed over it.

'You came.' His blue eyes glinted, sending little bolts of excitement through her. 'You will dance with me?'

She blushed. 'Surely there are other ladies who should take precedence.'

'Not tonight. Do you realise we have never yet danced together?'

'I do.'

She was filled with exhilaration at the idea but when he went to lead her on to the dance floor she held back.

'I would have no misunderstandings between us, my lord. Your sister brought me, in Lady Blanchards's place.'

'Did she?'

'Do you not mind? You had advised them all to leave Brussels.'

'How can I object, since her staying means I can now dance with you?'

Mary flushed with pleasure, from her toes to the top of her head. She knew her cheeks would be pink and her eyes sparkling, but it no longer mattered. Let everyone see how she felt about the earl, how he felt about her. Tonight they would be happy and tomorrow… She would not think of the morrow.

They took their place in the set and as they waited for the music to begin Mary looked around, desperately trying to find something to say rather than merely smiling like a simpleton.

'I see Major Flint is here and looking very smart.'

Randall gave a short laugh, his eyes flicking quickly to his half-brother.

'Yes, he has been cutting me out with the ladies all evening, but I shall make sure I keep you well away from him.' He leaned closer. 'You are mine, Mary Endacott.'

His words and his glowing look sent a shiver of happiness through Mary. The music began and she danced in a joyful haze. At one stage she found herself standing beside Sarah, who took the chance to bemoan the fact that her twin was not present.

'I was sure Gideon would be here tonight, but Colonel Bennington Ffog says they only had a few invitations and the officers drew lots for them. I haven't the heart to refuse to dance with all those who have asked me, not when they will be going off to fight at any moment.' She pouted. 'But I really wish I could have spoken to Gideon.'

The movement of the dance separated them and Mary did not give Sarah another thought. She forgot about everything except the delight of being with Randall. They danced twice, three times and Mary protested that people would talk.

'Let them.' Randall replied carelessly. 'It does not matter who knows about us now.'

She laughed, giddy with happiness as he led her from the floor, but the little worm of anxiety gnawed away at her when she saw the number of officers bustling around Wellington. She was not surprised when Randall excused himself a few minutes later. She let him go with a smile. Not for the world would she add to his worries by tears or anxious looks.

Mary made her way around the edge of the room, but as she did so she became aware that she was attracting attention. Ladies glanced at her and lifted their fans to whisper to their neighbours. She tried to ignore it, but she knew what was happening. She had danced too often with Randall. People were remembering how often she had been in company with him, probably some had seen him entering her house, others might connect her with the veiled figure leaving his lodgings that morning. A sly look and laughing comment from one of the ladies she had met at the Appletons' party convinced her. Everyone now knew she was Randall's mistress.

She kept her head up and her smile in place. To slink away would be to admit shame and she felt none. She loved Randall and he loved her, let the world think what it wished.

Randall returned to the ballroom. The music was still playing, the floor still crowded with dancers, but if he had missed one set or two he had no idea, his mind was working on the orders he had received. He must find Mary and take his leave of her. He looked around, searching the room for her dainty figure in its white gown and deep red sash. At last he found her and hurried up to take her hands.

'We have our orders,' he said. 'I do not have long; I have already sent word to my lodgings.' He grinned, although it was an effort. 'I am prepared to ride directly to the battlefield in full dress, but I'm damned if I will do so in my dancing shoes.'

Someone tapped him on the arm, one of a group of gentlemen wanting to know what was going on. He was drawn into the crowd, everyone asking if there was any news. To the civilians he gave a vague reply, to fellow officers his answer was brief: the French were within hours of the city. It was time to move.

Mary made no effort to follow him. He would come back to her before he left, she was sure of it, but tonight he was a soldier first, and must do his duty.

'Mary!' She looked round to find Lady Sarah at her side. 'Is everything well? You and Justin look so, so *happy* together.'

Mary nodded.

'It is very well,' she said. 'My heart is so full, Sarah, I think it may burst. Randall—Justin—explained something, he wanted me to understand why he was so against marriage.' She clutched Sarah's hand. 'It was not easy for him, but I believe it was a testament to just how much he loves me.' Mary did not think her smile could grow any wider. 'I am so happy, Sarah, I am confident that Randall has fought his last battle.' She giggled, suddenly feeling quite ecstatic. 'And I am to be his countess!'

A movement close by made her look up and she saw Randall returning. She put out her hand, but even as she did so his attention was caught by someone across the room and with no more than a faint nod he turned and walked to the door. Mary's eyes followed him. Robbins was waiting for him in the doorway and looking very grim.

Mary's happiness was quickly dimmed by the thought of the bloody conflict to come, but she tried to hide it from Sarah. The girl had two brothers fighting and she did not wish to add to her distress.

'His last battle of the heart, at least,' she continued, trying to be brave. 'He knows that when he returns I shall be waiting for him.'

Damn. Randall veered away towards the door. He wanted to take his leave of Mary alone, not with his sister looking on. He would go back as soon as he had seen Robbins. Impatiently he followed his man back to the ante room and sat down to pull on his Hessians.

'Well?' he said, getting to his feet again. 'Where is the Latymor sword?'

Robbins coughed. 'I couldn't find it, my lord.' He looked up fleetingly at Randall. 'I've looked everywhere. It was in the trunk last night, my lord, that I'm certain of, because I had to move it to put in your buckskins that I had brushed clean. I haven't been to that trunk since.'

Randall stared at him. He rubbed his chin. It had been there this morning, because he had pointed it out to Mary. Then with crystal clarity, he recalled the words he had overheard her speaking to his sister.

I am confident that Randall has fought his last battle.

A cold fist squeezed his heart. He must be mistaken. He gave himself a mental shake and waved his man away.

'It doesn't matter, Robbins.'

'But, my lord, you always—'

'I have my dress sword; that will have to do this time. I must have moved the other one and forgotten about it.'

But he knew that was a lie. The words Mary had uttered so passionately echoed in his head.

I would give anything to have you safe away from here.

The conviction was growing, heavy as lead in his chest. He dismissed his batman and returned to the ballroom, his brain racing.

Mary was not from a military family, her parents had been radicals, her father a confirmed anti-royalist and a supporter of the revolution in France. She had told him that she was opposed to war, but he could not believe she would do anything to prevent him fighting. Yet he had not opened the trunk since Mary had left. No one else could have taken it. And what else could she mean by those words to Sarah?

I am confident that Randall has fought his last battle.

His eyes raked the room. Mary was standing by the wall. She was alone now, smiling and tapping her foot in time to the music as she watched the dancing. Could she look so happy if she thought he was going into battle? Nearer the door couples were saying goodbye, their faces sombre, distraught. A young wife was saying a tearful farewell to her officer husband and when he walked away she fell into her friend's arms, weeping. A stark contrast to Mary's seeming unconcern.

Randall felt a touch on his sleeve and turned to see Major Flint at his shoulder.

'You were looking for me, Colonel?'

'The game is on, Major. Ride back to Roosbos and get the men moving, quick as you can. I will meet you at Enghien.'

'You are not coming?'

Randall's mind was still on the missing sword. He remembered Mary standing in his room, cloaked and veiled, ready to leave. He went over their last meeting, moment by moment. She had sent him off to find Robbins, to ask him to summon a cab for her. He had only been gone moments, but long enough for her to take the sword from the trunk and strap it around her waist. And when he returned she had refused to let him embrace her. She had put out her hands and kept him at a distance when he had so much wanted to hold her one last time. Why should she do that, if not to prevent him discovering what she was carrying? His doubts were hardening into certainty.

He said grimly, 'Not yet. I have some unfinished business.'

Randall strode across the room, his temper rising. He recalled another occasion, when he had told her what he expected of his men.

Unquestioning obedience? I do not think I could give anyone that.

Suddenly it all made terrible sense.

As if aware of his eyes upon her Mary turned her head and he saw the smile falter. A look of pure terror flickered across her face. As well it might, if she guessed he had found her out. He had trusted this woman. Bared his very soul to her and this is how she repaid him.

The rein he had been keeping on his anger finally snapped.

'Well, madam, did you think that your actions would keep me from fighting beside my men?'

She was smiling again, but there was a shadow of doubt in her eyes and in her voice when she answered him.

'I thought by coming to the ball I would see you once more, my lord, was that so very foolish?'

'I am not talking about your being here, madam. I am talking about the sword.'

'Sword? I—'

He dismissed her words with a wave of his hand.

'Do not add lies to your treachery, Miss Endacott. I may have told you I would not fight without the Latymor sword, but that was merely a sop to soothe your feminine nerves. I do not believe in such superstitious nonsense.'

'I never for a moment thought—'

'Did you not?' His temper flared. He had never known a rage like it. Not only had she had betrayed him, but she would not admit it, even though he had heard her boasting to Sarah.

The pain went far deeper than anything he had felt before, because she had betrayed him. He should have learned his lesson with the contessa. Women were not to be trusted. He needed to lash out, to make her feel something of his pain.

'No doubt you saw your chance of becoming a countess slipping away, is that it?'

'No! You know I care nothing for your title.'

His lip curled. 'Strange, then, that as soon as I proposed you jumped at the chance.' He was being unfair and he knew it, but her betrayal spurred him on, he could not help himself. 'The idea that I might not return to marry you was too fearful to contemplate, so you thought you could keep me with you by stealing my sword. Well, it won't work, madam.'

She was staring up at him. A moment ago her cheeks had been delicately flushed. Now they were white as her gown. White. The colour of virtue. How wrong he had been.

'You think I would t-take your sword?'

She looked the picture of bemused innocence, the little crease in her brow, the confusion in her eyes, her voice little more than a thread. He had not realised what a good actress she was.

'I do not think it, I *know*!' His lip curled. 'Where are your fine, radical principles now, madam?'

The earl's blue eyes blazed, but it seemed to Mary that a stranger stood before her. She was dazed by the violence of his attack and could find no way to counter it. Her brain seemed to be moving very slowly, trying to make sense of his words. She heard Lady Sarah's breathless voice at her side.

'Justin, everyone is leaving. They say the French are upon us, is that so?'

For a moment Mary was free from that ferocious glare as Randall's eyes moved to his sister, but only for an instant, then they were back upon her, harder than ever.

'This was part of your plan, too, I have no doubt. To ingratiate yourself with my family in the hope of finding favour with me.'

Mary could barely think straight, but this last accusation was too much. She dragged her head up.

'I have no *plan*, as you call it, and did not ingratiate myself with anyone.'

'You are a jade, madam. A scheming, ruthless jade. I have no doubt now that you meant all the time to catch yourself a title.'

Sarah gave a little gasp. 'Justin, you cannot believe that?'

'Do not be fooled by her quiet demeanour, Sarah. This woman has done everything she can to worm her way into my life. She insinuated herself into Hattie's company, worked it so that I had no choice but to escort her to Brussels and since then she has been practising her deception, convincing me that she was reluctant to receive my advances. Hah! Pretty good work for an impoverished radical's daughter, was it not, Miss Endacott, to have an earl lay his heart at your feet.'

She flinched as his words and his scathing tone flayed her, but it made no sense.

'I have done nothing to deserve this,' she said quietly.

'Justin, I am sure you are wrong.'

Randall rounded on his sister with a snarl. 'She has fooled you, Sarah, just as she did me.' He paused. Mary watched the muscle in his lean cheek working as he controlled his anger. When he spoke again his voice was quiet, composed. Hard as steel. 'The duke has given orders that everyone is to prepare for war. Go back to Gussie, Sarah. Tell Blanchards he must take you both out of Brussels with all speed. And as for you...' he turned back to Mary, cold fury in his eyes '...I would advise you not to be in Brussels when I return.'

Reeling from his attack, Mary could only watch as he walked away, his back ramrod straight, his head high. Sarah touched her arm.

'What was that about, what has happened?'

'He thinks—' Mary put one hand to her mouth. She felt sick. 'He thinks I stole his sword. The one he always takes into battle.'

'The Latymor sword? But why?'

'He called it his lucky charm.'

'But Randall has never believed in that sort of thing.'

Mary shook her head, her eyes still fixed on the door through which Randall had now departed.

'No, but he believes I have betrayed him.' She could feel the tears welling up. 'I must go home. I must find a cab.'

'I shall take you.'

'No, no, Randall does not want you to associate with me any longer.'

'Oh, stuff!' Lady Sarah snorted. She put her arm about Mary's shoulder. 'Do not worry, when Justin calms down he will see that you did not take his silly sword. Robbins has probably mislaid it. My maid is always losing things and they always turn up again later. My brother will be back to beg your pardon before you know it.'

Mary knew that would not happen. Randall did not back down. He did not apologise. He had told her so himself. Why should a proud aristocrat humble himself for her? She allowed herself to be guided out of the ballroom and remained silent as they collected their cloaks and made the short journey back to the Rue Haute. She was still smarting from Randall's anger and the injustice of it, but her heart was squeezed by a greater worry, one that she could not share, especially with Lady Sarah. Randall had gone off to fight: what if he did not come back?

Chapter Ten

The groom was waiting with Pompey at the door and Randall threw himself into the saddle. It was a relief to be mounted on the big grey and riding through the night; it stopped him dwelling too much on Mary's treachery. He gave himself a mental shake. Enough. His personal concerns must wait, there was much to do, lives could be lost if he did not concentrate on his duty now. Reveille was sounding as he rode out of Brussels and his progress was slowed by the chaotic bustle of soldiers marching, officers riding to and fro and any number of aides dashing out of the city, carrying fresh instructions from the duke. His frustration was only increased by a succession of conflicting orders and the fact that his troop arrived at Quatre Bras too late to take part in the action.

The following morning everyone's dissatisfaction increased when they were given orders to retreat from Quatre Bras and make for Genappe. Flint and Bartlett's divisions moved off under the leaden skies, but a bad-tempered fight broke out amongst Sheffield's men, delaying their departure. Randall hesitated. He was loath to interfere, but Sheffield was the most inexperienced of his majors and might need his support. An aide raced up and addressed him hurriedly.

'Sir Augustus sends his compliments, my lord. He asks that you attend him with all haste.'

Randall could not ignore a summons from his commanding officer. The men were back under control and beginning to move slowly on to the road. Wheeling Pompey, he set off after the aide. He would have to leave Sheffield to it.

An hour later he was galloping in pursuit of his troop, cutting across the fields, but when he rejoined the highway where it emerged from a small town there was no sign of Major Sheffield or his artillery. They were clearly still amongst the houses. Randall glanced anxiously at the heavy clouds. If it started to rain it would become almost impossible to make much more progress today, as the poor roads would churn up into a muddy quagmire.

Randall cursed under his breath. Where the devil was Sheffield? He turned Pompey and galloped into the town, racing through the streets until he arrived at a large square, where he was met by a scene of chaos. British cavalry and French chasseurs were milling around in a confusing mass, swords flashing and hoofs ringing on the stone paving, while Sheffield's gun carriages were trapped in a narrow street leading off the far side of the square. Bennington Ffog was in the thick of the action and Randall's eyes quickly searched amongst the cavalry for Gideon, but he could not see him.

He kicked Pompey onwards, galloping around the fray towards the artillery unit. There was no sign of Sheffield, but he recognised the cavalry officer at the entrance to the street, shouting out orders to the Rogues.

Randall let out a roar. 'What in damnation is going on here?'

Gideon turned to him, his eyes shining with the light of battle.

'Lord Uxbridge ordered the artillery to follow him through the streets, but the French were waiting. Sheffield is dead. We need to retreat. I've given the order to reverse by unlimbering. It's damned tight here.'

Randall glanced around him. Each gun was pulled by a team of eight horses, difficult enough to turn in the open, but in the confines of the street it was well-nigh impossible.

'You are right,' he conceded. 'It's the only possible way. But where's Uxbridge?'

'Gone,' said Gideon tersely. 'To get reinforcements, I hope.'

Randall nodded. 'We have to keep the damned French at bay while the men get those guns away.'

'I am with you, Brother. We'll have to stop them here.' Gideon drew his sword. *'Semper laurifer!'*

They brought their horses side by side in the entrance to the street, ready to prevent the French from passing them. In the square the hussars fought bravely, but every now and again a group of chasseurs would break away and surge towards the artillery. Randall and Gideon held them back while behind them the men worked swiftly, manoeuvring the gun carriages and horses. Randall fought mechanically, his mind racing. His dress sword handled well, although he had never used it in battle before. He had noticed that Gideon's sword was not the usual curved sabre carried by a cavalry officer, but a straight blade. It took only a second, brief glance to tell him it was the Latymor sword. *His* blade, or rather, his grandfather's. Randall blocked an attacking blow from a French chasseur and parried with a deadly thrust of his own. Had Mary somehow given it to Gideon? It made no sense. And why was Gideon commanding the artillery? Four more chasseurs were charging towards them: no time for anything now but to fight.

At last the guns were limbered up and retreating back the way they had come. And just in time, for the French chasseurs were making a dash for the street. Randall had lost sight of Gideon. He looked round to see his brother had dismounted to help a fallen bombardier to his feet. Randall shouted a warning as he saw Gideon's horse trotting off behind the gun carriages. There was no time for more, the French charged upon Randall, who resisted furiously. The narrow street meant only a couple of chasseurs at a time could attack, but as quickly as he despatched one another would take his place. He held Pompey steady in the centre of the street and fought fiercely, but he could not keep them all back. At least two chasseurs swept past him, only to be brought down by Gideon who used his sword to deadly effect.

The French kept coming. Randall's arm was tiring when he heard the clear, ringing sound of a bugle. Behind the remaining Frenchmen he saw the welcome sight of British cavalry bearing down upon them. His assailants turned to face this new threat and Randall allowed his aching arm to drop. The rain that had been threatening all day began to fall in a soft, silent drizzle.

Breathing heavily, Randall looked back to see the last of the gun carriages lumbering away into the distance. A couple of French horses followed them, their riders lying lifeless on the ground. He wheeled Pompey, looking for his brother. Gideon was kneeling on the road, his sword still in his hand, his head bowed. Randall threw himself from the saddle and ran up to him.

'Easy, Gideon.' He caught the boy as he keeled over, easing him on to the ground and keeping one arm around his shoulders as he ran a practised eye over his body. Randall's mouth tightened into a thin line. Gideon's left arm hung down uselessly, slashed almost to the bone, and dark stains were beginning to spread over his red coat, which was cut to shreds.

'Did we save your guns, Justin?'

The words came out with difficulty, each word on a rasping breath.

'Yes, we saved them, Gideon, thanks to you.' Randall began to unfasten Gideon's jacket, praying the sword wounds had not touched any vital organs.

'Good. The men lost heart when Sheffield fell and Rawlins didn't seem to know what to do.' Gideon gave a faint laugh that ended in a gasp. 'Not so easy as it seems, this soldiering.'

'Indeed not. Try not to speak now.' He eased open the tattered jacket. The shirt beneath it was crimson as Gideon's life blood seeped away. Randall looked about him frantically. The artillery

had disappeared and the cavalry had drawn the
French back into the square to finish the fight.
There was no one to come to his aid, but in his
heart he knew from his brother's rattling breath
that he was beyond help.

'It's growing very dark,' Gideon whispered.

'It's the rain,' said Randall. 'The clouds are
very heavy.'

'It did not work for me, your lucky charm.'
Gideon's bloody right hand lifted the sword a few
inches from the ground. 'I took it. When I came
to see you on Thursday. Hid it beneath my frock
coat. Thought you'd not fight without it. Foolish
of me, to think that.'

'Yes. Damned foolish.'

Gideon dropped the sword and clutched at Randall's sleeve. 'I did it for Chalfont, Justin. Mama
would never tell you, but she is getting old. She
needs you to look after the estates now.'

'I shall do so, Gideon. As soon as this is over.'
Randall felt the grip on his arm weaken and added
urgently, 'Stay with me, boy. We will get you to
a doctor very soon.'

'No, I don't think so.' The voice was no more
than a thread. 'Damned bloody business, war.'

Randall did not reply. His throat felt thick and
too clogged even to cough.

'Justin, are you still there?' Gideon's eyes
stared up sightlessly.

'Yes. I am here.'

'I didn't do too badly, did I?'

'You did well. I am proud of you, Brother.'

'Good.' The boy relaxed. Randall looked round again, cursing under his breath.

'Where the devil is everyone?'

'Too late for me.' Gideon winced. 'Tell Sarah I died well, Justin.'

Randall bit his lip, but even as he tried to find the words to reassure Gideon the life went out of the boy and his head dropped to one side, as if he had fallen asleep. There was a flash of lightning and thunder reverberated through the air. The drizzle turned to a downpour and washed the blood and grime from Gideon's young face.

'Don't worry,' Randall muttered. 'I'll tell her she can be very proud of you.'

Above the noise of the rain Randall heard voices and running feet. Flint had arrived with a party of men. Randall laid Gideon gently on the ground and rose to his feet. He blinked rapidly.

'Confounded rain is in my eyes,' he growled to Flint, who was standing beside him.

Thunder crashed and rolled around the skies. Raising his voice to make himself heard above the storm, Randall gave orders for Flint to take care of the body, then he walked to his horse and rode away without a backward glance.

Gideon was right. War was a damned bloody business.

* * *

There was no time for Randall to dwell on everything Gideon had said, to do more than regret—bitterly—that he had stormed at Mary and changed the warm glow in her eyes to one of bemused horror and heartbreak. The unit had to retreat to Genappe to meet up with the other two divisions that were some way ahead of them. Apart from giving Rawlins a dressing down for letting another officer—even worse, a cavalry officer—take charge of his troop, he had said no more about the incident. At one point they came upon the main body of the cavalry drawn up beside the highway and Randall's eyes narrowed when Bennington Ffog broke away and cantered towards him on his showy black charger.

'Colonel Randall, sorry about your loss, old fellow. Your brother was shaping up to be a fine officer.'

Randall nodded, not trusting himself to speak. He was glad to give his attention to Pompey, who had taken exception to the black's posturing and swung his head to nip at the glossy flank that was temptingly close. Bennington Ffog was momentarily alarmed by the attack, but he was not going to be driven off until he had delivered the ultimate humiliation.

'Died a hero, though, what? I told him to follow Uxbridge, but instead he stayed and saved your artillery division from being captured by the enemy. I shall be making sure Wellington knows of it.'

Randall's eyes narrowed in response to the fellow's guffaw of laughter. He said coldly, 'If he had stuck to his orders, my brother might be alive now, Colonel.'

The laughter stopped immediately. 'What? Oh, yes—yes, of course. Well, mustn't keep you. You'll be wantin' to get your men settled for the night.'

Bennington Ffog saluted and rode off, leaving Randall scowling after him.

'What in damnation did he want?'

Randall did not have to look round to know that it was Major Flint who had ridden up. His angry tone was unmistakable and perfectly matched Randall's mood.

'Offering his condolences,' he said shortly. 'I might ask the same of you. Why are you here?'

'Bartlett's division and my own are already bedded down for the night on the far side of Genappe. I came back to find Rawlins and show him the way, to save him taking the artillery pieces into the centre of another town.'

'Very well. Let's find the lieutenant.'

He turned and Flint fell in beside him. Randall

noted that his half-brother was leaving a safe distance between them: not that it was Pompey who was likely to be the aggressor this time. Flint's brute of a horse was known to lash out at anyone or anything within range.

Something of a Latymor trait, thought Randall grimly. Certainly one that he and Flint shared. And Gideon? No, his younger brother had merely been foolhardy.

'He'd been sent ahead with Uxbridge,' he said suddenly. 'That's when he came upon Rawlins and his men trying to get the guns turned about.'

'And the damned fool wanted his moment of glory.'

'He had the Latymor sword. He must have taken it when he came to see me on Thursday.'

And Mary was innocent.

'The devil he did.' Flint shot a quick look at him. 'The men noticed you weren't wearing it yesterday. Your lucky charm—'

'It carries no more luck with it than that tree stump.'

Worse, it had caused him to lose her.

'With respect, Colonel.'

Randall frowned, knowing Flint was never in the least respectful.

The major continued. 'It isn't what you or I know, it's what the men *think*. I'd wager it was the lack of the sword that panicked Rawlins and his men once Sheffield was dead. It's why they were so quick to follow Major Latymor.'

"Well, I am wearing it again now,' snapped Randall, dropping one hand to the familiar, worn hilt at his side. His dress sword would be taken back to Brussels along with Gideon's lifeless body. 'Make sure the men are all aware of it.'

He dug his heels into Pompey's flanks and the grey responded by breaking into a canter. Damn Flint for being right. But it made Gideon no less a hero. If he hadn't been there to whip up the men, God knows what might have happened to the guns. He would have to keep a close eye on Rawlins until another commanding officer could be found. It wouldn't be easy, the Rogues were well named, every man of them a villain, but they'd perform as well as any unit in Wellington's army, under the right officer. Give them the wrong one and they were as dangerous as those plaguey rocketeers whose damned missiles could never be relied upon to go in the right direction.

The morning found the Rogues taking up their position on a ridge above the Nivelles road with a square of infantry behind them. Looking down at the corn growing on the slopes before them, Randall could see it was full of Frenchmen, but they were retreating in the face of the deadly fire of the riflemen advancing upon them. However, it was not long before Randall's troop came under fire from the enemy guns on the far hill.

'Go to it, Rogues,' he roared. 'Show them what you can do!'

Chapter Eleven

Mary lay in her bed, eyes closed. She had dreamed that she was dancing with Randall, that he was looking down at her, smiling, his eyes shining with love. The happiness faded as memory returned. If ever he had loved her it had been short-lived.

Two nights had passed since that dreadful evening at the Duchess of Richmond's ball and she had heard nothing from Randall. She had returned to the Rue Haute, dry-eyed, too distraught for tears. Randall had accused her of taking his sword. That he should understand her so little, trust her so little, wounded her deeply. She refused to allow Lady Sarah to stay with her lest she incur even more of her brother's wrath. Besides, Mary did not want company. No one could ease the pain within her.

The morning after the ball, streets that had

been noisy and bustling with activity throughout the night were eerily quiet. No bugles sounded, the cobbles did not ring with the sound of horses or marching feet. Mary had spent the day trying to come to terms with what had happened. Randall had left Brussels and he did not wish to see her again. It was the worst of partings, no soft words or tender looks to remember, just his chilling anger.

'I did nothing wrong.'

She uttered the words aloud more than once during the long Friday following the ball, while she roamed the schoolhouse, wandering aimlessly through the empty rooms. Jacques and Therese kept her informed of the rumours that were spreading like wildfire through the city. At first they said the French were repulsed; then that the British had been cut to pieces. Mary ignored them all and as soon as dinner was over she ordered Jacques to put up the shutters and she went to bed, but not to sleep. For a second night she lay awake for hours, at last falling into a fitful doze that was disturbed by dreams of Randall as she wanted to remember him, smiling at her, loving her. But with the dawn had come reality, and the pain was still there.

A knock at the bedroom door roused her. She sat up as her maid came into the room.

'I have brought your *chocolat chaud, m'amselle*. You slept well?'

'Yes.'

Mary lied. She could not tell her maid how she had lain awake in her bed, going over Randall's words, trying to work out why he had thought her capable of betraying him.

'Jacques went out early to see if there was any news.' Therese put down her cup and bustled about the room, chattering all the time. 'The thunder we 'eard yesterday, *m'amselle*, it was from a battle. At Quatre Bras.'

'Oh.' Mary felt nothing but a dull ache inside.

'Many of the English they are leaving Brussels now, *m'amselle*. Perhaps you would like me to pack your trunks today?'

I would advise you not to be in Brussels when I return.

Randall's last words to her cut as deep as when he had uttered them, but she would not run away.

'I am not leaving Brussels, Therese.' She sipped at her hot chocolate. Its soothing warmth put heart into her. 'Do you and Jacques wish to go?'

'*Mais non, m'amselle*. Brussels is our home.'

'But if the French should come?'

Therese gave a shrug.

'They have been here before. The French, the British, it makes no difference, we will endure.'

'And so will I.'

'*Tiens*, *m'amselle*, you would be safer in Antwerp.'

Mary wanted to cry out that she did not care what happened to her, but that would be foolish. When her sister's lifeless body had been dragged from the Thames, Mary had railed against her, furious that Jane had given in, had deserted her. Perhaps now she understood a little more why Jane had ended her life, but *she* would not do so. She would not give in to the aching misery that pressed upon her heart. After all she was the injured party, not the earl. She raised her head and spoke in a firm voice to her maidservant.

'I shall stay until we have reliable information on the situation.'

And news of Randall. He might not want to see her again, but she was still desperate to know he was safe. She dragged herself from her bed. She must throw off this lethargy. There was much to do.

Jacques was waiting downstairs for her, his face creased and anxious.

'*Mademoiselle*, there are those who say the French are coming,' he told her. 'It would be best for you to leave. If they discover you are English...'

She put up her hand.

'I am staying. I do not believe this is anything more than rumour.' But if it should be true? She might have to leave quickly. 'However, you can fetch my horse from the livery stables and put it in the little barn at the edge of the gardens. In this present climate I would not be surprised if someone made off with it.'

Jacques hurried away and Mary went into her sitting room. A number of letters lay on her desk, including three from outraged parents informing her that they had heard of her behaviour at the Duchess's ball and would not be sending their children back to the Rue Haute. She was not surprised. It would be all over Brussels by now that she had thrown herself at the earl, that she was his mistress. Acceptable for a high-born lady, perhaps, but not for a lowly teacher. She would have to close the school. Best to do it now, while only the dozen girls she had sent to Antwerp were still in her care.

Mary sat down at her desk. She must write to their families. Her staff would continue teaching the children in Antwerp until their parents could fetch them. In the meantime she would close up the Brussels schoolhouse and sell it, if she could find a buyer.

And after that? Mary stared at the blank sheet of paper on the desk before her. She had a little money, enough to live on for a while, until everyone had forgotten her. Then she would open another school. In Paris, perhaps. Her French was impeccable and she was confident some of her father's old friends there would help her. Or England. In the north country, far away from any of Randall's estates. What did it matter where she went now? What did anything matter?

A tear dripped on to the paper and she dashed a hand across her eyes.

'Oh, do not be such a ninny,' she scolded herself. 'This melancholy will pass soon enough and then you will care very much, if you have not made provision for yourself.'

She raised her head when she heard the knocker, and deep voices in the hall. Her heart leapt. It was Randall. Quickly she wiped her eyes and rose, shaking out her skirts.

'Oh.' Her soaring spirits plummeted. 'Bertrand. Good day to you.'

If he noticed her disappointment Bertrand Lebbeke gave no sign of it.

'I am on my way from the hospital and saw the schoolhouse was inhabited. You should have left Brussels by now, Mary.'

She spread her hands. 'As you see, I am still here. I sent the children to Antwerp, the school goes on there without me.' She invited him to sit down. 'Is there any news? Any *real* news, I mean, rather than the incessant rumours that Jacques brings me.'

'Well, the French are not yet at the gates,' he said, smiling a little.

'And was yesterday's action decisive?'

He shook his head. 'I do not think so. The Allies fought bravely, although the artillery did not arrive in time to protect them.'

So Randall did not fight yesterday. He was safe. Mary's relief was so great it made her feel light-headed and it was an effort to concentrate upon Bertrand's next words.

'Brussels is overflowing with wounded soldiers,' he said gravely. 'The hospital is full, we have been working all night, but the number of injured men requiring attention grows by the hour.' With a stab of remorse Mary realised how tired he looked as he rubbed a hand across his eyes. 'Many are being tended in the streets. The mayor has made an appeal for bedding and supplies to be brought to the Grand Place. Perhaps you have not heard. They need food, bandages, anything that can be spared.'

She said guiltily, 'I have not been out of doors since—since Thursday, I did not know it was so...' She sat up straighter in her chair. 'You could use this house, if you wish. The dormitories are empty, the beds are free. We could house a dozen or more here.'

'Do you mean it?' He brightened. 'It would make a difference.'

'Then it is at your disposal.' She stood up, glad to have something positive to do. 'Therese and Jacques will help me to clear away anything the girls might have left behind.'

'It is very kind of you, Mary. When do you expect your pupils to return?'

'They are not coming back. I am closing the school.'

'Ah. You are marrying Lord Randall.'

'No, that is not it at all.' She went back to the desk, avoiding his eyes as she straightened the pens and closed the lid of the inkwell. 'I have decided to move on, once the battle here is over.'

Bertrand was watching her.

'It is over, then, you and your English milord?'

She managed to say brightly, 'Oh, good heavens, it was never serious.'

'But I was told, you and he—on Thursday night—'

'Yes,' she broke in quickly. 'I was a little... reckless. That is why I must close the school. I did not behave as I ought.'

He came closer.

'Oh, Mary, I am sorry.'

'No, please, Bertrand. Do not pity me. I knew what I was doing, but it was very foolish of me, so I must go away.'

He took her hands. 'You do not need to do that. You could stay and marry me. I will—what is it you English say?—I will make an honest woman of you.'

'You are very kind, Bertrand, thank you, but, no.'

'Ah, because your radical beliefs will not allow it?'

She shook her head. She had been prepared to compromise to marry Randall and she was surprised at how happily she would have done so—clearly that was not the reason she could not marry Bertrand.

'Because I do not love you, you see, and I could never marry without love.'

Or trust. She could not marry a man who did not trust her, even if he was an earl.

'Of course.' He dropped her hand and stepped away. 'When will you go?'

'I do not know. When I have settled my affairs. When this war is over. In the meantime, please send your wounded soldiers to my house and we will look after them as best we can.'

'I know you will. Thank you, Mary, and remember, I will always be here for you, if you need me.'

With a little bow he was gone and she could only be thankful for his forbearance.

Within hours the first of the wounded men was being carried into the schoolhouse. Mary talked to the medical orderly who brought them in, trying to store in her memory all his instructions for their care.

She maintained her calm demeanour as she helped Therese to make the wounded men as comfortable as they could, but her thoughts were a chaotic jumble of fear and anxiety, not for herself but for Randall. The lack of information was agony, not knowing where he might be, if he was wounded. If he was alive. She threw herself into looking after the soldiers. It was gruelling work. Every bed was occupied and when a man was deemed well enough to leave or, more usually, did not survive, his place was immediately filled by another badly injured soldier. By the time Mary lay down on her bed in the early hours of the morning she was so exhausted that even the ceaseless patter of rain on the windows could not keep her awake and she fell into a deep, dreamless sleep.

Her fears were waiting for her as soon as she awoke. She rose and dressed mechanically, steeling herself to face another day. However the workload was a little lighter, because the teachers she had been obliged to lay off returned to help with the nursing. Thus it was that when Bertrand arrived later in the morning he found Mary preparing to go out. He teased her when she had told him her destination.

'You, go to church, Mary? I am aware you must take your pupils there, but I thought you did not believe in such things?'

'Given our present situation I will take help wherever it comes from,' she said frankly. And if he knew how hard she prayed for Randall's safety he would be astonished. 'The truth is, I thought I should go to the morning service, I might glean a little information.'

He stood aside. 'Then I wish you good fortune, *ma chère*.'

The streets were teeming. Army wagons were moving and as Mary made her way to the more fashionable quarter she noted that many of the houses rented by the English were now empty and shuttered, or had carriages waiting at the door. She could find no news and in desperation she made her way to the Rue de Regence, only to find that Lady Sarah and her sister had already gone to Antwerp.

A growl of thunder made her glance up. The sky was clear blue and for a moment she was puzzled until a second rumble, then a third, made her blood run cold. It must be cannon fire. Quickly she turned and hurried back to the schoolhouse. The battle to save Brussels was underway.

* * *

Randall dragged a grimy sleeve across his eyes. This was how he imagined hell would be. The heat was stifling, shells screamed in around them, bodies covered the ground while the men still standing returned fire, grim determination in their blackened faces. Then, just as Randall was about to send a man to reconnoitre the situation, one of Wellington's aides came galloping up. The duke's orders were breathlessly relayed and instantly Randall was astride Pompey and roaring out commands.

'Limber up, fast as you can!' He rode up to Major Bartlett, almost unrecognisable in his muddied uniform, one sleeve torn from cuff to elbow and flapping wildly. 'We are heading to the ridge yonder. You will recall we came in that way yesterday, past a place…what was it called?…Hougoumont. The French are massing their heavy cavalry between the château and the Charleroi road. Take up your position between the two infantry squares up there. And be quick about it!'

Having given his orders, there was nothing for Randall to do but to watch how efficiently the men set to work. He had to give Major Bartlett his due, he had whipped his troop into shape and they were now a respected fighting force. Pity the man was such a hardened libertine. Perhaps he hadn't yet met the right woman? Randall pulled himself up with a jolt. When had he begun to think that a man could change so drastically? He knew the answer, of course. It was Mary's doing. How much he had to tell her, if he survived this hell. If she would listen.

Sooner than he dared hope the gun carriages were on the move, lumbering across the sodden fields and up the gentle slope to the ridge. Somewhere in his mind, a tiny part that was not focused on the ensuing conflict, he was aware of his pride in the Rogues. They had not let him down. Neither had Mary, but if this bloody slaughter continued he might not live to tell her so.

Flint and Bartlett joined him on the ridge as the men struggled to manoeuvre the heavy guns into position. All around them was the thunderous roar and thick, acrid smoke of battle. The raised road that ran along the ridge afforded them some protection, but beyond it lay an open plain and as the smoke drifted away they could see the dark mass of French cavalry on the far hill.

Flint gave a low whistle. 'They'll be upon us before we know it.'

As if to ram home his prediction a cannon ball whistled between them and thudded into the ground, splattering them with nothing more dangerous than mud. This time.

'You'd better make sure you're ready,' was Randall's curt reply.

He did not doubt his men or his officers. They would meet this challenge as they had met all the others. He wheeled about and rode back down the hill, chivvying the stragglers. Returning to the ridge, he took a quick survey of the squares on either side. They were under constant bombardment, shells burst overhead and the squares shrank in size as the casualties mounted. The wounded were dragged inside the square, the dead pushed outside while the sergeants raced to and fro, ordering the remaining men to close up.

Men? They were boys, thought Randall, observing their pale, frightened faces. Untried, too, he suspected. His lips thinned. The duke's orders had been for his men to retreat into the squares when the cavalry charged, but he knew that if the Rogues ran for cover it would start a mass panic. The squares would not hold. Many of the infantrymen were looking his way. He had seen the hope in their faces as the big guns were brought up. He prayed their presence could put some heart into the squares.

Bartlett's division was the first to the ridge, but scarcely had they put their big gun into position than the cavalry were approaching at a trot. 'They are coming,' shouted Randall. 'Steady now, lads.'

Flint's nine-pounder was now ready for action and even Rawlins had brought his pieces up with commendable speed. Within seconds of each other the big guns fired their first rounds. Their canister shot skimmed low over the raised road and into the oncoming cavalry, mowing down the leaders. The first round slowed the densely packed mass to a walk. They picked their way over or around the fallen, but they kept coming. Randall recognised them as *grenadiers à cheval*: they were menacing enough in their plain blue uniforms and buff cross belts, but with their huge caps they looked like giants on horseback.

'Dear lord, they'll charge right over us,' cried a voice somewhere behind Randall.

Bartlett's snarling response was no surprise. 'Not Randall's Rogues, they won't. Remember the motto—Always victorious!'

'Aye,' roared Randall, drawing his sword and raising it. '*Semper Laurifer!* Ready, Rogues… *fire!*'

His arm swept down, the blade glittering in a sudden shaft of sunlight. The deafening thunder of the guns shook the ground. Randall kept his sword in his hand, ready to fight to the death as the advancing cavalry charged towards them. His fingers tightened about the hilt. He felt rather than saw the hesitation in the approaching mass and at the last moment the leading riders wheeled away. But not all of them, some could not stop. Those with horses wounded and maddened out of control charged straight through the lines and on to the rear, making no effort to attack the gunners as they swept past.

Smoke enveloped everything. The Rogues were nothing more than ghostly shapes as they constantly reloaded. Again and again the guns spewed their deadly fire. When the smoke did lift momentarily Randall glanced across the road and saw that the French were swarming, but they were not advancing. He could see the columns at the rear pushing forward while those before them tried desperately to retreat and get away from the incessant barrage of round shot and canister that ripped through their ranks.

Randall's ears continued to ring long after the firing ceased and the enemy had withdrawn. He heard the cheers going up from the much-reduced infantry squares, but the jubilation was short-lived. Skirmishers filled the void left by the cavalry and opened fire on the ridge. Again the slight rise of the road protected them from the worst of the assault, but some of the shots found their mark. The sergeants were once again working to keep the shrinking squares intact while Randall's more experienced troops prepared their guns, giving no more attention to the musket shot flying about them than they would to a swarm of troublesome insects. Occasionally a man would go down and his comrades would carry him quickly to the rear. Randall knew they were itching to retaliate, but they couldn't waste ammunition when the cavalry would be returning any minute. Nevertheless the skirmishers continued to irritate and, having recovered from that first cavalry charge, his men were growing restless. He turned Pompey and urged him up on to the road, where he trotted along in front of his men. Foolish, perhaps, to put himself on show, but he knew the old saying, 'The nearer the target, the safer you are.' Pompey snorted but never flinched, too old a campaigner to be disturbed by the brattle of muskets. Shots whistled past, one ripped through his sleeve, grazing the arm and another was so close he felt the air move against his cheek, but he continued to ride. His phlegmatic demeanour had its effect on the Rogues.

The cavalry was moving again, even before the sniping ceased. Randall's keen eyes followed the skirmishers as they slipped away. The grass and crops had been flattened by the cavalry charge and it was easier now to follow their retreat. He watched them making for an old barn in the distance. It was within range of his guns. Maybe he'd have Rawlins turn his nine-pounder in that direction. But that was for later. Now there was a much more urgent problem.

'Here they come again, my lads,' called Randall. 'Hold your fire, don't waste your shot.'

'As if we would,' shouted one of the bombardiers. 'Don't you know yer bleedin' Rogues by now, Colonel?'

Randall's lips twitched, but he kept his face straight and his eyes on the approaching cavalry. They came on in a steady, solid mass, so many that the rear columns stretched out of sight. Amidst the smoke and roar of the battlefield, Randall was struck by the silence of the advance, no shouts, no cries, they moved forward with a steady determination. The ground reverberated beneath the hoofs of their horses, like the distant, continuous rumble of thunder, ominous and deadly, coming ever closer. An unstoppable force.

Randall looked back at the Rogues. They stood ready by the guns, port fires spitting and glowing behind the wheels. He glanced at the infantry squares. They, too, were standing firm, their eyes fixed on the Rogues. *Hell and damnation*, thought Randall, *if we break, so will they.*

The enemy were so close Randall could see the detail on the leading officer's uniform, the single row of gilt buttons running down the centre of his chest, yet still he kept his sword raised. Experience told him the first salvo could mean the difference between victory and defeat. The tension was palpable. The ground shook with the oncoming charge; his men were braced, tense and ready for action.

Eighty yards, seventy. Then, when the deadly mass was no more than sixty yards away, he dropped his arm and the guns roared their defiance. They belched flame and smoke as the deadly volley flew at the enemy. The first rank of cavalry fell immediately, slowing the advance, while the shot continued to punch through the column, spreading mayhem. Yet the charge was not halted, they were pushing on, slow but inexorable. The Rogues reloaded with steady, trained efficiency and the guns roared again and again while the squares kept up a constant barrage of fire against the oncoming enemy.

Bodies of horses and men littered the ground but still the French pressed on, leaping over the dead only to fall at the guns' muzzles. Randall rode forward to intercept one *grenadier* who was charging towards the gunners. He despatched the man speedily and wheeled about looking for another assailant. The attack was growing less frenzied. Many of the cavalry were retreating, the rear column peeling away rather than face the deadly salvos. At last Randall gave the order to cease firing.

As soon as the cavalry withdrew it was replaced with artillery fire, the enemy guns soon finding their range and raining down shot and shells on the Rogues. Randall galloped quickly along the lines, assessing the damage as the smoke cleared. He brought his horse to a stand by Bartlett's guns and was about to speak when a shell whistled in and exploded.

Everything went black. The noise and heat faded away. The darkness became a comfortable cocoon and he wanted to give himself up to it. He felt Mary's arms about his neck, heard her soft whisper.

I believe in you, Randall.

Randall forced his eyes open. He was on the ground, winded but unhurt. Somehow he had managed to jump clear of Pompey, who was lying close by. Randall scrambled up and raced to the grey, but Pompey was already dead. He had taken the full force of the blast.

'Killed instantly, thank heaven.'

He rested his hand briefly on the smooth neck. Another faithful friend gone.

'Colonel!'

Randall climbed to his feet as Bartlett came up. The major's face was black as a chimney sweep, making his green eyes even more catlike. A memory swept through him of another pair of green eyes. Of Mary looking at him with shock and dismay as he ripped up at her.

'I am unhurt, Major. And you?'

It was a mark of the man that he answered for

his division. 'We've had a few losses, sir. Evans has lost a leg, but we've taken him back to the surgeon. I hope he'll live.' He grinned. 'Hot work today, sir.'

'Hot work indeed,' replied Randall. Glancing over the ridge, he drew his lips back into a humourless smile. 'Here they come again. To your post, Major Bartlett!'

This time the Rogues sensed the charge was half-hearted and went in for the kill, responding with an even deadlier salvo. The smoke was thick, a dense low cloud just above head height, a heavy grey blanket glittering with scarlet from the fragments of scorched wadding that drifted slowly to the ground. Randall could not see the squares—everything was reduced to a small scenario—only the noise did not diminish, a deafening, screaming roar, as if all the demons of hell had been let loose.

Then there was no enemy within sight. Peering through the half-light, Randall made out a few riders wheeling about on the far side of the road and he strained his hoarse throat to roar out one final order.

As the guns fell silent he dragged his sleeve across his eyes, suddenly exhausted. A party of horsemen was approaching slowly on the road along the ridge. He blinked and looked again at the leading rider. His profile was familiar, that hooked nose—even more prominent than the

Latymor nose!—the Duke of Wellington. He closed his eyes. Thank God they had ceased firing. The duke looked grim, riding slowly and ignoring the remains of the French cavalry still wheeling in confusion only yards away.

The Rogues began to cheer and Randall's deafened ears picked up the thud of a drumbeat, soft and steady. He looked back. To the rear of his men a thin, straggling line of infantry was coming up the rise towards him. They marched past the squares and the guns, across the road and proceeded steadily down the slope towards the enemy. The gunfire from the far hill continued, taking down a few men, but soon the guns fell silent and that ragged line continued to advance. What was left of the squares on either side of Randall's troop dissolved into lines and followed, their weapons at the ready.

'By God we've done it,' said a voice at his shoulder.

'Aye, Major Flint. We've done it. But at what cost?' Randall saw a stray saddle horse trotting by and shouted to a passing sergeant to catch him.

'Heavy, but we expected that,' returned Flint gruffly. 'They say Bartlett's wounded, but it doesn't sound serious.'

'The tomcat's used up another of his lives, has he?' said Randall. He saw the momentary gleam in Flint's eyes, surprise that his colonel should know the major's nickname, but he made it his business to know everything about his men.

That's why the losses were so painful.

He said shortly, 'Clear up here, Major.'

The sergeant ran up with the horse and Randall mounted stiffly. He would be bruised later from his fall. And just when did he get that gash on his leg? His pantaloons were ripped open along the thigh and there was dried blood mixed with the mud and grime on the skin, but it was no longer bleeding so he could afford to ignore it for a while. He nodded to Flint.

'Tell the men well done.'

'They'd rather hear it from you, sir.'

'I'll do that when I return.' He wheeled the horse about and trotted off.

With most of the firing ended the smoke began to disperse and as it did so Randall's head started to clear. A last glance at his troop had shown him the devastation they had suffered. The men were exhausted; those that had survived the battle were lying against the gun carriages, too tired to move. He doubted they had sufficient horses to draw away all the guns. He would deal with that later, if Flint had not already done so by the time he returned. Good man, Flint. Got things done. He'd be a good choice to take over the Rogues, he'd make a success of it. Or anything else he put his mind to, come to think of it. Wouldn't do to tell him so, though. Prickly devil, his half-brother.

Randall galloped away from the carnage of the main battlefield in the direction of the building he had spotted earlier. A small group of soldiers was coming towards him and he drew rein. Their dark green jackets proclaimed them riflemen.

'You are coming from the barn yonder?' he said, nodding towards the dilapidated stone structure behind them.

'Yes, sir.' The leading rifleman raised his hand. It was a lacklustre salute, but they looked as exhausted as Randall felt and he was in no mood for formality. 'It was full of Frenchies. Still is,' he added. 'But now they're dead Frenchies.'

Randall nodded. That was all he wanted to know. He'd had visions of that thin line of infantry being picked off by the French *tirailleurs* if they passed close to the barn as they swept up the remnants of the enemy. With that worry out of the way he could return to his men. He rubbed a hand across his eyes. Not yet. A raging thirst had come over him and he realised he had not taken a drink all day. His borrowed horse had no water bottle hanging from the saddle. Randall looked towards the stone building. He could see now that there was a small orchard behind it and a line of lush green growth and reeds snaked past, suggesting a stream. He kicked the horse on. He'd take a drink then get back to his men. The silence of the barn did not worry him, nor the knowledge that it was filled with dead Frenchmen.

He had no intention of going any closer than necessary. There was indeed a small stream, little more than a trickle running between the high reeds, but it would suffice. He dismounted and dropped to his knees to slake his thirst. The water was sweet and cold and he splashed his face with it. All day the smoke of the battle had hung over the land like a grey raincloud, but now it was lifting and he could see that it was going to be a fine evening. Sitting back on his heels, he unbuttoned his jacket to allow the breeze to cool him. He might even make it back to Brussels tonight. It would be late, but perhaps not too late to call on Mary. He needed to make his peace with her. He could not rest until he had done so.

Randall glanced up at the blue sky. Would she see him? Would she forgive him? He closed his eyes. If he was in her place he would not do so. Dear heaven, how could he have been so mistaken? He should have known he could trust her. He had always considered himself a good judge of men, but this woman had wrong-footed him from the start. If she'd listen, give him another chance…

He was preparing to rise when movement

caught his eye. There was someone near the barn. Cautiously he raised his head. It was a child, a French drummer boy. How he had come there was a mystery, but he was heading for the barn doors. Randall could imagine the gory scene inside. No child should see that.

He jumped up and ran forward, shouting to the boy to stop. He did so, but only for a moment. When he saw an English officer running towards him he took to his heels and dashed away. Randall wanted to give chase, but exhaustion had caught up with him. His legs buckled and he stumbled and collapsed on to the ground just in front of the barn. When he looked up again the boy had disappeared. He gave an inward shrug. The lad should be all right. The Allied army was victorious and therefore in good spirits, which made them magnanimous, most of them. He could only hope someone would look after the boy.

He stood up. His legs were still unsteady and he put his hand on one of the doors. As he did so something glinted in the reeds, very close to where his horse was grazing peacefully. Randall swung round. His hand went to his sword as a loud retort echoed and he felt a sudden hammer blow to his ribs.

'What the—?'

A French *tirailleur* rose up from the reeds. So not all the sharpshooters were dead. Randall saw the fellow grab the horse and swing himself into the saddle. Damned impudence! He became aware of a pain in his chest and slid a hand inside his open jacket. There was no mistaking the warm stickiness on his fingers. He glanced down to see the stain blooming on his white shirt.

Wine red. The colour of the sash on Mary's dress.

'Mary.' He swayed, uttering her name as the blackness closed around him.

Chapter Twelve

Looking after the wounded left Mary little time for her own troubles, but throughout the day Jacques came in with conflicting reports of how the battle was going. Thankfully those soldiers who were able to speak were confident that Wellington would win the day and their optimism more than countered her manservant's gloomy predictions. Bertrand stayed until late in the afternoon, doing what he could for the injured men and when he left he promised to send word if he heard anything of the battle. Mary settled down to a lonely dinner. She forbade Jacques to go out again, saying that whether the news was good or bad they would hear it soon enough and besides there was nothing they could do about it.

Dawn was breaking when she was roused by the sound of someone banging on the front door.

Dressing quickly she found Bertrand in the hall. He came across and briefly touched her hand.

'The French are beaten, Mary. Brussels is safe.'

She closed her eyes for a moment, uttering up a thankful prayer.

'But we need to use your classrooms now,' he continued urgently. 'I have a wagon outside, full of men with injuries the most serious.'

'Of course.' She hurried across to the door and threw it open. 'I had Jacques clear the schoolrooms yesterday, just in case.' She stood beside him as dishevelled soldiers in filthy uniforms carried in the wounded. She smiled down at each man and uttered a few soft words of greeting. Not by the flicker of an eye would she betray her dismay at their battered and bloodied appearance.

'Are there many more?' she asked quietly, when the last man had been taken in.

'Too many. They fill the streets, but they are the lucky ones. Hundreds, *non*, thousands are still on the battlefield. Every hour they remain untended lessens their chances of survival.'

'Have—have you heard how the artillery fared?'

Bertrand would know that she was really asking about Lord Randall, but she could not help herself.

'Alas, *non*. I have no news for you.'

She nodded, pressing her lips together. There

was nothing she could do. If they had not quarrelled Randall might have sent her a note, telling her he was safe. Or asked one of his officers to inform her, if it was bad news. Now she could expect nothing from him.

'Very well,' she said at last. 'Let us get to work and make these poor men comfortable.'

'*Mademoiselle*, there are soldiers at the door, asking for you.'

'Thank you, Jacques. Tell them I shall be with them in a moment.' Mary finished tying the bandage around what was left of one man's arm and hurried to the hall.

She expected to find more orderlies there with another wagon full of hideously wounded men. Instead she saw five soldiers gathered outside the door. Their blue uniforms were torn and muddy, but she recognised them as artillerymen. Her heart racing, Mary hurried forward, but before she could utter any of the questions bubbling to her lips, one of the men spoke.

'Beggin' your pardon, Miss Endacott, but we was wondering, if, well, if Lord Randall was here?'

She stopped. 'Lord Randall? Why should he be here?'

The men shifted awkwardly and glanced at one another.

'What Sergeant Hollins means, miss, is that we can't find 'im,' said a soldier with a badly tied and grubby bandage wrapped around his head. 'He rode off yesterday once the Frenchies were beat and we was expectin' to find 'im back here in Brussels, but there ain't no sign of 'im.'

'Oh, good heavens!'

Mary swayed, putting a hand against the doorpost to steady herself.

'Oxton's right, miss,' affirmed the sergeant. 'We've tried all the 'ospitals, even the military one at Mont Saint Jean, but he ain't there, and we thought, like, since you and the colonel was friends, he might've come here. And to be honest, we don't know where else to look for 'im.'

She closed her eyes for a moment. They did not know that she and Randall were no longer friends and they had brought her the news she had feared, that he was missing. When she opened her eyes again she found the men were regarding her hopefully.

'I am very sorry,' she said. 'He is not here.'

'Then he must still be on the battlefield,' replied Sergeant Hollins, 'but I'm dam—I'm dashed if I knows where.'

'Then you must find him, there is not a moment to lose,' she replied, recalling Bertrand's words that morning. If only the doctor was here, she would beg him to go with them, but he had returned to the main hospital an hour since. Her eyes went again to the ragged binding wrapped around the head of one trooper. 'Wait! I shall come with you. If Lord Randall is wounded you may need me. I have been helping Dr Lebbeke here and at least I know how to dress a wound now. '

The men looked at one another.

'It ain't that we don't *want* you to come, ma'am, but we ain't got a mount for you and there's not a spare horse to be found in Brussels. They've all been commandeered by the mayor. Or the army.' The sergeant pointed his thumb at the horses standing in the street. 'We, um, *commandeered* these ourselves this mornin'. French cavalry 'orses they are, a real handful and no lady's saddle, either.'

For the first time that day a genuine smile tugged at her mouth. 'Do not worry about that, I have a horse of my own hidden away. Jacques, bring these men some refreshments while I get changed. And saddle Marron!'

Mary scrambled into her riding gown, trying not to think of the last time she had worn it, riding out with Randall. She could not afford to be sentimental. She must concentrate on what might be needed to save Randall, if he was still alive. Once dressed she raced downstairs and filled a saddlebag with the things she thought might be needed to tend a wounded man. At last she was ready and she went out to join the men waiting at the gate. Jacques was there, holding Marron, and she gave him one last instruction. He ran inside, returning a few minutes later with blankets and two long poles.

'We have no wagon to bring Lord Randall back to Brussels,' she told the astonished artillerymen. 'You must take these so we can make a litter.'

The men exchanged looks, then with a shrug, two of them took the blankets and strapped them behind their saddles while two more took a pole each and tucked it under one arm. Dirty and unkempt as they were, they reminded her of a couple of jousting knights. She thought how much Randall would appreciate that image of his Rogues. She bit hard on her lip to stop the tears welling up: if she ever had the chance to tell him.

Mary was about to mount Marron when she heard a series of loud barks. A large shaggy black dog was racing towards her, followed by a lady on a white horse. Mary's spirits fluttered. Perhaps Lady Sarah had news of Randall? After all she had the company mascot with her. The animal made straight for the Rogues, frolicking and jumping around them as if they were long-lost friends, but Mary's hopes that Randall might be safe were soon dashed when she observed Sarah's dishevelled appearance. Her hair was disordered and her pale blue riding habit was caked in mud, as if she had been rolling on the ground.

'What has happened?' cried Lady Sarah wildly, 'Is it Justin? I know he is alive, but where is he?'

Mary took a moment to compose herself so that she could speak calmly and explain the little she knew to Randall's sister. Sarah's conviction that Randall was not dead was heartening, but totally without foundation, as was her assertion that Fate had brought her and the dog to the Rue Haute in time to accompany them. Mary shook her head.

'I think you would be better returning to Antwerp,' she said. 'You are in no fit state to come with us.'

'I have been looking for Gideon and I will not, cannot, give up my search,' replied Lady Sarah, clearly trying hard not to cry. 'I cannot go back until I know what has happened to my brothers.'

Despite her own worries, Mary recognised that Sarah was distraught, but if Randall was alive he would not thank her for allowing his sister to visit the battlefield. She was about to say as much when she noticed that the men were looking considerably more cheerful.

'Dog's got a good nose, ma'am,' said the sergeant, scratching the animal's shaggy head. 'He'll find the colonel for us, I'm sure.'

Mary took another glance at Sarah's determined face. If she argued they would waste more time, so she gave in with as good a grace as she could muster. When she was mounted she brought her chestnut hack alongside Sarah's showy mount.

'Here.' She held out a large pocket handkerchief. 'Take this. I have drenched it in scent; we may need it when we get to the battlefield. I have a house full of soldiers with the most appalling wounds, and sometimes the smell is—' She broke off, just the thought of it turning her stomach. 'Luckily I have prepared more than one.'

'Thank you.' Lady Sarah gave her a tremulous smile and Mary realised how hard and practical she must appear to a society miss like Lady Sarah Latymor. Perhaps she was, but she feared they would both need nerves of iron to get through the coming ordeal.

The road to Waterloo was teeming. Carts and wagons jostled for space with crowds of ragged soldiers. Nearing the battlefield they saw signs of freshly dug graves and soon they reached the bloody killing fields themselves. She held the scented handkerchief to her nose as soon as the now-familiar smells of death and decay rose up. After the past few days Mary thought she was inured to the sounds of men screaming in agony and the sight of their bloodied, lacerated bodies, but nothing could have prepared her for the hellish landscape around her. There was nothing but devastation wherever she looked. What she had not bargained for was the sound of gunfire. She looked a question at the sergeant, who replied through gritted teeth.

'They're shooting the wounded, ma'am. Those that ain't got no chance of surviving. Putting them out o' their misery.'

Dear heaven, don't let Randall be amongst them.

Forcing her mind to the task of finding him, Mary said briskly, 'We should start where you last saw the colonel.'

They took her to the ridge and clattered along the raised road. Mutilated bodies and broken wagons lined the way, and when they reached the spot where the artillery had been stationed the signs of carnage were everywhere, muddied corpses of horses and men lay where they had fallen. She glanced behind. Lady Sarah was looking very pale and Mary felt a quick stab of sympathy for her desperate appearance. She had not asked, but she hoped Sarah had suffered nothing worse than a muddied habit while she had been riding alone, looking for her brothers. One of the Rogues was riding with her now and the shaggy dog was loping along beside her horse so Mary turned back, concentrating on keeping her own fear and nausea under control. The sergeant stopped and turned to the gunner riding beside him.

'You saw him last, Brent,' he barked. 'Tell the lady.'

'He went off just after the duke had passed by,' said Brent. 'Followed the infantry down there, he did.'

'Then that is what we shall do,' declared Mary.

Turning her horse from the road, she made her way towards the plain spread below them. She imagined it had once been a rich green, or perhaps golden with corn. Now it was nothing more than a vast and muddy expanse, littered with the dead. Mary forced herself to look at the horror surrounding them, searching for Randall. The recent rain had softened the ground and now it was saturated with blood and it sucked noisily at the horses' hoofs. In the distance people were walking amongst the corpses. Looters, possibly. She was suddenly very thankful for her ragged escort.

There was a discernible road leading down to the plain and they followed it until they reached a fork. The sergeant started along the route that led them towards the very heart of the blood-sodden plain. Mary choked back a cry of dismay. It was unthinkable that there could be anyone alive in that hell, yet even from here she could here men groaning, see movement amongst the carcases.

'No, not that way!' Lady Sarah's urgent cry brought them all to a halt.

Looking back, Mary saw that the dog was running to and fro along the other road, the one leading away from the battlefield. She said nothing while the men debated which way to go, but in the end Lady Sarah had her way and they took the less bloody road. The dog bounded ahead of them and in the distance Mary could see a building, some sort of barn. The ground on either side of them was green, although patches of flattened grass and telltale bloodstains showed there had been fighting here. It was only as they approached the building that Mary saw the bodies piled against its outer walls.

'Oh, dear heaven, they are using this as a charnel house!'

The dog was whining and scratching at the barn doors.

'Justin is in there,' cried Sarah. 'I know he is.'

'We shall see.'

'Careful, miss,' cried Sergeant Hollins, but Mary had already dismounted.

Leaving Sarah with the horses, she strode towards the barn. The dog had pushed his way in between the rickety doors and she heard him bark.

'Well he's found something,' exclaimed the sergeant. 'Dawkins, Cooper, you two stay with Lady Sarah while we has a look.'

Mary swallowed. She had come this far, she would know the truth, however painful. Steeling herself, she reached out and pulled open one of the doors. The heat and stench billowed out to meet her, making her retch. Quickly she turned away while she tied the scented handkerchief over her mouth and nose. It helped, a little.

The sergeant and two of the Rogues pushed the barn doors wide. The sight that met their eyes made Mary recoil and even the men were cursing softly under their breath. There were bodies everywhere, scattered over the floor and piled carelessly on top of one another against the back wall. Desolation swept through her. Nothing moved. If Randall was here, he was dead. The dog was sitting just inside the entrance, staring into one dark corner behind the door, his tongue lolling out as he panted noisily. Mary stepped closer, peering at a small patch of grey amongst the shadows. She gave a cry.

'Randall!'

The dark uniform was encrusted with dirt and almost black in the gloom, but the jacket was undone and it was the white of his shirt that she had seen. It wasn't until she fell on her knees beside him that she saw the bloodstain on his chest. As her eyes grew more accustomed to the shadows she saw the bloody gash on his head. It grew even darker as the three artillerymen ran up, adding their shadows to the gloom.

'My Gawd, he's dead!' cried one of them.

'Well, you two fetch those poles to make the

litter,' growled the sergeant. 'Dead or no, we're taking the colonel back to Brussels.'

Mary stared at the motionless figure stretched out on the floor and her eyes filled with tears. He couldn't be dead. Not this way. Not without saying goodbye. She reached out and touched his fingers. They did not move, but they were pliant. Trembling, she stripped off her gloves and took his hand again. It was warm.

Snatching the handkerchief from her face, Mary wiped her cheeks and moved closer, placing her fingers on the skin of his neck. She held her breath, hardly daring to believe that she could feel the faint beat of a pulse.

'He's alive,' she said, her voice not quite steady. 'He lives.'

'No.' Sergeant Hollins gave a low whistle. 'Well, bless me!'

The two artillerymen who had gone to fetch the poles, rope and blankets to form the makeshift stretcher returned in time to hear the news and crowded round her.

'And he's still got that old sword at his side,' muttered one of them. 'Always said it was lucky.'

The sergeant stepped up, saying tersely, 'It won't be lucky if he stays in this hellhole, Gunner Stubbs. Let's get him out of here—'

'No.' Mary stopped him. 'We must not move him yet, Sergeant. First I need to see just how badly he is hurt.' She had heard Bertrand say often that carelessly manhandling a patient could make injuries much worse. 'Stand back a little, if you please. I need as much light as possible.'

She forgot the stench and the corpses around her as she began to examine Randall's inert form. She was no expert, but in her years as a teacher she had dealt with any number of accidents and she had learned a great deal more in the last couple of days. She could find no broken bones. One sleeve was ripped, but there was no more than a graze on his arm and the gash on his leg was no longer bleeding. Of more concern were the wounds on his chest and temple. Mary used the clean water from the flask she had brought with her to damp a cloth and wipe away the blood from his head. The cut was not large, but it had bled profusely and the skin around it was badly bruised.

'Not a sword cut, that,' opined the sergeant, watching her work. 'P'raps he bashed his head when he fell.'

'Very likely,' she said.

It would need to be bandaged, but first she had to turn her attention to the most worrying sign of injury. With trembling fingers she unfastened his shirt. The blood was still oozing from small neat hole in his chest.

'He has been shot,' she said, trying to keep the

panic from her tone. She folded one of the cloths she had brought with her into a pad and held it over the hole. 'Help me to lift him, Sergeant Hollins. Carefully, now.'

After a few moments she said, 'I c-cannot see that the ball has come out at the back. It must be still in him.'

Gunner Stubbs stepped closer. 'Can you take it out, miss?'

In other circumstances the soldier's faith in her ability would have made her smile. Sadly, she shook her head.

'No. I will bandage his wounds, then we must get him back to Brussels.'

'Are we going to carry him all the way back?'

She shook her head. 'Not exactly, Sergeant. I thought we might lash the front of the poles into the stirrups of the quietest horse. Then we will only need two of you to hold the other ends. It is important that we move Colonel Randall as carefully as possible.'

'It'll have to be your horse then, miss,' replied Gunner Brent. 'None of they cavalry horses would bear having anything behind 'em.'

'So be it.' Mary rose and shook out her skirts. 'Fixing the poles might be more difficult to a lady's saddle, but we shall manage. Let us get to it.'

She prayed it would work. It took a little time to fix the poles to Marron and lift Randall on to the makeshift litter. It was only when they were preparing to leave that Mary realised Lady Sarah was missing.

Sergeant Hollins scratched his head. 'Must've taken off while we was busy in the barn.'

'Dawkins and Cooper's gone, too, miss,' remarked Gunner Brent.

The sergeant shook his head when he saw Mary's horrified look.

'I wouldn't vouch for all the Rogues, but those two wouldn't do her no harm, miss, especially knowing she's the colonel's sister.'

'She was looking pretty queer last time I saw her,' offered Gunner Stubbs. 'P'raps she was feeling so ill she wanted to go home.'

'That could be it,' said Mary doubtfully. She looked around. There was no sign of the three riders, nor any indication which way they had gone.

Sergeant Hollins batted away a fly.

'Dog's gone with 'em,' he remarked.

Mary gave a little sigh of exasperation.

'Well, we cannot waste time looking for her. Lord Randall must be conveyed back to Brussels as quickly as possible and I shall need you all to help me.'

The little party set off. It was slow work, for they could only go at walking pace and Mary was anxious that they avoid jarring Randall's battered body. She was desperately worried about the wound to his chest. She said nothing to the others, but she was fearful that if the ball had entered some vital organ all their efforts might yet be in vain.

She walked beside the litter, occasionally wiping Randall's face and forcing a little water between his parched lips. Occasionally her eyes went to the sword still strapped to his side. He had found it. He must know now she had not taken it. It was a small consolation and seemed trivial compared to the task of getting Randall back to Brussels alive. He showed no signs of consciousness and she kept putting her hand to his neck to reassure herself that the faint pulse was still there.

It was dark by the time they reached Brussels. The sergeant ordered Gunner Stubbs to run ahead so that when they arrived at the Rue Ducale, Robbins was ready for them and helped to carry the seemingly lifeless body upstairs to the bedchamber.

'Lieutenant Foster is on his way,' said the manservant, regarding his master with worried eyes.

The sergeant touched Mary's arm.

'You'll stay and nurse him?'

She glanced at Robbins, wondering if he would object to her presence, but she read only worry and consternation in his face.

'It would help to have another pair of hands, Miss Endacott.'

'So you'll stay?' Sergeant Hollins said again. 'You've been nursing other soldiers, you'll know what to do.'

Their confidence in her was touching. She only hoped it was not misplaced.

'I will stay, Sergeant. Perhaps you will take Marron back to the schoolhouse, and ask my maid to pack a bag for me and send it here? Tell her to pack my grey gown; it is the most suitable for nursing.' It was also extremely plain. Not the gown any mistress would wear. There must be no misunderstanding of her role here. Mary was bone-weary, but she summoned up a smile for the men who were crowded together near the door. 'Thank you, gentlemen, you have been magnificent. You may be sure your colonel shall know of your efforts, when he comes round.'

She would not admit the possibility that Justin might not live, even to herself. The men looked pleased if a little uncomfortable to be addressed as gentlemen. They shuffled out and soon it was only Robbins and Mary left in the room. For a while they stood in silence, staring at Randall.

'I will not leave him,' said Mary. 'Not until he is out of danger. One way or another.'

'No, ma'am.' Robbins coughed. 'I believe there

is a small room next door that is not in use. I will ask the landlady to prepare a bed for you.'

'Yes, thank you.'

'I will do it now,' he continued. 'And I shall bring water and a nightshirt for his lordship.'

When he had gone Mary felt very alone. The silence pressed in on her, the fears she had refused to acknowledge throughout the day now mocked her and she could not keep back her tears. She fell to her knees beside the bed.

'Oh, Randall, don't die,' she whispered, clutching at the bedcovers. 'Don't leave me. Even if I never see you again I could not bear for you to die.'

Her words disappeared into the silence. No one responded, there was no comfort to be had from Randall's breathing, so shallow and quiet that it was hard to believe he was still alive.

When Robbins came back Mary's momentary weakness had passed. She was on her feet, her calm demeanour restored, and she helped Robbins to undress Randall. They worked steadily by candlelight, cutting away the tattered uniform and washing the blood and grime from his body. Mary gently cleaned and bandaged the wounds on his head and leg as Bertrand had shown her, but the ominous little hole in his chest she left for the brigade surgeon.

* * *

Lieutenant Foster arrived an hour later. He was looking pale and drawn, dark shadows beneath his eyes hinting at a lack of sleep. He frowned when he saw Mary standing by the bed.

'Miss Endacott, is it not?' His cold disapproving manner told Mary he knew that she was Randall's mistress. *Had been* his mistress, she corrected herself. 'I do not think we need detain you any longer. Robbins and I will look after his lordship.'

Mary bridled as his dismissive tone.

'Since I fetched Lord Randall from the battlefield I consider I have a right to be here, Lieutenant.'

'But this is no place for you.'

She lifted her chin and glared at him. Let him try and dislodge her!

'If I might say so, sir…' Robbins gave a deprecating cough '…Miss Endacott knows a bit about nursing, Lieutenant Foster. I could do with her assistance, having no one else here to help me.'

After a brief inward struggle the surgeon shrugged.

'Very well. Perhaps, Miss Endacott, you will bring those candles a little closer and I will see what I can do.'

'The wound to his head is not serious, neither is the cut to his thigh.' The surgeon washed his hands, his examination of Lord Randall finished. 'I have bled him and bound him up, but apart from that there is very little I can do. The earl has a musket ball lodged in his chest. It does not appear to have touched any of the vital organs, but it is very close. However, he has survived this long and there is no reason why he should not make a good recovery.'

'You are not going to remove it?'

'Good heavens, no. One slip of the knife and I should kill him for sure. No. It is best we leave it to God. I know of cases where men have gone on for years with a bullet in them. Young Lord March, for example. Took a ball in the chest at Orthès two years ago and lived to fight in this engagement. He is very well, save for a tendency to pass out if there is a sudden drop in temperature.

'No, leave well alone is my advice. The first forty-eight hours are the most dangerous. Lord Randall must be kept as still as possible. You will also need to be vigilant. If he shows any signs of fever, call me and I will bleed him again. I do not foresee any difficulties, however. The colonel is very strong; he has a good chance of survival.'

'I do not want him to have a good chance,' said Mary, trying to stay calm, 'I want him to have the best.'

'Of course you do, madam, and if you follow my advice I think you will find that Lord Randall will pull through. I have some experience of these matters, you know.'

His comfortable tone set Mary's teeth on edge and she almost expected him to pat her on the head before he left the room.

Mary and Robbins shared the night-time vigil of sitting with Randall. He did not wake, but Mary was encouraged when, towards dawn, he became restless. Rather than lift him she dipped a sponge into water and held it against his lips. His eyelids flickered but did not open fully and after a few minutes he sank back into unconsciousness again. Mary resumed her seat by the bed, reaching out to take his hand and hold it between her own. It was a tiny comfort.

There was no future for them together, she knew that now. She could never forget his lack of trust or the hateful things he had said to her. She had thought of little else since that horrid ball, when her world had fallen apart. How long ago was it? She glanced at the window, where the grey dawn was lightening the sky. It must be Tuesday. Five days that seemed like a lifetime. She had lived in a twilight world of unhappiness, grieving and anger over Randall's unjust tirade, and at the same time feeling agonisingly fearful for his safety. Now he was here, wounded but alive, and she was at his side, nursing him. She would stay as long as he needed her, then she would leave him and begin to make a new life for herself. A life alone.

Randall was conscious, but he was lying at the bottom of a deep, black pit. It was warm and comfortable, as long as he did not move. Everything was quiet. He could remember the heat and noise of the battle, the thunderous roar, the shouts, screams, but it must be over now. The comfortable blackness lifted a little. He became aware that his body ached, his head was throbbing and there was the tightness of a bandage on his thigh. His ribs, too, were tightly bound so that he could not take a deep breath.

He lay very still, eyes closed. He was no longer on the battlefield. He must be in bed, and a town, because he could hear the faint ring and clatter of horses and wagons in the street. He tried opening his eyes and recognised his lodgings in the Rue Ducale. Someone was moving quietly about the room, but it was not Robbins, it was a woman. She had her back to him and all he could see was the dull grey gown. A nun, perhaps? No, her head was uncovered. He recognised that dark hair, it was strained back into a tidy knot but he had seen it falling in glossy waves over her shoulders.

Mary. That was not right. He had sent her away. They had argued. No. He had been angry. She

had said nothing, just looked at him, her eyes full
of pain. His brain was sluggish; he struggled to
make sense of the thoughts and memories that
were flooding in. He had accused her of taking
the Latymor sword, but she had not done so. It had
been Gideon. And Gideon was dead.

There had been no time to mourn in the midst
of battle, but now the memory of his brother's
death cut through Randall like a knife and he
shifted in the bed, as if trying to evade its sting.

That small movement made Mary turn to him.
Her face was pale and anxious. He wanted to say
something, to drive the shadows from her eyes,
but he could not speak.

'I am helping Robbins to nurse you,' she said
quickly. 'There are so many wounded men and
Lieutenant Foster can spare no one.'

Why should she need to explain her presence
here? He would rather have her here than anyone
else. But they had quarrelled and she would not
know that. He must tell her.

'I know it is not ideal,' she went on, not meeting his eyes. 'I am sorry if my presence distresses
you. I shall leave as soon as Robbins can manage
on his own.'

No, he did not want her to leave. Randall struggled. The words were in his head, but he could
not yet command his voice. He frowned, concentrating hard in an effort to speak, but when Mary

glanced at his face she misunderstood his scowl and thought he did not want her there.

'I will send Robbins in,' she said hurriedly.

Randall wanted to protest, to shake his head, to reach out, but he could do none of these things. It was all too much effort and he found himself sinking once more into the deep, warm pit of oblivion.

Mary hurried out of the room, blinking rapidly. What had she expected? He had told her quite plainly he did not back down, did not apologise. Yet she had hoped he would be pleased to see her. Perhaps it was not just the sword. Perhaps he truly believed the other accusations he had thrown at her, that she had schemed to marry him, that she wanted him for his fortune and his title. After all, he had been hurt before.

Summoning all her strength, she went in search of Robbins and asked him to attend to Lord Randall, who had at last opened his eyes, then she returned to the sitting room and allowed herself the luxury of shedding a few hot tears.

She looked up as Robbins came into the room.

'He is sleeping again now, miss.' He gave her a reassuring smile. 'He seems pretty comfortable.'

'I wonder if we should find someone else to look after him with you.' Mary got to her feet, clasping her hands tightly in front of her. 'He did not look at all pleased to see me here.'

'He's not himself, miss.'

She shook her head. 'If you had seen his look—' She broke off, unable to trust herself to say more without more tears.

'Looking black, was he? Oh, I've seen that, miss, often and often,' replied Robbins in a comfortable tone. 'He has a way with him that makes grown men shake in their boots, but it don't mean anything.'

'He accused me of taking his sword.'

'Did he now? Yet he was wearing it when you found him, wasn't he?'

'Yes.'

'Then he must know the truth now, miss. He must know you didn't take it.'

'But it wasn't just that.' She hesitated. 'He thinks me a fortune hunter.'

'I've never had you down as that, miss, and I don't think his lordship really believes it, either, whatever he might have said in the heat of the moment. He's had enough caps set at him over the years to know the difference.'

She tried to smile.

'You make it sound so simple, Robbins.'

'It is simple, Miss Endacott. His lordship ain't a great one with words, but if he's wronged you he'll be as sorry as he can be. Only you must give him time to tell you so, in his own way.'

'But if he doesn't want me here—'

'If you will excuse me for saying so,' he interrupted her, 'Lord Randall is in no position to know what is best for him at the moment. Besides, where am I going to find another nurse to look after him as you do? The whole of Brussels is like one big hospital now. They are even nursing the wounded on the streets.'

'That is true, I suppose.'

'Of course it is. Now you go back in and sit with his lordship and I'll brew a dish of tea for you. I managed to buy some black bohea when I went out this morning.'

'Especially for me? Oh, how kind—thank you, Robbins.'

The manservant flushed a little and shifted uncomfortably.

'Aye, well, it *is* for you, because his lordship would never drink such stuff.'

'Well, perhaps he will do so now,' returned Mary, smiling. 'It might be quite beneficial to his recovery.'

She went back into the bedroom, comforted by the manservant's support.

When Randall opened his eyes again he found Mary sitting beside his bed.

'So you are awake at last, my lord.'

'How long have I been here?' Every breath was painful and his voice seemed to be little more than a thread.

'We fetched you from Waterloo yesterday.'

'We?'

'Why, yes, sir. Sergeant Hollins and some of your men came to the schoolhouse yesterday, looking for you.'

A delicate colour tinted her cheeks and she wouldn't meet his eyes when she explained this. He cursed silently. So even the Rogues believed she was his mistress. How could he have been so irresponsible?

'You went to the village, to Waterloo?'

'We found you on the battlefield.'

The information made his blood run cold.

'I would not have had you see it, Mary.'

Her shoulders lifted slightly.

'We found you, that is all that matters.'

'My indomitable Mary.' The flush on her smooth cheek deepened. He reached out for her, but she rose quickly, ignoring his hand as she straightened the sheets. Did she think he was still angry with her? 'Mary, we must talk.'

'Not yet, my lord. There will be time for that when you are better.' She raised her head as voices sounded from outside the door. 'Lieutenant Foster is here to see you.'

Mary hurried from the bedroom, thankful to put off the tête-à-tête a little longer. She did not want to hear what he had to say; she had made her decision, it was the only solution and she would not allow him to talk her out of it. She would not admit to herself how much it would hurt if he did not even try.

Chapter Thirteen

The brigade surgeon appeared quite satisfied and when he saw Mary in the sitting room he told her that rest was all the earl needed now.

'His lordship is already sleeping,' said Robbins when Lieutenant Foster had left. 'I'll watch him now, miss, and you can get some rest.'

But Mary was too on edge to lie down. She had asked for her embroidery and her writing box to be sent over from the schoolhouse, but plying a needle left her far too much time to think, so instead she went through her correspondence. There were several letters from parents of her pupils, giving notice that they would not be sending their children to the academy again. They had obviously been sent before they had received her own letter, telling them that she was closing the school. None of them gave a reason, but it was quite clear from their tone that they had heard she was the mistress of an English milord. There was also a note from Lady Sarah that required an answer. It would be difficult to respond. Mary knew she should be thankful that Sarah was safely back in Brussels, but she could not help thinking that if Sarah had not persuaded her to go to the ball, Randall might never have said such wounding things.

Quickly, she pushed aside that thought. He would still have thought her a thief and a fortune hunter even if he had not had the opportunity to accuse her to her face. That is what hurt most, that Randall should be so quick to condemn her. She could not forgive him for his lack of trust. Perhaps she had been too hasty in putting aside her own principles when he had suggested marriage. He was still an earl, a member of the nobility whom she despised. Even love could not change that. She just managed to wipe away a tear before it splashed on to the paper. She did not want anyone, especially Lady Sarah, to know of her distress.

Thankfully she had quite recovered her composure by the time Major Flint barged in some time later and she stoutly refused to give him more than five minutes with his colonel. He looked shocked at his half-brother's appearance, but at least that prevented him from asking her too many questions about her presence there. Not that it mattered. Her reputation was in tatters.

Randall slept so much that it was a simple matter for Mary to avoid being with him when he was awake. It was necessary for her to help Robbins to wash the earl and ease him into a clean nightshirt, but she scurried away as soon as she could, determined not to be alone with him.

She managed to get some sleep in the early evening, ready to relieve Robbins at midnight, but when she went into the earl's room she found him awake. He stared at her with sombre intensity.

'I believe you have been avoiding me.' He spoke quietly, so unlike his normal, brusque tone that she felt the tears sting her eyes again.

'No, my lord, I—'

'Don't lie to me.' His voice was weak, but she discovered it had lost none of its power to command.

'Very well,' she said. 'Yes. I have been avoiding you.'

'I know now that you did not take the Latymor sword.' His fingers plucked at the bedcovers. 'It was unforgivable of me to accuse you.'

'Yes.'

'What can I do to make it up to you?'

'Nothing, my lord.'

'Mary—'

'Please, my lord, there is no need for you to say anything else.' She sat down beside his bed and folded her hands in her lap. 'I wanted to put off this until you were stronger, but perhaps it is best if we discuss it now.'

'You mean while I am too weak to argue with you?'

His flash of humour stabbed at her, but it did not shake her resolve. She continued in a calm and measured tone.

'I am closing the school and leaving Brussels. It is impossible for me to stay here.'

He closed his eyes, a shadow of pain flickering across his face.

'That is my doing,' he said. 'Mary, let me make it right. My hand—and my heart—are yours. Nothing has changed.'

'Everything has changed. I know now it would never work.'

There, she had said it.

His eyes were on her face again. 'Go on.'

She met his glance steadily.

'I cannot marry you, Randall. It was always an impossible dream, an earl and the daughter of a radical. I was too quick to jump at your proposal and did not think it through. You are a peer of the realm, an ancient order that I cannot support. You are also a soldier and I am opposed to war.'

'I am well aware of our differences, Mary, but they are not insurmountable—'

'That is not all,' she interrupted him. 'Can you not see what has hurt me most of all? Your lack of trust. You thought I would steal your sword to keep you by my side. You did not question it; you did not come and ask me if I had taken it. You assumed I would stoop to such a trick. That I was selfish enough to put my own desires before everything that you hold dear.'

'It was wrong of me, I admit it, but will you not give me a chance to put it right?'

'It cannot be done.'

'You are certain of that? You have appointed yourself judge and jury and have decided there can be no possibility of our finding happiness together?'

Misery welled up inside her, clogging her throat. She could only shake her head. The silence pressed around them and for Mary it was filled with unshed tears, unspoken words and unuttered, anguished cries.

'Where will you go?' he asked at last.

Her wretchedness deepened. He, too, knew it was over and did not attempt to argue.

'I do not know yet.'

'Will you tell me, once you have decided?'

'I think not.'

She wondered if he would press her, make one last attempt to persuade her to stay, but there was a knock at the door and Robbins looked in.

'It is time for my lord's laudanum, miss, if you would like me to help you?'

'Yes, yes, please, Robbins.'

She let the manservant lift Randall's shoulders while she held the cup to his lips, but all the time the earl's blue eyes were on her, peering into her soul, seeing the anguish deep inside. When they were alone again he spoke, so quietly she had to lean closer to hear him.

'I want you to be happy, Mary.'

'And I you, my lord.'

His hand caught hers, his grip surprisingly strong.

'When will you leave?'

'As soon as Robbins no longer needs me to help nurse you. Tomorrow, perhaps. Lieutenant Foster says you are mending well.'

'Yes, he told me that. Since I have no fever he thinks I may live comfortably with this musket ball in my chest.' He lay back on the pillows, watching her. 'But I cannot live comfortably without you, Mary.'

His eyelids begin to droop. The laudanum was taking effect.

She said softly, 'You will learn to do so, my lord.'

His eyes closed and the grip on her hand went slack.

'You will learn to do so,' she whispered again, pulling her fingers free. 'And so shall I.'

* * *

By the following morning Randall was showing a marked improvement. When Mary carried his breakfast into the room she found him propped against a bank of pillows. Robbins had just finished shaving him and he looked so much like his old self that her heart turned over, first soaring with love for him before it plummeted down into the depths of despair. He no longer needed her to nurse him, she must go. It was with the greatest difficulty that she kept her tears at bay and greeted him with a cheerful good morning.

'You are looking much better today,' she remarked, putting the tray down across his knees.

'I do not feel it.' He paused until Robbins had gone out and closed the door. 'You are determined to leave me?'

'Yes, Lieutenant Foster says you are out of danger.'

'Mary.' He caught her wrist. 'I told you once I am no good with soft words, but please, stay and talk to me.'

She stiffened, staring at his hand until, reluctantly, he released her.

'There is nothing to say, my lord.'

'But there is. You must listen to me.'

'Must?' She bridled instantly. 'I am not one of your minions, Lord Randall. There is nothing I *must* do where you are concerned.'

'Then let me plead. I *beg* you to listen to me.'

'*No!*' She put her hands to her temples. 'I have made up my mind. We cannot make each other happy. Our worlds are too different, my lord. It is best we part now.'

'I do not believe that,' he exclaimed. 'I will *never* believe it. Beneath it all we are a man and a woman, Mary. We are in love. There *has* to be a way.'

She gave a little sob. 'Oh, why must you make this so difficult?'

'Because it has taken me thirty years to find you, Mary Endacott. I do not intend to let you slip away so easily.'

Not trusting herself to reply, she hurried out of the room. Robbins was waiting in the sitting room and he gave her a searching look. Fearing he might ask her questions that would make her cry, Mary spoke quickly.

'When is Lieutenant Foster calling?'

'Noon, miss. Plenty of time for you to get some sleep and I'll wake you when he comes. Not that I think he will find anything wrong with his lordship now. Looking very much more his old self this morning, I thought.'

'Yes, he is, Robbins. So you will not be needing my help any more, will you?'

'Well, as to that, miss…'

She gave him her brightest smile. 'I am sure I

can be of more use back at the schoolhouse now. I shall collect up my things, and as soon as the lieutenant has confirmed Lord Randall is recovering well I shall remove myself. I have no doubt you will be relieved not to have me fussing around you.'

'I shouldn't say that, Miss Endacott. I couldn't have managed without you and that's a fact.'

This unexpected praise from the taciturn manservant made Mary's heart ache even more and, muttering her excuses, she went to her room. It did not take her long to pack her bag and afterwards she lay down on the narrow bed. It would break her heart to leave Randall, but it must be done. His treatment of her at the ball had shown her just how far apart they were. He had blamed her for the loss of his sword and for leading his sister astray. She was innocent on both counts. Robbins had told her the thief was his own brother and as for Lady Sarah, Mary did not think she had ever held any influence over her at all. And what Randall would say if he found out Sarah had accompanied her to the battlefield she did not like to think.

Mary turned on to her side and curled into a ball. Really, with the exception of Harriett every member of the Latymor family was arrogant and overbearing. She would never find happiness with them; she had been foolish to ever think she might. But it did not stop her shedding a few more tears into her already damp pillow before she eventually fell asleep.

She awoke some hours later to the sounds of commotion. She sat up quickly, rubbing her eyes. Surely that was not Randall's voice she could hear, raised in anger? Shaking out her skirts, she went to her door and opened it, in time to see a flash of uniform and hear the clatter of boots on the wooden stair. When she entered the earl's apartment she found Robbins coming out of the bedchamber, his face even more sombre than usual.

'Was that Major Flint I saw leaving?'

Robbins carefully closed the door behind him.

'Aye, it was, miss. Came to tell his lordship about his sister.'

'Lady Sarah?'

'Aye, miss. It seems she's, er, taken up with Major Bartlett and his lordship ain't happy about it at all. In a rage, he is, shouting about court martials. It was as much as we could do to keep the master from getting out of bed and going after her, there and then.'

A sudden roar was heard from the bedroom.

'He wants pen and ink, miss,' Robbins explained. 'To write to Lady Sarah.'

He hurried away and Mary stood for a moment, one hand pressed to her cheek. How could Sarah be so thoughtless? She should have known her actions would enrage her brother. Randall would doubtless put this, too, at her door, and blame her for encouraging Sarah to kick over the traces. She heard the earl's angry voice calling for his man and she went into the bedroom. Randall glared at her, his eyes blazing.

'Where is Robbins?' His voice was full of suppressed fury.

'Gone to fetch pen and paper, as you requested.' She went a little closer. 'Please, Randall, this anger is not good for you. You should be resting.'

'Hah, how can I rest when my sister is, is *consorting* with one of the most notorious libertines in Europe? Robbins, bring that pen and paper. Now, man!'

She noted with alarm that his colour was mounting.

'He is on his way.' She paused. 'If you will permit me to say so, Lady Sarah is no longer a child to be ordered about. In fact, I had the distinct impression there is a will of iron beneath that soft exterior.'

'Oh, you did, did you?' He glowered at her. 'And what would you know about it?'

Her temper snapped. 'A great deal more than you give me credit for! It is a Latymor trait that I have come to recognise, my lord.'

'Well, by God, I do not intend to let her ruin

herself,' he exclaimed furiously. 'In fact, I will go
and find her myself—'

He threw back the bedcovers and swung his
legs over the edge of the bed, but even as Mary
protested he stopped, a spasm of pain crossing his
face and his colour draining away.

'Randall!'

He did not hear her, but fell back against the
pillows, his face a deathly white.

'Randall!'

Her second cry brought Robbins hurrying in
and together they eased the earl back into bed,
flinging away the pillows and laying him flat. An
erratic pulse was beating in his neck, but that and
his ragged breathing were the only signs of life.
Mary took one of his hands and began to chafe it
between her own. It was a very inadequate gesture, but she did not know what else to do.

'Thank heaven the surgeon's due here any minute,' muttered Robbins. 'I'll go down to the door
to look out for him.'

'Yes, do,' said Mary. 'And bring him here as
quickly as possible.'

She had barely finished her first prayer when
she heard footsteps on the stairs and moments
later Lieutenant Foster came in. Mary stood back
to allow him room to examine Lord Randall, but
she hovered at the end of the bed, clasping and

unclasping her hands as she explained what had happened.

'He seemed so well this morning,' she said. 'Then he flew into a rage when Major Flint called upon him and he tried to get out of bed.'

'Ah. Then the musket ball has moved,' said the lieutenant. 'It will be pressing upon some vital organ.'

'Then it must be removed.'

'Not by me. We must hope it will shift again.' Mary stared at him and he shook his head at her. 'To remove it would be far too dangerous. The ball entered the chest with remarkably little harm. To take it out again we would have to cause considerably more damage. Why, I should have the whole of the Latymor family clamouring for my head if he was to die under my knife.'

'But he cannot live like this.'

He sighed.

'I agree it is unlikely he will survive, but operating would undoubtedly be fatal. This way— well, we can pray for a miracle, Miss Endacott. That is my professional opinion.'

Helplessly Mary looked at Randall's immobile figure lying in the bed. She glanced at Robbins. He was almost as pale as his master and he fixed her with troubled eyes, as if looking to her for a solution. She breathed in deeply and drew herself up.

'Would you object, Lieutenant, if I called for another opinion?'

The officer looked almost relieved at the suggestion.

'Not at all, miss, but I think the answer will be the same.'

'We shall see. Robbins, you must go and find Dr Lebbeke for me.'

It seemed an eternity before Bertrand arrived, although the chiming of the church clock told Mary it had not been an hour. Lieutenant Foster had gone, declaring that he had many patients to visit that day and could not wait. However, he had written a note before he left and Mary thrust it into Bertrand's hands as soon as he came through the door.

Bertrand read it in silence while Mary carefully removed the bandages from Randall's body. The wound was nothing more than a small, dark hole and looked quite insignificant in the broad, powerful chest. Bertrand's examination did not take long.

'And what is it you expect me to do for him, Mary?' He looked at her gravely. 'The army surgeon explains the case most carefully.'

She fixed her eyes upon him.

'If the ball stays in him he will die.'

'I am afraid that is almost inevitable.'

'But if the musket ball were removed?'

'What you are asking, *ma chère*, is an operation of the most delicate.'

'But could you do it?'

'*Bien sûr*, but I cannot guarantee the colonel will survive.'

'At least he would have a chance and that is more than he has at the moment.'

'Perhaps.' Bertrand waved towards the surgeon's letter. 'Lieutenant Foster has counselled against an operation.'

Mary fixed her eyes on the figure in the bed.

'He has to live. He *has* to.'

'Because you wish it?' said Bertrand. 'Because you love him?

She met his eyes.

'Yes,' she said softly. 'I cannot marry him, and once this is over I will never see him again, but...' she blinked away the threatening tears '...I c-cannot bear the thought of a world without him.'

'Then we must try to save him for you, Mary.'

Once the decision was made there was no time for regrets or second thoughts. The room was prepared, the bed stripped of blankets and a table placed beside it, upon which Bertrand spread a fearsome array of instruments. Mary fetched a clean sheet which they used to cover Randall from the waist down. As she straightened it carefully over his lower body she thought that it would very likely be his shroud, if things went wrong.

Outside the ordinary sounds of the city life continued. The cries of the street sellers, the barking dogs, the rattle of wagons all floated in through the window as Bertrand worked. Mary could only watch. When she saw the sweat gathering on his brow she wiped it away with a damp cloth, then she stood back again, watching silently as he slowly, delicately probed the wound.

Time lost its meaning. She did not hear the clock chime, did not notice the square of sunlight moving across the floor, her whole attention was fixed upon Randall. She felt quite helpless and she knew Robbins was outside the door, equally anxious, equally keen to go anywhere, do anything that might help the earl to live.

After what seemed like eternity Bertrand gave a little huff of satisfaction.

'Enfin.'

Mary stared at the bloody musket ball he held between the jaws of the forceps. It was such a tiny object, yet it could fell a man. She shifted her gaze back to Randall.

'He lives still,' murmured the doctor, as if reading her mind. 'We will clean the wound with spirits and then cover it again. No salves, just clean bandages. And then we wait. If there is no fever, no infection, then he may survive.'

It was another hour before they had finished and by that time the light was fading. While Bertrand cleaned and packed away his surgical tools Mary looked doubtfully at the figure in the bed.

'He has not regained consciousness at all,' she said, biting her lip and trying not to sound anxious.

'But his pulse is steady.'

'Perhaps you should bleed him again.'

'*Mais non*, it is your English doctors who like to drain the life blood out of a man. We will let him rest for another day at least. Now, I must go. I am needed at the hospital.'

'You are working tonight?'

'*Mais oui.* There are many more wounded that need my attention. When he wakes or if you become anxious, send for me.' He gripped her shoulder. 'I have done all I can, Mary.'

'I know. And I am very grateful, especially when you have so many injured men to attend.'

'Ah, but this one, he is special to you, Mary.'

Chapter Fourteen

Another night-time vigil at Randall's bedside left Mary exhausted. She slept away the morning and spent her waking hours catching up on correspondence, including replying to another enquiry by Lady Sarah with a curt note, in which she did not minimise Randall's critical condition.

She felt a surge of irritation. It should be Randall's family who were here, nursing him. The thought occurred only to be instantly dismissed. Lady Sarah had been brought up to a life of ease and privilege; she would know nothing of nursing a sick man. And Randall's only other female relative in the country was Lady Blanchards, whose delicate condition would preclude her from attending the sickroom.

No, the Latymors could not help her and agonising as it was to spend hour upon hour sitting at Randall's bedside, Mary knew it was where she wanted to be, as if her loving him might make a difference to his recovery.

Bertrand called the following day, took one look at Mary and ordered her out of the house to get some fresh air.

'You are too pale,' he told her. 'It does you no good to be in the sickroom all the time.'

'I am not here all the time. I share the nursing with Robbins.'

'And when do you ever leave the building?'

She spread her hands. 'I want to be here with him, just in case.'

'Nothing is going to happen to Lord Randall while I am here, Mary. *Maintenant*, you will go out, if you please. The sun is shining, you might walk in the park. The sight of the flowers will lift your spirits.'

She shook her head. 'I would rather not. The proud English ladies will look down their noses at me. But there is something I could do; there is a notebook here that Major Flint left behind on his last visit.' The visit that had enraged Randall so much that he had tried to get out of bed. The visit that had almost killed him. She knew she was being unfair, but misery and a lack of sleep had stretched her nerves to breaking point. 'I will return the major's book to him. That will get me out of your way for a while.'

She put on her bonnet and set off, but even the sunshine could not dispel the anxiety that constantly pervaded her thoughts. While Randall was ill, while there was some doubt whether he would recover, she could stay and nurse him. She could coax the tiny amounts of honeyed water between his lips, lovingly smooth his hair from his brow. But when he recovered—or otherwise— she would have to leave and the future stretched out before her bleak and empty. Yet there was no question of staying with Randall. She could not forget the look in his eyes when he had accused her of stealing his lucky sword. She could not forgive his lack of trust. It would always be there, ready to be recalled, to come between them whenever they had a disagreement.

When she arrived at the major's lodgings the door was opened to her by a young woman with striking red-gold hair and hazel eyes. She was slightly taller than Mary and dressed simply, like a servant, but there was something about her that made Mary think she was—or had been—a lady.

Mary held out the small, leather-bound book.

'I have come from Lord Randall's lodgings. Major Flint left this when he called there.'

'Thank you.' The woman put out her hand. 'He told me that Lord Randall was injured in the battle. How is he now?'

There was genuine concern in the woman's eyes and the kindness in her voice almost over-set Mary. She struggled for words.

'I, that is, he...' It was too much. She dare not express her fears. 'We are hoping, praying—excuse me!'

She hurried away, dashing a hand across her cheeks. She would not cry. It was a sign of weakness and she despised such emotions. Besides, it would do no good. She must think of the future.

Bertrand had gone by the time she returned to the Rue Ducale and Robbins was pottering around Randall's room. When he heard her in the sitting room he came out to join her.

'How is his lordship?'

'The sawbones says he is going on well, miss.' The manservant's cheerful smile was heartening. 'He woke up while the doctor was here and he was perfectly lucid. Cursed me roundly, he did, just like his old self.'

'Oh.' Mary removed her bonnet and set it carefully on the table. She said casually, 'And did he ask for me?'

'No, miss, but he was only awake for a little while and Dr Lebbeke's examination seemed to tire him. But his heart is beating strongly now and the doctor sees no reason why he shouldn't make a good recovery.'

'I hope so, Robbins.'

'I'm going to prepare a little broth for when he wakes up again. He'll be very pleased to see you here, miss, if you don't mind my saying so. You've been like a tonic to him and that's a fact.'

'I have?' She managed a smile. 'Well that is good. But I have always said I should leave as soon as we were sure he was out of danger.'

The manservant shook his head, saying confidently, 'He'll be needin' you for months yet, miss.'

'It is kind of you to say so, but we both know that isn't true. Lord Randall will recover perfectly well without me.'

Robbins looked troubled and Mary guessed his thoughts. They had worked closely together over the past few days and had come to respect each other, too much for the manservant now to lie to her. Instead he said diffidently,

'Very stiff-rumped, his lordship…'

'And so am I stiff…er…rumped!' Mary stumbled a little but was determined not to be mealy-mouthed about it. 'I was wrong to think we could ever be anything to one another. I do not agree with the earl's principles or his station. I would be going against everything my parents taught me if I were to remain. As I shall tell him in my note. I will write it now and then I can be gone.'

'No!' The manservant looked startled. 'You can't leave us just like that.'

'I can and I think I should.'

'No, miss, not tonight. At least say you will stay until the morning. His lordship has only come round the once. The sawbones might not have got it right. He might have another turn and then where should I be if you was gone?'

Mary bit her lip. Robbins would manage, he had been with his master too long not to be able to cope with any situation, but his concern was touching and the temptation to stay near Randall was too great.

'Very well, I will remain a little longer, just to make sure he is doing as well as you say, but you must tend him. If he does wake again I do not want to see him.'

That was a lie, of course. She wanted to see him more than anything in the world.

'Very well, miss, if he asks for you I'll tell him you are sleeping.'

Mary sat down at the little desk to write her letter to Randall. She could hear Robbins moving around in the bedchamber. Her pen spluttered when she heard the low murmur of voices. Randall was awake. Robbins came hurrying out and went downstairs, returning a few minutes later carrying a tray containing broth and a glass of wine. He went back into the room, closing the door carefully behind him.

Mary waited, the ink drying on her pen. Would

he ask for her? Would he demand that she come and see him? Robbins could hardly refuse a direct order. She strained her ears, but the muffled sounds from the next room could not be distinguished. Her last hope died when Robbins came out of the room again with the empty dishes and carefully closed the door behind him. He grinned at her.

'Took the lot he did, miss, even the wine, and looks the better for it. The effort tired him, though. I think he'll sleep like a log now.'

Mary nodded. 'That is very good news, Robbins.'

How could information be so welcome and yet so bitter?

Swallowing a sigh, she dipped her pen in the ink again and finished her letter.

The food put heart into Randall. He felt as weak as a kitten, but a good night's rest should put that right. And in the morning he would see Mary, make his peace with her. Robbins had told him she was still here, that surely was a good sign. Sleep came quickly, but it was disturbed by dreams. At one point he dreamed he woke up. It was very dark and someone was standing by the bed. Mary. He recognised the smell of her, the no-nonsense scent of fresh linen and soap with just a hint of sweet herbs. He did not move as she leaned over him, her lips brushing his temple and he heard her soft words.

'Goodbye, my love.'

'Good morning, my lord. I took the liberty of bringing your breakfast.'

Randall opened his eyes and peered blearily at Robbins. It took him a few moments to realise where he was and how he felt. He had had his first night's sleep without laudanum and for once his head was clear. He felt hungry, too. Robbins eased him up on to the pillows before setting the breakfast tray across his legs.

'Thank you, Robbins. Since it was you who brought my supper I thought Miss Endacott might be tending me this morning.'

'Miss Endacott has gone, sir.'

'The devil she has!' He remembered his dream. 'When did she leave?'

'Around midnight, sir.'

Goodbye, my love.

'She left a letter for you.' Robbins drew a folded paper from his pocket and held it out. After a moment's hesitation Randall took it and scanned its contents. Suddenly having a clear head was no advantage. She had spelled out the reasons why they would not suit all too well and ended with an instruction—nay, a plea—that he did not try to find her. Carefully he folded the paper and put it down on the covers.

'My lord, if I may—'

'No, you may not!' He clenched his teeth together, holding back the anger and frustration that boiled within him. 'I beg your pardon, Robbins, I should not snap at you. Leave me now, if you please. I will call you when I have broken my fast.'

Robbins went out, closing the door behind him quietly, as if trying not to exacerbate his master's already frayed temper. Randall stared at the tray before him. His appetite was quite gone.

For three days Randall held off from writing to Mary. He was too weak to get up, but he found he could deal with most of his military business from his bed, having made up his mind to quit the artillery and return to England. There was much to do to put his affairs in order. The army had moved on to Paris, chasing Bonaparte, but he was kept busy writing reports and composing letters of condolence to the families of his men who had died in battle—those Rogues who *had* a family. Officers came and went, to report or carry away his orders. It was tiring, but nothing like as difficult as his first visitor, his sister Sarah.

The girl seemed to have grown up a great deal during the past few days, she was much more self-assured. Randall wanted to rip up at her about her liaison with Major Bartlett, but his first words brought a flash of fire into her eyes and he held his tongue. Mary's words came back to him. Sarah was a woman now with a mind of her own. And besides, who was he to reprimand her? However, when she asked how Gideon had died he made no attempt to fob her off. She deserved to know the truth. In the retelling of it he was obliged to re-live the terrible moment of cradling his younger brother in his arms as the life went out of him. Not only that, but Sarah berated him for his treatment of Mary. He deserved it, he knew that only too well, but when Sarah told him how Mary had led the search for him, how she had entered into the barn to look for him amongst the dead, the agony of what he had lost, how he had wronged her, was more painful than any sabre cut.

The injustice of it worried away at him and eventually he wrote a note for Mary. It was re-turned, unopened, together with the information that Miss Endacott had left Brussels and would not be coming back. Randall crushed his care-fully worded letter into a ball and hurled it across the room.

'Fine lady, Miss Endacott,' remarked Robbins, in response to the stream of quiet invective flow-ing from his master's lips. He bent to pick up the mangled paper. 'Quiet, like, but very determined, in her own way. It was quite an eye-opener, I can tell you, the night they brought you back here, to see how the Rogues deferred to her, as if she could make everything right. And then she wouldn't take the brigade surgeon's word for it that there was nothing to be done for you, but insisted on bringing in her own doctor—'

'Yes, yes, all right!' Randall sighed and cast a rueful eye at his batman. 'I handled it very badly, didn't I?'

'I'm afraid you did, sir.'

'And now she's left town and gone heaven knows where.' His clenched fist struck the bed-covers. 'If only I wasn't tied to the bed, weak as a cat, I'd go and find her, wherever she may be.'

Robbins grinned, saying cheerfully, 'One step at a time, my lord. We'll get you out of bed today and it won't be long before you're on your feet again, I'm sure.'

Randall knew his man was right. A few hours in the chair was all he could manage that afternoon.

When Dr Lebbeke came to see him the following day he demanded irritably how long he could expect to be incarcerated indoors.

'You are making an excellent recovery,' replied the doctor when he had finished his examination. 'I see no reason why you should not go out of doors tomorrow, if you feel up to it, although I expect going down the stairs to the door will be enough for you.'

'Damn, I must get further than that!'

'All in good time, my lord. If you try to do too much too soon, then all my efforts might be in vain.' The doctor shrugged himself into his coat. 'I must leave. I go to the Rue Haute. There is a patient at the schoolhouse who concerns me.'

'So she left you in charge, did she?'

'*Mais non.* Mademoiselle Endacott is still in command.'

'I thought she had left Brussels.'

'She is in Antwerp for a few days, but she returns at the end of the week. I still have several patients at the schoolhouse, men too ill to be moved, and Mademoiselle Endacott will remain to supervise their nursing. I consider her presence is necessary to their recovery.'

Randall frowned, a demon of jealousy rising inside him. 'You asked her to stay?'

'I suggested she should do so and she has agreed.' Lebbeke picked up his bag, saying carefully, 'I think she was glad to have an excuse to remain in Brussels.'

There was something in the doctor's tone and in the look he cast at Randall that made the demon subside again.

'And…er…how much longer do you expect your patients to be at the schoolhouse?'

'Oh, I have no intention of moving them for some weeks yet. If that is all, my lord, I shall be on my way.'

Lebbeke gave a little bow and went to the door.

'Doctor?'

Lebbeke turned, brows raised. Randall met his eyes.

'Thank you.'

Mary sat at her desk, but her eyes did not see the columns of figures in the open ledger. It was more than three weeks since she had left Randall at the Rue Ducale, but he still occupied all her waking moments. She wanted to forget him, to have nothing further to do with any of the Latymor family. She had returned to the Rue Haute and had immediately written a brief note to Lady Sarah, telling her that Randall was recovering. That should have been the end of it, but Lady Sarah had turned up on her doorstep the very next day, begging to be allowed to help with nursing the wounded soldiers.

Mary knew she should have turned her away, even though there was plenty of work to be done. Having a Latymor in the house was a constant reminder of the past, a perpetual knife in her heart, but looking into Sarah's eyes, so like her brother's, she could not refuse. The lady was obviously suffering, in her own way.

Randall, too, had written to her, once, but Mary had returned the letter unopened and sent Jacques to deliver it, together with the message that she had quit Brussels. It was not a complete lie; she had gone to Antwerp to finalise the closure of what was left of her school. The last of the pupils had gone home and the teaching staff had been paid off, then she had returned to the Rue Haute.

She had intended to pack up her belongings and move out, prior to the sale of the schoolhouse, but Bertrand had persuaded her to stay, convincing her that her presence was very necessary to those wounded soldiers still remaining in the house. Dear Bertrand, he had been a rock during the past weeks, treating her as a comrade, a friend, and never censuring her for her recklessness in throwing herself at the earl. Bertrand had involved her in the nursing of the sick, tried to distract her thoughts, but always, at the back of her mind was Randall. She missed him so much it was a physical ache, not just at night, when she would recall his kisses, the way they had made love together, but his companionship.

She had teased him for being so serious, but more and more she had begun to see that glint of humour in his eyes. That last week, when she had shared his bed, she had felt so comfortable with him. She had never had to explain herself, he had understood her, or at least she had thought so, until that last disastrous confrontation. Perhaps Randall was right; they were merely a man and a woman in love, for despite all her good intentions she could not shrug him off. He was like her shadow, constantly with her. Sometimes she felt that if she could turn her head just a little quicker she would find him there, at her shoulder.

Mary put down her pen and rubbed her eyes. It had been a mistake to stay in Brussels. She should not have allowed Bertrand to persuade her. There were too many painful memories. However, Bertrand had promised her that the last of the patients would be gone by Monday and she was determined that she, too, would leave then. Jacques and Therese would oversee the sale of the schoolhouse while she made a new life for herself away from here. Away from Randall.

No matter how often she told herself it was for the best, and that their worlds were too far apart, it made no difference to the ache within her and today the pain was so great she felt the hot tears welling up just thinking about it.

'Oh, do not be so foolish,' she told herself. 'It is something you are going to have to live with. Think about the dreadful suffering you have seen over the past few weeks. If men can survive such terrible injuries, you can live with a little heartbreak!'

She took up her pen again. When she left on

Monday she must give her business ledgers to her lawyer and the accounts would need to be in order. She tried once more to add up the column of figures, but tears filled her eyes. She heard her maid in the hall and the door opening, but she dared not look up. She said, with as much brightness as she could infuse into her voice,

'Is that my morning coffee, Therese? Thank you. Put it on the desk, if you please.'

She kept her head bent, her pen hovering over the ledger as if she was concentrating on the figures while all the time she was blinking rapidly to clear her vision. Dear heaven, it seemed to take the maid an age to approach. Why did she not put down the cup and leave her in peace? A shadow fell over the desk and a hand—a large, long-fingered male hand—placed something on the open ledger.

Blinking rapidly, she saw it was a single red rose.

Chapter Fifteen

Mary kept her head bent and her gaze fixed on the rose while she found her pocket handkerchief and wiped her eyes. When at last she did look up she saw Randall standing before her, regarding her solemnly. A rush of emotions battered her: joy, pain, fierce desire, misery. She knew she would have to make him leave, quickly, before her resolve disappeared. She pushed herself to her feet, keeping her fingertips on the desk to support her trembling body. She must remember how he had treated her at the night of the ball. The injustice of it. As she had hoped, anger lent an edge to her voice when she addressed him.

'What are you doing here?'

'I have come to see you.'

'That much is evident,' she retorted. 'I, however, do not want to see you. You may have forgotten what you said to me at the ball, sir, but I have not.'

'No, I have not forgotten anything.'

'You should go, now.'

When he did not move she went to the door and turned the handle. It did not open.

'It is locked.' She turned to glare at him. 'Where is the key?'

'It is in my pocket.'

His cool tone infuriated her.

'How dare you. Jacques!'

'It is useless to shout. I told your manservant we were not to be disturbed. He has gone off to attend to something at the other end of the house.'

'You have been giving orders to my servants?' She gasped with indignation at his effrontery. 'That is outrageous!'

'It is an advantage of the rank and privilege you so despise.'

She almost stamped her foot at that.

'How dare you tease me? Unlock this door immediately and leave my house.'

'Not until I have said what I came to say.'

She crossed her arms and glared at him.

'I do not want to hear it.'

'But I am afraid you must.' He waved towards a chair. 'Will you not sit down? No? Very well.'

Mary watched him as he stripped off his gloves and laid them with his hat on the table. He had done that before, she remembered how he had stared at the bouquet Bertrand had given her and said then that he would never bring her flowers.

Her eyes strayed to the rose lying on the desk. It was a potent sign of how he had changed.

'Pray say what you must, then be gone,' she told him, shrugging off the thought and concentrating upon her anger.

'Did you know that it was my brother Gideon who took the sword?'

'Yes. Robbins told me. He also told me how the story has been corrupted. It is said you gave him the Latymor sword to carry in his first engagement.'

Randall nodded. 'It has already passed into the Rogues' folklore. They say because he was carrying the sword he was able to prevent the French capturing the guns and thus save the company's honour. An action that cost him his life.'

'I heard that, too.'

She looked at the carpet, keeping her lips firmly closed. She would not sympathise with him over the loss of his brother, she dare not allow him any hope that she was weakening. She heard the little cough; the one Randall gave when he was nervous.

'I wanted you to know how very sorry I am for the way I treated you. I humbly beg your pardon.'

An apology? Randall never apologised.

'And you think this will do the trick?' she asked him, when she could command her voice.

'No, but it is a start.'

She risked looking up and for the first time

she noted that he was wearing his morning coat of blue superfine.

'You are not in uniform.'

'I am no longer a soldier.' He came towards her. 'I am going home, Mary, to Chalfont. And I would like you to come with me. You need not fear that the family will not receive you. Word has already reached my mother of the part you played in my rescue. I should not be at all surprised if she were to fall on your neck and call you the saviour of the Latymors.'

When she did not speak he hurried on.

'You cannot know the agony I have suffered since you left me. I was a fool not to trust you, I know that now and I do not expect you to forgive me for it, but if you will give me time, I will try to make it up to you.'

He dropped to one knee before her. Her hand went out when she saw him wince and before she could snatch it back he grasped it. She could no longer avoid looking at him and he held her gaze.

He said urgently, 'Marry me, Mary. Let me spend the rest of my life showing you just how much I love you. You were right when you said I was afraid of life, but you have changed that. You taught me to laugh, Mary, and to love. Now I need you to teach me how to live my life without the Rogues. Recovering from the bullet wound has given me time to think. I never knew love, real love, until I met you, Mary. I told you of my boyish infatuation and you know that I have not lived the life of a saint, but all that is in the past now. I am begging you to marry me, my dearest love, because I know that without you there is no future happiness for me.'

The naked anguish in his eyes tore at her heart. She could not hold back a sob.

'Oh, Randall!'

With an agility that surprised her he sprang up and dragged her into his arms. She surrendered to his kiss, her lips parting, senses swimming as the familiar longing rushed through her from her hair to the tips of her toes. The blood was singing in her veins, but even as her body thrilled to his touch she remembered her resolve and she struggled to free herself, taking care not to push against his chest.

'Randall, I cannot marry you. Please do not ask it of me.' She hung her head. 'I explained it all to you in my letter.'

He gathered her hands in his own, holding them tightly.

'Would you mind if we sit down?' He added apologetically, 'I am not yet fully recovered.'

Immediately she was all concern.

'Oh, yes—yes, of course.' Mary guided Randall to a sofa, but as he pulled her down beside him she recovered her wits sufficiently to say hotly, 'And what in heaven's name was Jacques thinking of to let you in? You may be an earl, but

I gave specific instructions that if you called he was to say I was not at home!'

'Do not blame your man; Lebbeke insisted I should be admitted.'

'Bertrand?'

'Yes, he was crossing the hall when I arrived.' He grinned. 'He *is* my doctor and realised my situation was most grave.'

She forced herself not to smile and gently disengaged her hands.

'I am very sorry, Randall, but your coming here can make no difference. I cannot marry you. I have thought about it constantly since the night of the ball and I know it would never work between us. I must refuse you, my lord.' She hunted for her pocket handkerchief. 'Please do not try to change my mind.'

'Very well.'

Mary wiped her eyes and tried hard not to feel disappointed. He sighed and leaned back against the sofa.

'War is a simple thing, compared to love,' he said. 'In war we know the enemy and pound away until they, or we, are defeated. To love someone is a very much more subtle and difficult thing. The object of our affection becomes the most important person in one's life, their happiness is paramount, even if it means you have to sacrifice your own. You say our worlds are very different and that is true. I was born a peer of the realm and I am a soldier. I am trained to fight against revolution, you were raised to fight for it. What was it you wrote in your letter? To marry me would be a betrayal of all your parents believed in. But is it a betrayal of what *you* believe in, too?'

'Yes—no.' She bit her lip. 'I thought it was, but I have changed, since knowing you.' She waved her hand. 'But that is beside the point now. Even though I love you we are too different. We should be in eternal conflict.'

'Would we? Your parents taught you that only love can bind two people together, did they not? Love and a *commonality of intellectual interests*, is that not what you told me when we first met? Have we not discovered these past few weeks that we have many things in common? Our dislike of pretension, for example, and abhorrence of injustice. Think back on the time we have spent together. There has been no lack of conversation, has there?'

'No,' she murmured. 'Although I have no idea what it was we found to discuss.'

'Nor I. You must remember that I am a soldier, Mary, so you will forgive me if I refuse to give you up without one last battle. We have our differences, but I do not believe they are irreconcilable. I believe we can be happy together, and I know I am asking you to risk a great deal more than I, but I am willing to spend my life trying to make you happy. The world is changing, Mary, and I must change, too. I am going back to England, to take up my responsibilities at Chalfont Abbey. It is time I looked after my family. Gideon is dead, Hattie and Gussie are happily settled, but there are the boys, who have not yet left school. And Sarah, of course. You pointed out to me that she is no longer a child. She will go her own way, with or without my blessing, but I want her to know I shall always be here to support her, whatever she does.

'I have left the running of the estates in Mama's hands for too long. She believes in the old order but I believe in a new one, so it will not be easy, there will be battles along the way. I cannot change the world overnight, but I can give my people education and better housing. I also want to make some form of reparation to my father's natural children. Flint has an independence—'

'I think he will need it,' put in Mary meditatively, 'when he settles down.'

'Flint, settle down?' Randall frowned at her. 'What makes you think he will do that?'

'Oh, something Lady Sarah said. And I saw someone at his lodgings. A lady. Softly spoken, but there was steel in her, I thought.' She flushed a little, trying to hide a smile. 'It is just a feeling. Female intuition, perhaps.'

'I thought you did not believe in such things?'

Her gaze slid away from the teasing light in his eyes.

'I am a little less certain now of my beliefs.'

She was relieved that he did not question her, he merely nodded.

'If it is so I wish Flint good fortune. He no longer needs my help, but many of my father's natural children have been sadly neglected. I shall do what I can for them. And I shall take my seat in the House. Perhaps I can make a difference on a larger scale.' He turned and reached for her hands. 'It would be much easier if I had you beside me, Mary, helping me to do the right thing.'

She saw the love shining in his eyes and looked away.

'Don't, Randall. How can I resist you when you look at me like that?'

'You are far too strong-minded to be swayed by any argument I might make, my dearest love, but I thought perhaps that you might be able work with me, to advise me on the best ways to improve the lives of my people.'

'Unfair, my lord,' she exclaimed, caught between laughter and tears. 'You promised not to try to persuade me!'

'With your excellent education, my love, you must know the playwright John Lyly wrote that rules of fair play do not apply in love and war.' He pulled her into his arms. 'Your parents married to protect you and your sister, knowing the world is a cruel and unforgiving place for those born out of wedlock. I want to marry you, Mary, to give you the protection of my name and my fortune, but if your conscience will not allow it, then I will live without a countess. I have two more brothers to carry on the succession so it is not imperative that I marry. You and I will live together in a union of love and common interests, if you prefer. Only, don't leave me, Mary, not like this. I want you to stay, whether as my wife, my mistress or merely a friend.' His arms tightened. 'So tell me, do you think you might be able to help me, in any one of those guises?'

She put her hands on the lapels of his coat, suddenly shy.

'If it were possible, I would like to be all three,' she said, addressing the folds of his neckcloth. 'I would like to be your wife, your mistress *and* your friend.'

He gave a triumphant laugh.

'What an excellent answer, my indomitable Mary. I should have known that you would confound me.'

His lips sought hers and she clung to him, all the doubts and uncertainties swept aside as she returned his sizzling kiss with all the fervour she could muster. At last he raised his head.

'Does this mean you will marry me?' he asked, gazing down at her.

'I think it does.' She smiled up at him mistily, but even through her tears his relief and happiness were evident. 'I will marry you, Randall, because I want to bind you to me in every way possible, because I have discovered these past weeks how much I have grown to love you. And for another reason, too.' She put her hands on her stomach. 'For the sake of our baby. It is very early days, but my courses have not begun.' She saw he was staring at her and she gave a tremulous smile. 'Yes, Randall—Justin, I am afraid we were not as careful as we thought.'

'Oh, my dearest girl, if you are carrying our child then you will make me the happiest man on earth.'

He drew her to him again. This time the kiss was longer, deeper and when Mary next opened her eyes she found herself lying against the arm of the sofa, head thrown back while Randall pressed delicate kisses along the line of her throat. She gave a sigh.

'I cannot believe it will be so easy,' she murmured, shivering deliciously as his lips caressed her collar bone. 'Your mother will be horrified by my beliefs.'

'She already loves you for saving my life and will love you even more for your strong principles,' he replied, nibbling her ear. 'And I am convinced she will be only too delighted that I am marrying a respectable woman. And I intend to marry you as soon as we get to England.'

'England.' Mary sighed, then gave a little gasp. 'We will have to return on your yacht. Randall, I refuse to be manhandled again—'

He put his finger against her lips.

'You may relax, dearest, there will be no need for me to do so. You shall wear a pair of sailor's trousers. Jack the cabin boy is about your size.'

'W-wear trousers? That would be scandalous!'

'You will look adorable.' He kissed her again, heating the blood in her veins.

'Is this wise?' she protested half-heartedly. 'Randall, you have only just recovered.'

'Be quiet,' he ordered, pushing her back down on the sofa. 'I am going to show you just how well I am recovered!'

* * * * *

Don't miss the second story in the fabulous
BRIDES OF WATERLOO *trilogy,*
A MISTRESS FOR MAJOR BARTLETT
by Annie Burrows
Coming June 2015

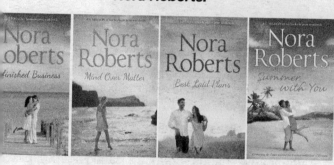

MILLS & BOON®

It's Got to be Perfect

IT'S GOT
TO BE
Perfect

UNCORRECTED
PROOF COPY

HALEY HILL

* cover in development

When Ellie Rigby throws her three-carat engagement ring into the gutter, she is certain of only one thing. She has yet to know true love!

Fed up with disastrous internet dates and conflicting advice from her friends, Ellie decides to take matters into her own hands. Starting a dating agency, Ellie becomes an expert in love. Well, that is until a match with one of her clients, charming, infuriating Nick, has her questioning everything she's ever thought about love…

Order yours today at
www.millsandboon.co.uk